The One That Got Away

island girls: 3 sisters in mauritius

zee monodee

Zee Monodee

First Published in Great Britain in 2022 by
LOVE AFRICA PRESS
103 Reaver House, 12 East Street, Epsom KT17 1HX
www.loveafricapress.com

Text copyright © Zee Monodee, 2022

Also available as ebook

Island Girls: 3 sisters in Mauritius

The One That Got Away
How To Love An Ogre
Falling For Her Bad Boy Boss

Blurb

Eldest sister of the Hemant sibling trio, Lara Reddy, returns to Mauritius as a divorcee and must contend with Indo-Mauritian society's outdated views about marriage and the modern woman. In the middle of this dumpster fire, she comes across Eric Marivaux, the white French-Mauritian man she loved as a teenager and gave up because their interracial, mixed cultural relationship would not stand a chance on this island. But here comes a second chance: Eric wants her back in his life, and he will stop at nothing to win her back. Will Lara be her own worst enemy and thus end up unhappy ever after?

Chapter One

Come on, Lara. You can do it.

It's only your mother.

Thirty-two-year-old Lara Reddy gripped the steering wheel tighter as the thoughts raced in her mind. Her left foot itched to slam onto the clutch so she could reverse out of here before her mother realised she'd made it close to the family home in Curepipe, one of the biggest towns on the island of Mauritius.

But she'd simply be delaying the inevitable.

Why, oh why, hadn't she thought of this before she'd left London? True, the lure of the job had been immense. The possibility of running her own state-of-the-art international conventions centre on the island. It had been nowhere close to her position as Events Manager at a renowned business hotel in London. For someone in her early thirties, life didn't get much better than this, career-wise. If she'd stayed in the UK, she'd probably wave menopause goodbye without making it any higher up the corporate ladder.

A once-in-a-lifetime opportunity. Not to mention that the company had head-hunted her.

She'd jumped … without giving due thought that she'd be plunging into the deep end of the local pool where the sharks dwelled.

No child of Mauritian origin who'd grown up in England or elsewhere in the world would choose to come back there to live. Too much gossip and drama. People poking and prodding into personal lives. Mauritius and its Indian-origin society reminded her of a fishbowl, where any foreigner was a goldfish. The locals ranged from piranhas to barracudas, in between which swam killer whales and every kind of shark. Proof of the pudding—her mother was one of the worst social predators ever.

She gulped and tried to unclench her hands from the steering wheel.

The urge to smoke hit her from nowhere. She'd given up cigarettes exactly three years, two months, one week, and five days earlier. Ever since that God-awful argument with Roy—

Lara closed her eyes tight. No, she wouldn't think of him. She'd ponder anything else.

Like a smoke?

She slapped the thought away and forced in a deep breath. Damn it, she hadn't thought of smoking in weeks.

Not true, sing-sang that little intruder again.

She'd thought of it just that morning. In the no-smoking international airport, when she'd lifted her head because there'd been a prickling along her nape. Then, she'd seen him. The tall, big white man with the long, shaggy blond locks and shoulders that seemed wide enough to take on all the concerns of a woman's world.

A gasp escaped her once more.

Eric.

The boy she'd loved as a teenager, when she didn't even know what the word love entailed.

The one that got away.

He left, remember? Without a word.

Rooted on the spot, the air had hitched in her throat. She'd sent furtive glances around, looking for an equally blond and even more beautiful woman in his vicinity. His French wife. Pain had ripped her heart when she'd wondered if she'd also have to see their child—probably children, by now—as well.

Her gaze had landed on the board announcing all the flights. The only other arrival besides her London Gatwick one had come from Johannesburg.

Eric Marivaux lived in France—why would he return to Mauritius from South Africa?

Her panic had alleviated then.

It wasn't him. Couldn't be him. The Eric she'd known had been tall but not as imposing or brawny. He'd also hated having his hair longer than an inch. This man had locks any shampoo company would kill to feature in one of their adverts. Must be an Afrikaner who bore a striking resemblance to him.

Still, with her hands clamped tight on the handle of her luggage trolley, she'd crept backwards until she'd tumbled out of the air-conditioned lobby through an automatic sliding door. The cloying, humid heat of the January summer had wrapped around her, crushing the breath inside her chest and further addling her brain.

It wasn't him, she told herself again now as she eased the car into first gear and crawled along the street she'd called home during the two and a half years she'd spent on the island.

The air from the vehicle's fan turned cooler. For once, rain wasn't falling in a steady drizzle over Curepipe. When they'd first moved there, she and her sisters had marvelled at how much the climate in this spot at one of the highest altitudes on the island resembled British weather. Minus snow in winter, Curepipe was a perfect contender for dark, gloomy, and wet climes. Except on days when the sun shone, when everything looked sharp and crisp, bathed in a clear glow while the temperature soared to a pleasant, tolerable heat—like today.

Massive houses with well-tended lawns and front gardens dotted both sides of the mile-long road into the quiet and affluent residential area. She remembered what the family home looked like, but she took her cue from the sight of the low, pruned tea bushes rounding Lees Street into a cul-de-sac. When the dark-green plantations came into view, she slowed the car before turning left into the open driveway of the Hemant residence.

Gravel crunched under the tyres, the sound of chirping birds in the big, leafy maple tree in the front yard contributing to the blissful peace.

Not for much longer.

A whiff of hot cooking oil touched her nostrils. Her stomach rumbled upon registering the scent of frying *bhadias*, those little cakes made from a batter of gram flour and herbs. The distinctive blend of coriander and chillies floated on the edges of the aroma. She glanced at her watch. Three o'clock, meaning teatime, and why her mother was frying savoury cakes. And that also meant—

She winced as she cut the engine and heard the strident sounds of feminine chatter coming from the opened kitchen window. Damn. Company.

Please let it not be a cluster of aunties.

A horse-like chortle screeched through the air. Lara closed her eyes in despair and let her forehead touch the steering wheel. Neighbourhood gossip and busybody Auntie Ruby was here. She'd bet her life the other member of the Terrible Three—as she and her sisters had dubbed their mother and her two best friends—would be here, too. Auntie Zubeida from next door. Of course, her mother would have her two besties around. Didn't Gayatri Hemant suffer from obsessive-compulsive talking disorder and the need for a permanent audience around her?

She shouldn't have come. The sound of her mother's high-pitched voice crept over the din, asking if someone had heard a car stop in the driveway. They'd come out in the next minute.

Picking up her courage and wishing it were the Dutch kind despite not being a drinker, she tore her fingers and head from the wheel and threw the door open. She then peeled herself out of the vehicle as a chorus of gasps resounded in the garden.

All three older women were suddenly on her like a bad rash. Hugging her and kissing her cheeks, holding her face in their hands while they exclaimed how beautiful she had become. All of which were simply tactics to lull her into complacency before they'd really pounce on the meaty topic—her recent divorce.

With their deceptively frail-looking hands on

her shoulders, they pushed her towards the back door to the kitchen. A memory assaulted her—of being pushed towards the altar on her wedding day, a glittery gold and red veil over her eyes.

She stopped in her tracks, the forgotten pain returning to slice through her heart. Because she'd believed in Roy, had offered him her heart on a platter that day. He'd thrown it back in her face ten years later ...

The biddies must not have noticed her stilling. They simply continued to steer her inside until she was seated at the table. A plate of towering hot *bhadias* appeared in front of her, along with a bowl of *satini cotomili*—the coriander, tomato, and chilli paste-like dip Mauritians ate with all their fried foods.

Auntie Ruby, the resident gossipmonger, lived up to her reputation. She was the first to mention Lara's failed marriage before they made it back into the house.

The sound of the grating voice droned on. Lara chose to ignore it before her mother gave her a slight slap on her shoulder.

"You wicked girl. You said you were coming on Monday, and here you are surprising us now."

A sigh escaped Lara. This was code for "*how could you have kept this a secret and made me lose face in front of everyone when I told them you are coming on Monday?*" Her mother lived for hearsay, and the general idea of "what will people say?" like most people in Mauritius. Whoever said the *ton* and its silly rules had died in the Regency era had not taken a trip to Mauritius in the year two-thousand-something.

"But my poor little girl," Auntie Ruby said in a cajoling tone, bringing nothing but danger to mind. "Of course, you wanted to come home earlier. Who wouldn't? Look what that awful, awful man has done to you."

Translation: *"And here's your cue to air out the laundry, from the sheets to the knickers, you silly goose."*

Other than saying they'd had irreconcilable differences—the same reason listed on their divorce papers—she'd kept mum about the whole business. Roy's family had had a field day dirtying her name, but she hadn't fallen to that level.

The same couldn't be said about her relatives, though.

"Our hearts went out to you, dearest girl, you who are like a daughter to us," Auntie Zubeida chimed in. "We never saw this coming. How could you not have told a soul you and that scoundrel were having problems? We would've spoken to him, set him right, showed him this is not how he is supposed to treat our daughter."

"Tsk-tsk. And what a beautiful couple you two made. How could anyone have thought you would break up?" Auntie Ruby added.

Beautiful. She huffed. She and Roy had been pretty faces. Young, sexy, rich, with prosperous careers in London and a flat right next to Tower Bridge. No wonder they'd been the envy of everyone here. Maybe said envy had cast the Evil Eye on the couple they'd made.

Lara shook her head. Silly of her to heed such notions as the Evil Eye. People made their own futures, and she and Roy had made their beds. She might not be at fault, but she'd had her hand in these irreconcilable differences. Maybe if she'd made an effort, if she'd changed. If Roy had given her time—

"Tell us what happened, Lara *beti*. You cannot keep shouldering that burden alone!"

Lara forced a small smile. As if they really cared about her, calling her the tender affectionate moniker for 'daughter' in Indian tongues.

"I'm doing fine, Auntie," she said. "That's what matters."

All three women watched her with narrowed eyes. No way was she doing away with the Inquisition. She should've thought of that before coming.

She should've ensconced herself in her newly-bought semi-detached in a gated community in Grand-Baie, the farthest northern tip of the island, content to while the days staring at the brilliant blue sea from the upstairs veranda.

"How can you be fine?" Auntie Ruby screeched. "We have been so preoccupied with your plight. How on earth are you going to get along? How will your parents bear all this? To think they still have an unmarried daughter on their hands. Now, they are ending up with two daughters. Oh, what fate God has dealt them."

Lara bit her lip to keep from answering back. Right, the *ton* must've been more solicitous than this. The aunts were simply nosing for gossip. But then, that's what Jane Austen wrote in her subtext, too. The concern was merely a polite way of enquiring about tattle in their society.

When the coppery taste of blood registered on her taste buds, she took deep, calming breaths to keep her temper in check. The urge to suck on a lit cigarette gnawed at her insides. While smoking was not the answer, one inhale would be terrific stress relief right now.

The relentless rambles picked up crescendo around her. Growing physically sick, she jumped to her feet.

"For God's sake, Auntie! We only got divorced. It's not the end of the world."

Silence blanketed the room. The women stared back at her with eyes like saucers and utter disbelief etched on their features.

At the transformation, laughter welled up in her throat. The three faces appeared so pinched that face-lifts couldn't have stretched their skins so well. She choked down the chuckles before they erupted since she'd merely throw oil on the fire if she burst out laughing.

However, her mother seemed to be choking on another emotion as her fair, wrinkle-free face went all red.

Lara squirmed around from one foot to the other as a sinking feeling settled in her gut. She had asked for trouble with her outburst. However much she'd told herself she wouldn't give in, she'd done it. Let her mouth run off. If there was one thing her mother disliked more than anything, it was being spoken back at, especially by her own children. When they'd been little, such behaviour had earned them a sharp backslap to the mouth.

"What are you giggling about?" her mother

asked as she stood and brought a hand onto her heart. "We are trying to make good lives for all of you. But our struggles and worries are not your concern, are they? How can they affect you so little? You just lost a husband."

Lara shut her eyes. Inwardly, she also closed her hearing. For goodness' sake, it had been three years ago! Roy had even moved on—getting remarried, his wife expecting their first already. His mother, the sick witch, had proudly shown Lara all this back when she had still lived in London, in the family house she'd won in the proceedings.

She'd lived on top of a gunpowder keg in the past few years with a fuse just waiting to be lit.

Her mother had just lit said fuse.

Lara'd had enough. Enough of the woman's outdated views about marriage and the Indo-Mauritian woman. How much longer did she have to stay to avoid being impolite?

She'd like to meet her sisters and her father, but her mother had her wanting to run for the hills before she'd seen anyone else.

"Mum, please," she said softly as she glanced at her parent. "Not now."

Her mother had the grace to appear contrite and shut up.

"Of course. You must still love him, and—"

"I don't love Roy anymore."

Not after he'd betrayed her. No, he hadn't cheated, but he'd done worse. He'd wanted a bride with Indian origins yet a modern take on life and career. She'd been all that ... until the day it became everything wrong with her.

The women blinked.

"Well, I say, if my husband had run off with another woman who doesn't even have the decency to be fairer-skinned than I am, then I, too, wouldn't love the dog anymore," Auntie Zubeida said.

And here we go again. It always had to come down to fairer looks in the Indian world.

Auntie Ruby gasped. "That home-wrecker is darker than Lara? How could he? Men really have no taste, do they?"

"Haven't you heard?" Auntie Zubeida asked in a hushed tone. "She's the niece of Mrs Morea, the woman with the shop across from Spar. Her sister's daughter. And we all know everyone from their family has skin as dark as burnt *halwa*."

"Shame on him. You poor thing, Lara. You must be seething. How could he have fallen so low?"

Anyone listening would think Lara had skin as white as snow. Of course, she didn't, having inherited her father's nut-brown, olive-toned colour. But she'd been considered a good prospect, thanks to her family name and their fortune. Exactly like in the *ton*, with the added bonus of her perfect scores at school and the subsequent formidable career outlook.

"He didn't cheat on me, Auntie. We separated, and that's when he met the girl he married."

When his mother paraded that girl in front of him. Once, she'd paraded Lara in front of him that same way.

Her mother huffed. "It's what he wants you to believe. How do you know he wasn't doing the dirty with her behind your back?"

She'd asked herself the same question, only to

slam into a brick wall. Never a masochist, she had dropped the query. What would it change if he'd cheated? He'd hurt her way more by attacking her very soul.

"You're not even a woman, Lara. You're a damn robot!"

Although those words had stuck, they hadn't been the worst slur.

"You stink like a chimney sweep!"

Considering Roy had lit her cigarettes in the past, those words had been bull's eye.

She'd quit her addiction the same day, cold turkey. To be fair, she'd become a robot, throwing everything into her job and working her way up from simple hotel event planner to event manager within a year.

"But now you're here, and we'll take care of you. Good thing I got your room readied in advance."

Lara winced as another realization crashed in. She had yet to inform her family she would not be staying with them. "About that ..."

"How have you crammed all your suitcases in such a tiny car?" her mother asked. "I've never known you to travel light. Your shoes alone come in a trunk."

The trunk would arrive by cargo along with most of her stuff from London.

How would she worm out of this revelation alive?

If only she hadn't been so eager to escape Roy and his pregnant missus. Yes, the sight had hurt because she *had* loved him. Not a mad, crazy passionate love, but she had agreed to commit her life to him. How much more steadfast could someone get?

She'd thought they were in this together.

How wrong she'd been. One day, he'd said he wanted a child, and it was high time she got her priorities sorted so they could have a family. No discussion, no compromise. A shock, considering he had always been easy-going and malleable. Headstrong, she'd said no, and that had been the end of them. He'd left their flat the same night to go to his parents' and never returned. A week later, a legal clerk had served her the divorce papers at work, in the hotel's busy lobby.

She wasn't cut out to be a mother. He'd known and appreciated that she'd never had any hang-ups about it. The sight of babies scared her the way other people had clown phobias. While she could get on with little kids, she'd seen herself as the slightly batty old hag auntie every family had. She didn't trust herself around babies, not even with the prospect of her own. Maternal instincts must've passed her genetic makeup, and she'd always gone after the things she was good at. Motherhood not being one of them, she'd scrapped it. Roy had also never said he wanted children. His career as a hot-shot actuary had been his sole focus.

So how could they have gone so wrong all of a sudden? She still had no clue.

A piercing wail sliced through the air. The roar of a kitten, thinking it was a fierce lion, came on the coattails of the screech, along with loud sobbing.

The kitchen door flew open, the sole of the little kid who'd kicked it still in the air. Lara gazed over the mini-man with the Mohawk before sliding to the side onto the pigtailed little girl with tear-stained cheeks. A stretch of dull grey stood behind the children. *Seriously, this couldn't be ...*

Her mother tore out of her seat to march towards the door. "*Bon dié o*, Neha. What have you done to this poor baby to get him to scream so?"

Lara blinked. What happened to beautiful Neha who looked like the muse for a serene Renaissance painting? This was not the woman she had met four years ago during her last visit!

Their mother deftly ripped the swaddled lump from Neha's arms. With a rocking motion, she got the baby to stop screaming.

"This is how you do it, Neha. I would believe you'd know by now."

Neha bit her lip before she nodded.

She still allows herself to be bossed around.

Her poor sister ... Maybe with her being here now, she could help? Provide a shield against their mother. She and Neha had never really been close, but maybe—

Hold on, was she imagining this, or did Neha just give her a false smile?

"Lara. We weren't expecting you before Monday," Neha said.

"It was a surprise," she replied.

Another forced smile. What was wrong with her?

A loud kick resounded from the kitchen door. Lara leaned to the side to catch sight of the little boy practising karate chops on the wood panel. "That's Kunal, innit?"

She turned to the still-sobbing girl. "And you

must be Suzanne. Look how you've grown."

Terrors, the lot of them. She shivered when she imagined this could've been her fate if she'd given in with Roy.

"And why is *she* crying now?" Auntie Ruby asked. "Anyone would think you terrorize the poor child, Neha."

Neha lowered her eyelids, and a faint blush crept over her pale cheeks. "I can't get her to stop," she said in a low voice. "Since her father left for Madagascar this morning, she hasn't let up."

Feeling sorry for her sister at the defeated tone, Lara had an idea. "Wait. I know exactly what will cheer her up."

She dashed out to the car, pulling out the large shopping bag full of gifts. And with her head stuck inside the potpourri-scented vehicle, she took a deep breath and gathered her thoughts. Hopefully, Neha's arrival with the children would be distracting enough for the aunties, and they'd leave her alone.

Fat chance, but she could hope. *Hope is what idiots live on*, as the French saying went.

With the handle in her grip, she traipsed back to the kitchen, rummaged into the bag and pulled out a wide, flat case which she handed to her niece. "This is for you."

The sobs stopped, and the little girl gingerly reached for the offering. She blinked once she closed her hands on the box, then let out a screech loud enough to burst an adult's eardrum.

"It's got all the Disney princesses, even Elsa and Anna! Thank you, Auntie Lara."

Lara had to smile at the unbridled enthusiasm.

At the corner of her vision, she saw the little boy stealthily approaching. Reaching into the bag again, she extracted a large carton of Avengers action figures. "And this is yours."

His eyes grew wide, and he jumped up and down. Lara didn't know when he wrapped his bony arms around her neck. In his eagerness, he nearly snapped her neck in two as he pulled her to his level. Then, just as abruptly, he released her and plopped himself down on the rug in front of the dining-room door, where Suzanne was tearing out the contents of her gift.

Finally, Lara handed a blanket wrapped in a package to her sister. "This for the baby."

"His name is Rishi," Neha said in a clipped voice.

"For Rishi, then."

Another squeal ripped through the kitchen as the back door slammed open. Lara glanced up only long enough to brace herself for the energy bolt heading straight for her.

"I can't believe you're here already!" her youngest sister, Diya, shouted as she hugged Lara and made them both hop like bunnies on steroids.

Lara reeled to get her balance back when the girl released her. How could such a petite woman who could pass for a life-size doll pack so much energy and zest into her tiny body? She became drained simply from listening to the teenager talk a mile a minute.

"Oooh, is this the goodie bag?" Diya asked. "Please, please, please tell me you got the game I asked you for. I wasn't sure you got my last email—"

"I got it," she said, simply to make the girl shut up.

"And the Body Shop basket? And the Boots hand cream? Oh, and tell me you made the Boxing Day sales and got me those killer sandals from NEXT—"

"Yes, yes, and yes." She pulled out the latest *Assassin's Creed* PC game case from the bag. "Here you go. The rest is coming by cargo."

"Oooh, you're the best!" Diya grabbed the thin plastic box before she hugged Lara again. "Okay, gotta be off. Everyone will kill to be in my shoes when they see I got this."

"And where do you think you are going, young lady?" their mother asked.

"Meeting with some friends at KFC. Be back for dinner, or ask Daddy to pick me up when he gets home from work. Oooh, look what Suzanne got. No, sweetie, wait. That's not how you apply blusher."

Neha gasped. "You got her makeup?"

"It's kid-friendly. I double-checked after the salesgirl at the Disney shop assured me it was safe."

"She's eight years old. Much too young for all this."

"Oh, don't be such a ninny, Neha. I started wearing makeup when I was her age, and I'm none the worse for wear, am I?" Diya asked with a roll of her dark eyes.

"That's what has me worried," Neha said under her breath, but loud enough for Lara to hear. "And I can't believe you got Kunal dolls."

"They're action figures, sis," Diya said as she breezed past them to the door. "Take a chill pill, will you? Tata, ye all!"

The quiet in Diya's wake felt strangely anticlimactic as if all the air in the room had been sucked out. Neha kept her reproachful glare on Lara, who, to escape the malevolent scrutiny—after all, what was her sister's problem?—turned towards their mother and the aunties.

Bad move.

"We better get you settled. Not yet one hour since your return, and you three are already back to bickering like children."

"We aren't bickering—" both Lara and Neha said simultaneously.

"Are, too," their mother said with finality in her tone. "Now, go get your suitcases, and let's get you upstairs, Lara."

Here it is. The moment of truth.

"About that," she said again. "I won't be staying, Mum."

"I beg your pardon?"

"My stuff's at my place in Grand-Baie. Didn't I tell you? I bought a house there."

She kept her voice nonchalant and averted her eyes from her mother's unnerving stare.

The numb shock reverberating in the still kitchen told her she had another think coming. The silence lasted, but unfortunately, was short-lived.

"You mean you're going to be living alone?" her mother asked in a burst of righteous indignation. "But it is just not done. Absolutely not proper. What will people say? You are a single woman, Lara. It is not right for you to stay alone. And you've still got us, your family. People will say we don't want you at our place, that we're ashamed of your divorce, which couldn't be further from the truth. There'll be so much talk. It'll undermine all your future prospects."

The voice seemed to carry concern and care, but all she heard were recriminations and barely-concealed disbelief. Nothing more than an attempt by her mother to save face because, all her life, her mother had always made appearances and conventions come first. There was no concern for her there, for the daughter she and the aunties claimed to love and support.

Everything was about them, and them alone. Exactly like Roy had done with her. Nobody cared about her.

Her mother opened her mouth again.

Lara sighed. She didn't want another fight. Thinking of Roy always made her feel low, and no one could argue with Gayatri Hemant when feeling low, for she'd run the person down like a bulldozer. Nonetheless, steely resolve filled her. She'd come here for a purpose, a job. Anything else was negotiable.

She wasn't putting up with her parents again. She'd left home at nineteen and wouldn't return at thirty-two. After thirteen years of living on her own, she wouldn't give her mother the pleasure of monitoring her movement with detention-centre rigour. Living under the family roof would mean just that.

And, she could win this with logic. Hadn't she thought the pitch out? She took a deep breath. "Mum, I'm a Managing Director now."

The older woman brightened, pride glowing on her face. Lara gained confidence.

"As such, I need to be present and available at very short notice."

Her mother slowly nodded.

"I need to be close to work. This place is more than an hour away from the centre. I cannot be available and be so far, right?"

Her mother continued nodding.

"So it's better if I live at this new house in Grand-Baie."

With a sudden jerk that made her worry about the possibility of whiplash, her mother stopped nodding. The dark, almost black, gaze—made more striking by the kohl liner contrasting with perfectly smooth, milky skin—stared Lara straight in the eye.

"You'll be living alone, and that's not done."

Reproach dripped from the words.

She sighed to conceal a snort. She was losing the calm and the battle. Worse, she didn't want to hold on to patience any longer. She wanted out ASAP. For goodness' sake, she would have scores of people working under her authority. Surely, she could reason with her mother.

Couldn't she?

"Mother, it's my final word. I'm going to live there, whether you like it or not. You forget I lived alone in England."

"Yes, but that was the Western world. This is just not done here. Also, you're all alone. Single."

The aunties nodded and echoed the sentiment. Even Neha looked at her with concerned eyes.

If she hadn't been on the brink of a mental

breakdown when her husband had left her, then today, the urge to crash would have caught up with her. How would she survive here?

By staying as far away from her society-proper family as much as possible. By finding another temporary addiction to help cope with them. Her new boss was gonna love her.

Though this was Mauritius, where one could travel from one tip to another in two hours. She'd never be far enough, truth be told.

All for the job, she told herself. She deserved this.

She'd committed her life to Mauritius but had forgotten to check her sanity when she'd crossed into this backward society. A mistake she hoped to never make again, but from here on, she was doomed.

Highway to Hell, we meet again.

Chapter Two

Eric Marivaux closed his eyes and let the back of his head touch the fluffy cushion on the sofa on his family home's veranda. Crickets chirped in the garden, the sound coming through on a gentle breeze belying the oppressive island summer. On the hillsides of Floreal, an affluent neighbourhood next to Curepipe, summer was definitely the best season, with none of the scorching heat and humidity of the coastal areas. Where he lived, in the north, the air-conditioner stayed on constantly.

This felt like bliss, and he sighed. If he let himself go, he could easily fall asleep and wake up with a crick in his neck. Those sofas were decorative more than functional.

He didn't have to ponder long over this—a backhand slap landed on his shoulder. The cushion next to him seemed to groan with an exaggerated huff when someone plopped on it.

He forced an eye open, smiling when he saw his younger sister, Angélique. She always made him smile, but tonight, even more so as she positively glowed with happiness.

"It's your fault," he grumbled. "You just

couldn't wait, could you?"

She back-slapped him again. "Cut it out, Eric. Do you know how long I've been sitting on this?"

"Three weeks. That's how long I've been in South Africa. It can't be more than that."

"*Ayo*, you're no fun! *Maman* was adamant we had to wait for you to be here before I could bring Patrice home."

He tore both eyes open to stare at the young man and his father sitting at the patio table and sharing a glass of Perrier. Good choice—the guy would be driving back to his home in Bel-Ombre, the farthest southern tip of the island, later tonight.

"Thanks for the consideration, Ange," he quipped. "You were ready to bring him home with me out of the country."

She poked her tongue out at him. "At least that way, you wouldn't have been able to find fault with him."

He winced—he had been a bit uncompromising regarding his baby sister's boyfriends. She'd never brought one home until today, which made him scrutinise the man who had won his sibling's heart. Big and brawny, Patrice Laroche looked like the rugby front-row prop he was for the national team. The baby face belied the savage air, though. Eric hoped the man had the mental fortitude of a full-back, as well, because he'd need it to deal with wilful Angélique.

"Seriously, Ange. A deer breeder?" he jest.

She poked him with an elbow in his ribs. "He's not a deer breeder, silly. His family owns the biggest *chassé* on the island, which happens to have the biggest deer population of the whole place."

He laughed as he pulled her to him. "I know. I was just having fun at your expense."

"Hmmph," she snorted into his side.

"You're happy?" he whispered close to her ear.

She nodded. "Yes."

"Then that's all that matters."

His sister pulled away to stare at him with big grey, wide-open eyes. "You mean that?"

He ruffled her dark hair, which prompted her to evade his touch. "Of course I do. He makes you glow, *ma puce*. As long as he keeps doing that, he's okay in my books."

She threw her arms around him to hug him, then got up and left to go back to the table, where she plopped down on Patrice's lap. The poor guy seemed to lose his breath.

Eric smothered a laugh and relaxed against the sofa again, closing his eyes. However, two seconds later, the cushion dipped next to him, in a more dignified manner this time.

He opened his eyes to find an older version of brunette Angélique sitting next to him.

"So that's why you couldn't have me miss dinner tonight, even though I just got home after a twelve-hour delayed flight," he told his mother.

She smiled, threading his arm with hers and resting her head against the back of the sofa. "She has been driving us crazy, you would not believe."

"I can imagine." He winced.

"So, what do you think?"

He raised an eyebrow. "What do I think? I thought I didn't have a say in these things, seeing how the elders always weighed in on those matters."

"Oh, you're insufferable," she said with a slight slap to his shoulder. "I mean it, Eric."

He sighed. "Can you ask me that when I'm not jet-lagged and carrying the weight of three weeks of intensive training and surgery on me?"

She rubbed his shoulder. "I'm sorry, *poussin*. Jet lag doesn't bother you usually."

He groaned at the endearment. Seriously, being called 'baby chicken' stopped being cute after he turned thirteen, over a good twenty years ago.

"But this was too good an opportunity to miss," she continued. "To learn besides one of the best paediatric surgeons in the world. I knew you'd be perfect for it."

A niggling doubt insinuated itself in his mind, and he frowned as he sat straighter. He'd always wondered how he had gotten the traineeship. True, he was one of the few paediatricians on the island who also specialised in paediatric surgery, but still ...

"Did you have anything to do with me getting that placement?" he asked.

His mother rolled her eyes. "Of course not. Your credentials spoke for themselves."

But how had said credentials gotten in front of Dr Bekker's eyes? He tried to put two and two together.

"Hold on. You are good friends with Pastor Van Ryk, no?"

She shrugged. "So?"

"And he also happens to be good friends with Dr Bekker."

This was starting to look more and more like a

setup. He hated setups.

His mother huffed. "What do you want me to say? Yes, Pastor Van Ryk enquired if you were a paediatric surgeon, to which I replied yes. What wrong was there in that?"

Nothing per se, and if there had been, she wouldn't see it as such, either. His mother lived by her very own code of conduct.

But he had to admit the traineeship had improved his position as an authority in paediatric surgery on the island and in the Indian Ocean region. Was he looking a gift horse in the mouth here? Things tended to have a price tag with his mother involved, one he might not be willing to pay.

"Look at her, Eric."

He turned towards the table, where Angélique had thrown her head back in laughter.

"She's happy," he said softly.

His mother nodded. "And such a good match, too. I really couldn't believe it. The Laroche family is one of the oldest blood on the island."

He tightened his jaw. She'd always paid heed to these notions about family lines, pedigree and whatnot. It had driven him crazy in his youth. Still did, in fact.

If she hadn't been so inclined, would he have considered—

No, he couldn't think of it, of her. He'd vowed to stop seeing her everywhere.

Sometimes, it happened, slipping under his guard, like this morning at the airport. There'd been the tell-tale prickle along his nape, and he'd glanced around. So many brunettes around Customs and

Baggage Claim, but the only young woman with straight jet-black hair had been Chinese.

Not Lara Hemant.

"The official engagement party will be in two weeks," his mother continued. "Your grandmother is coming from France."

He turned back to her. "Seems you've been busy during my absence."

"Your sister sprang this on us. Believe me, to make a half-good engagement party, you need to get started months in advance. *Dieu merci*, Patrice's father has offered us the lodge at their Bel-Ombre *chassé* as the venue. I don't know how we would've gotten a decent club or hotel booked on such short notice."

Ange and Patrice should elope. Seriously. If he ever tied the knot one day, that's what he would do.

That's what he'd thought to do with Lara. They would've flown to Vegas, why not, or even just gotten married on the neighbouring Reunion Island, where his French passport made him a national. Anything to get away from stifling family stuff.

But things hadn't worked out.

"And speaking of your grandmother, Eric." She paused, taking a breath. "Sophie might be coming with her."

A nerve ticked and hurt his cheek as he clenched his jaw. He didn't want to hear that name, hadn't wanted to since he'd left her begging and crying back at Château Armont, his mother's family estate in France. Sophie de Maivière was the goddaughter of the matriarch of the aristocratic Armont clan. Of course, she'd worm her way in.

"She's coming with husband number what? Three now?" he asked through gritted teeth.

"Don't be so harsh, Eric. You know her husband died last month."

Her third husband. The Italian count had been so old, his dentures always fell into his soup bowl at formal meals.

"You two were good together," his mother added in a light tone.

Sophie had thought so, and she had made his family believe it. She was a simpering fraud who'd used him as a conduit into the prestigious Armont family through his grandmother's favour.

She'd never turned his heart because the organ had belonged to Lara. But she'd sucked his time, and he'd lost a year in her stifling clutches, consequently losing Lara.

The hurt squeezed his chest, and he tightened his fist on the fluffy fur ruffle on one of the decorative cushions.

"*Maman*, please. Don't talk about Sophie to me," he said as he stood. "If she comes to Ange's engagement party, you can count me off the guest list."

She grabbed his hand and stood, too.

"I'm sorry. It's a sore spot. I shouldn't have." She paused and squeezed his hand. "I just want you to be happy."

He glanced at his sister and her fiancé, then turned to his parent. "Correction, you want to see me settled down, especially now that your youngest child is tying the knot, and this makes it even more obvious that the eldest is still entirely unattached."

She sighed. "Eric, *mon chéri*. You're thirty-three. Isn't it time you settled down, though?"

No, it wasn't. Not yet. And it wouldn't be the right time until he could settle down with the one and only woman he'd loved.

Lara.

The one that got away.

But she was happily married in London, and here he was, thousands of kilometres away, still pining for her. He couldn't fault her for what she'd done. He was the one who hadn't given proof of life for close to a year after leaving for France.

Maybe seeing his sister so happy with a lovesick idiot Patrice brought home Eric's loss more viscerally. Was a little bit of such happiness in his life so out of reach?

He'd never have a whole heart—the ship had sailed, but he could have something …

For the first time in fourteen years, he wilfully pushed the thought of Lara Hemant—now Reddy—aside and turned to his mother.

"Okay," he said. "I'll think about it."

Chapter Three

Sometimes, you have to hit rock bottom before climbing back up.

True in Lara's case.

She'd hit the abyss floor more than once recently, but the mini-breakdown one week after her arrival had helped her spring back into top shape. True to form, her mother had strong-armed her into attending a family wedding. That day, Lara had been bulldozed by her parent, had received a very cold shoulder from Neha when she'd asked for help to tie a sari—because Western clothing was just not 'done' at family gatherings—all before walking into the lion's den.

Well, make that whole pride of lions, in an arena similar to the Coliseum. Her divorce had still been the talk of the town, and everyone, from the aunties she'd never met to the cousins she didn't know existed, had taken their turn to make her feel like a pile of poop.

Running home hadn't been an option so she'd borne it all, and she'd been sorely tempted to hand in her resignation letter and book the first flight out of this viper's nest as soon as she'd stepped foot home.

Reason had finally prevailed, after a pint of

Haagen-Dasz had disappeared into her stomach and the condensation had ruined Neha's prized silk sari. She'd come to work the next morning and had thanked the heavens when Markus Hendrickson, the head honcho, had officially handed her the reins to the conference center that morning.

Since then, work piled up on her. For the first time, she didn't bemoan her boss acting like a borderline slave driver because she needed the exertion to forget about the other aspects of her life. The packed schedule also gave her a perfect excuse to avoid going to her parents' place. In the past three weeks, she'd deftly fielded calls from her mother, avoiding numerous invitations for lunch or dinner.

One month down—so many more to go.

The hectic career made time fly. Perhaps she could sail through her existence here.

Lara tore her eyes from yet another incomprehensible report and reclined in her chair. Their first conference loomed ahead, less than a fortnight away. What she'd handled in England was nothing compared to her new responsibilities. A handful of corporate portfolios, at best, there while here, the enormity of pulling off a weeklong conference rested solely on her capacity and direction. She, and the centre, would be toast if she failed at this baptism by fire.

A loud knock resounded in the office. *Please let it not be another manager needing a meeting with me.* She usually loved being the social butterfly at work, but her position in the hierarchy worked against her. She sighed. They saw her as a foreigner, and worse, since she was of Mauritian origins, she should've been one of them … but she wasn't. She was 'other', even more so than their fully expat boss.

Everyone dealt with her with formal reserve, the legendary Mauritian welcome and good-naturedness there, but again, slightly held back. She tried to befriend them and find out more about their personal lives to strike a rapport. Apart from her personal assistant, she wanted to believe she was eroding their aloof manner chip by chip, but she'd be kidding herself. She needed a popularity coup to end up on the staff's good books.

Not right now. Not with her first conference looming like a behemoth about to crash into her and the centre.

Stop the defeatist thoughts!

Seconds later, Doris Li, her PA—a middle-aged Mauritian woman of Chinese origin—strolled in with a steaming black mug in her right hand.

"Here's your coffee, and there are four messages, all from your mother," Doris said.

At the mention of her mother, weariness gripped her, and all the energy drained from her body. Despair overwhelmed her, sapping her muscle control, and her head fell onto the desk's surface.

A soft bump resounded when her forehead hit the cold glass. As heat formed on her skin where it lay against the cool surface, a thought crossed her mind. *The glass is very solid.* She'd already bumped her head at least a dozen times on it through the past month. Each time because of her mother.

She lifted her head to stare into Doris' doughy face. Lara never failed to be amazed how the other woman could appear so soft and serene all the time.

But that was a tricky assumption, she'd realized after less than an hour in the woman's presence. Doris was as tough and unyielding as she looked gentle and precisely the right person to handle Lara's mother.

Lara was lucky to have such a hardworking force of nature as her second in command. She straightened and rubbed the sore spot on her forehead with her left hand. With the other, she grabbed and took a sip of the scalding hot brew.

"What does she want now?" she asked as she put the heavy porcelain mug down.

"Oh, the usual." Doris shrugged. "For you to call her back ASAP as it's urgent."

"God, she's gonna run me dead." She moaned with a shake of her head. "But forget it. Just please continue to stave her off for me. Oh, by the way, has your daughter reached Melbourne safely?"

"Yes. She got there right in time for the new semester."

Her cell phone rang, interrupting their chat. When Lara saw the caller ID, she let her head drop onto the desk again in despair.

Does she ever let up?

Puffing a breath, she swiped the screen and brought the phone to her ear without bothering to lift her neck from its tricky angle. She didn't know if she'd be able to, anyway.

"Hey, Mum." She tried to keep her voice flat. Hopefully, her mother would take the hint and not linger for hours.

"Hello, darling." The shrill voice almost sang. "That awful secretary of yours keeps saying you're in meetings every time I call."

The effervescence tone turned to a whine during the diatribe, eradicating her patience.

"It's because I *am* in meetings all the time, Mother. It's my job."

"Oh, never mind. You'll never guess. Kamini's just had a baby, and it's a boy," her mother said in an excited rush. "She had an emergency C-section when her labour just wouldn't progress this morning after the whole night she spent at the clinic. She's done good, that girl. A male heir for her first born."

What on Earth was her mother talking about?

"Kamini? Isn't she the one who just got married? She sure didn't look ready to pop at the wedding."

Wrong thing to say, she realised too late. Her mother did *not* have a sense of humour.

"Oh, Lara, don't be silly. How dare you say something so shameful? Pregnant on her wedding day." Gayatri Hemant huffed. "Anyway, I'm not talking of that Kamini. I'm talking of the *other* Kamini, Lalita's daughter."

There was only one Lalita in their family, and she'd met the woman's son at the wedding. Vishal, as he was called. The only person who hadn't thrown a stone at her. He'd reminded her of an eager puppy, but she'd clung to his kindness like a life raft that evening.

"Your father is busy as always, and visiting hours at the clinic start at three o'clock. I know you're finishing at one o'clock today since it's Saturday, so you can come pick me up and take me to visit her."

Lara groaned and tried her best to keep her mother from hearing it. "Mum, the poor girl's just had a baby. She must be tired. Let her rest. You'll go see her tomorrow."

She winced and held the phone at a distance from her ear with the ensuing outburst.

"But that is just not proper. What will Lalita say? That I'm not concerned at all about her first grandchild. No, we have to go today."

Lara closed her eyes. She didn't trust herself to reply and took deep, calming breaths to steady her nerves. But air wasn't what she needed. She craved a cigarette. Bad. If things remained constant, she'd never be rid of the debilitating urge as long as she let her mother get to her.

"Lara, are you still there? Never mind, I'll wait for you this afternoon. Don't be late."

The beeping of the cut call resounded in her ear, and she itched to slam the phone down to ease some of the pent-up frustration gathering in stormy spirals inside her. But she kept herself in check. It wouldn't do for the Managing Director to be caught vandalising her own office. Her mother wasn't worth that kind of career self-destruction.

As she took in the wide expanse of her office, or her domain, as she called it, the calm refused to come.

"Damn," she said with a sigh. The desire for a burning drag on a cigarette welled up, making her wish she'd broken something. At least then, some of the fury would've vented off and not flared through her like fire attacked defenceless paper.

I need a smoke. No way around this certainty. One wouldn't hurt, right?

However, to keep herself in check, she went into the adjoining bathroom, locking the door behind her. There, in the privacy of the white-marbled loo, she removed her shoes and kicked the punching bag she'd stealthily installed in the middle of the cold space.

Blessed relief filled her as her shins took the brunt of the onslaughts, and dull pain radiated in her bones. As she'd found out, work plus kickboxing had proven to be the best antidote against cigarette cravings and encounters with her mother lately.

***

From the spot where she stood next to her car in the clinic parking lot, Lara was awed by the grandeur of the imposing structure of solid concrete.

Once inside, however, she had to admit the cosy interior made one forget that medicine and life-and-death decisions occurred within the premises. The whole place pulled off a light green and yellow palette, with touches of contrasting colour added by the many painting replicas hung on the walls. Overstuffed and comfortable-looking furniture made up strategic corners, with glossy marble underfoot. On the whole, the tasteful, understated elegance of the place could pass for a hotel.

She could not hope to remain in the car waiting for her mum's return, so she cut her losses and put up no fight to follow her parent around the rambling corridors. Her mother barged into the halls of the maternity ward as if she owned the place while Lara trudged behind. At the nurses' station, they learned Kamini's room number, and after a short walk down a narrow hallway, they found the location. The door lay wide open, and relatives overflowed from there.

Amidst all the bodies and faces, she caught a glimpse of the new mother, whom her mum embraced with exuberance. Kamini's weary gaze travelled around, meeting with Lara's. Lara nodded at this cousin she didn't recall ever meeting. Yet, the washed-out girl returned a genuine, albeit faint, smile.

Sympathy overwhelmed her heart. The poor creature seemed absolutely knackered as if she wanted nothing but to sleep. Kamini probably longed for the support of her husband, who'd been relegated to a corner. And she could've done without her mother and mother-in-law fussing and clucking like geese on crack around her.

A fresh wave of empathy gripped Lara. She could so easily relate to her cousin. Both of them were prisoners of their society and its way of life.

She approached the bed and reached out to clasp the hand to which an I.V. line was attached. The girl, who couldn't be a day older than twenty, returned the gesture with a squeeze, and a bond formed between them. For how long, she didn't know. But at that moment, it existed, and both women shared it with a touch.

A fresh wave of relatives arrived, making her itch to leave the stuffy room. Disgust and revulsion filled her like a rush of burning bile up her throat when she had to fight her way out of the maze of people. Nausea kicked in, her head going light. The air conditioning was barely adequate with so many people around. Despite the lingering tinge of disinfectant and the sickly smell of hospitals, she was grateful for the cleaner air in the corridor outside.

Every step she took away from the room toned down her feelings of revolt. Yet, she couldn't keep the injustice and the insensitivity out of her head. How could all these people be so obtuse and narrow-minded? Didn't they see their presence was awkward at such a time and in such a cramped space?

Lost in her thoughts, she rounded a corner of the hall, slamming into someone's side. Disoriented and dizzy with confusion at the jolting oomph of impact against a solid form, she stumbled, losing control of her legs. The walls moved up rapidly, but a strong pair of hands grabbed her arms before the back of her head hit the floor.

"*Bon sang, mademoiselle! Où courez-vous comme ça?*" a rich, deep masculine voice asked in the sharp yet lilting accent of white French-Mauritian natives.

Where are you running to, miss? she figured out from her rusty French.

Away from you. Something inside her acknowledged the danger before she could process his words. She knew that voice. Her head spun again, yet her mind remained so very alert.

Could it be …? No, it couldn't.

Her brain had to be playing tricks on her. The sound with its particular accent belonged to the very distant past. How was she hearing it at this moment? Had she fainted?

That's it. She wasn't conscious, and since she'd probably worked herself to exhaustion, the condition had triggered all sorts of switches in her muddled consciousness.

The image of the man from the airport burned

itself into her mind, and she gasped. *No!*

"Is everything okay?" The chuckle had gone from the tone, replaced by worry.

Solid strength still held her ribcage, the back of the hands warm and smooth where they touched her arms. Their heat went to her head, churning all coherent thought into a jumble.

Your eyes won't betray you. They'll see the truth.

She risked a glance up beneath her lashes. She had to be certain. To know if this was all a trick of her imagination ...

A tall form with broad shoulders outlined in a short-sleeved shirt filled Lara's vision. The lapels of the opened collar framed a strong jaw, and a wide mouth was set in a worried line above a square chin. A fine, straight nose sat above those sensual lips.

She had to gulp back the ominous lump wedged in her throat. Her heart hammered in her chest, and her mouth went dry. Her suspicions looked dangerously close to being confirmed, and the nagging notion played havoc with her thoughts. She closed her eyes.

When she opened them, she found herself staring into a pair of blue irises. A blinding flash went through her head, plunging her heart to her knees. She'd recognize those irises anywhere. Deep-set, bright, and laughing eyes the colour of the deepest ocean. The heavy, golden locks brushing his forehead accentuated the frown knitting his eyebrows.

Locks that had somehow broken free from the thick, brushed-back hair. She itched to sweep them back, to run the tips of her fingers along his smooth skin, like she used to in the past, onto the soft buzz of hair he used to keep so short.

Her mind went into a crazy spin, and all her senses reeled as everything became a vivid kaleidoscope of colours. Her stomach heaved, and her knees went weak as her body became limp.

But the man's firm grip was still on her, and he kept her steady on her feet.

"Are you okay? I think you better sit down here," he said.

The voice made its way into her perception, and she couldn't suppress the relief that flooded her. His voice had always had such power over her.

He still hasn't recognised me.

She'd changed a lot in the past decade, and with her head still bent forward, her hair shielded her face. She wanted to escape. To close her eyes and then open them to find it had all been a dream. Or a nightmare.

But this was real, and how long could she remain incognito? Lara swallowed with difficulty. Of all the people from her past, Fate had had to choose that precise person to shove along her path.

She allowed him to lead her to a sofa. Her saviour lowered her into her seat with extreme care and gentleness and sat next to her, turning to her. The smell of his aftershave—fresh, spicy, and very elusive—filled her nostrils and made its way into her foggy mind.

He still smells the same. Like a cool sea breeze wafting through the unique musk of a man's warm skin.

Lara took a deep breath and gathered her courage. There'd always been a risk of coming across him on the island. She'd preferred to hide from the probability, but she couldn't run anymore.

So, she lifted her head.

A frown marred the broad forehead. As devastatingly handsome as ever. Or maybe, even more than ever. His features were arresting, masculine, adult. No longer those of a teenager.

Her mouth went dry again, and her heart beat faster when the straight line of his lips broke into a large smile a few seconds later. His eyes lit up and widened.

"I'll be damned! Lara? Is it really you?" he asked, switching effortlessly to English.

She forced a smile and took a deep breath. "Hello, Eric. How are you?"

She couldn't have sounded more like a cold, distant bitch if she'd tried.

He stared at her for long seconds. Would he brush her off, get up, and leave her stranded again? After her stilted greeting, he'd be well within his rights to do so.

"Well, isn't this a surprise," he said.

His low tone and the lack of sarcasm or irony comforted her. He wasn't angry, thank goodness.

"Yes, it is," she replied before biting her tongue.

"I'm good. How about you? It's been a long time ..."

The way he paused, she didn't dare peer up to witness the emotion playing on his face in those too-beautiful eyes.

Yes, it has been. She didn't say the words, knowing they'd open a can of worms best left untouched. No point in rehashing the past. They were where they were. Since she couldn't stand up and run away, she should switch topics.

"What are you doing here?" *When you're supposed to be in France, married, and already a father.*

Before he could respond, a nurse approached them. "Excuse me, Doctor Marivaux. There's a call for you."

"Thank you. I'll be right there." He nodded at the woman before turning his attention to her again.

The exchange made its way into her hazy mind. "You became a doctor, after all."

He smiled in reply. His mouth had retained the easy manner of breaking into a sunny smile.

Her insides melted to jelly as she allowed her gaze to travel over him, to notice the casual ease that had replaced the stiffness in his body.

Dangerous. Comfortable territory with him would mean her doom.

"I'm a paediatrician."

"Oh."

The words didn't pierce through the internal bashing she subjected herself. She simply couldn't allow Eric Marivaux to see how his actions fourteen years earlier had completely altered her life. That a part of her still cared for him. He'd been her first love, after all.

He smiled again, and amusement danced in his eyes. The unconcealed joy on his face wrapped her in a trance. Could he be happy to see her?

Damn idiot—he's married!

She threw a glance at his left hand. No ring. But something glinted on his right, and her heart sank at the sight of the thick silver band on the third finger.

She couldn't kid herself because, sometimes, European men wore their wedding bands on their right hands.

"Are you sure you're okay?" he asked.

"Huh?"

She blinked out of her stunned state. Eric was not for her. He'd never been and never would be. She wanted to shake herself out of her crestfallen spirits, but couldn't, which infuriated her.

"Back there," he said with a nod. "You didn't seem too well. Is something wrong?"

"Oh, that." What could she tell him? That she'd been bowled over by seeing him again? "Heatstroke, nothing worse."

A warm blush spread into her cheeks, and she averted her face from his view. Out of the corner of her eye, she noticed her mother pacing the corridor's far end. Now *that* would be trouble.

She shot to her feet in a lightning-quick move, and her head spun. She swayed, and Eric caught her with his arm on her waist.

"Lara, what's wrong?" His tone was low, concern heavy in the words.

Yet, what registered more in her desperate, love-starved brain was his touch on her back, on the flimsy silk blouse. Tingles shot up her skin from the point of contact, and heat spread throughout her muscles in the surrounding area.

She made the mistake of glancing up then. His head was a few inches from hers. If he lowered it any more, he could kiss her.

She parted her lips, a puff of hot air escaping her mouth. She couldn't miss how his eyes darkened, and he tensed his strong jaw. How they must appear to the world, like a couple in a sensual embrace.

And how far from the truth such an assumption would be. Nevertheless, Lara would be in trouble if her mother saw them like this. She rolled her shoulders and tried to shrug away his touch.

Except he wouldn't let her. He tugged her closer, and she had half a mind to offer no resistance so she'd land against his solid chest. Would it feel as hard as it looked?

Get a grip on yourself! Eric dumped you.

She averted her face once more.

"I'm fine, Eric. It's just, uh, the sun and the heat. You know how bad it gets here in summer, even in Curepipe ..."

Humiliation flooded her as soon as the words blurted out of her mouth. She had to get away, by any means. Still, the burn of shame trickled inside her at her idiocy. What was she chiding herself for? Her stupid reply, or her sillier reaction to him?

She pulled out of his arms when he loosened his grip. Head down, hair shielding her face, she vowed not to look at him again if that's what it took to hang on to what little remained of her sanity.

"I'm sorry, Eric. I have to go. But it's been nice to see you."

Better leave it at this. She didn't intend to meet him again.

"It's been nice to see you too, Lara. You ... You're on vacation here?"

Better not let him know she was here for good.

"Something like that," she mumbled.

He nodded. "Take care, okay?"

She'd already taken a step away from him when something in his voice stopped her. Was it regret? Sadness?

Probably wishful thinking on her part, she reasoned, dismissing the notion. Why would Eric be sad when he was the one who'd done the leaving all those years before?

She gave him a small smile. "I will. You take care, too."

"Bye, Lara."

"Bye, Eric," she added softly.

She hadn't been able to resist saying his name aloud again.

Lara allowed her still-yearning-for-Eric gaze to linger on him for a second longer before turning on her heel and walking away. He moved, too. She sensed his movement even though he wasn't in her eyesight, that tiny prickle niggling at the back of her neck.

Exactly like in the past. And exactly like at the airport. She couldn't kid herself anymore—it had been him that day …

She reached her mother right before the older woman turned the corner to the spot where Eric's and her paths had collided, glad her mum hadn't noticed him. Or his touching her. God knew how many questions would arise then. She would never live it down. Eric was not an Indian man. He was white—his status thus way above what anyone from her family could aspire to. Akin to breaking into the aristocracy, or a commoner snagging a prince. She was no Kate Middleton or Crown Princess Mary of Denmark.Things like that happened to one girl in a billion every decade. She wasn't so lucky.

Hadn't that been one of the reasons she'd never allowed herself to dream of a future with him back in the day because she'd known already 'they' could never exist? Kids got away with it. Adults? A whole other kettle of fish she hadn't been prepared to touch.

For once, she welcomed her mother's incessant babbling. Gayatri Hemant, as usual, launched into an endless flow of talking as soon as she had a pair of ears in range. The senseless ramble took Lara's focus away from fruitless memories.

"What a snob Lalita is. I cannot believe it. This clinic charges a fortune, and she had to have her daughter admitted into this very one. She doesn't know what to do to show off her money."

Pointless to remind her mother how Neha had given birth to all three of her children in the same clinic. It hadn't been showing off then but affording the best care.

"Now, Vishal. What a pleasant young man. Such a fair complexion, so handsome. And I also heard he makes a lot of money. He's got a very good job, apparently ..."

Half an hour later, she was glad to be rid of her mother when she dropped her off at the family house. Not feeling fit enough to bear her parent's ramblings for longer, she declined the invitation to stay for dinner.

Instead, she burned the asphalt as she sped towards Grand-Baie. She craved the quiet and peace of her own home to be able to force a semblance of order and resignation into her muddled brain.

Not an easy task since she had the meeting with Eric on her mind.

Eric, the man she had loved like no other.

***

Eric stood in his private practice office, staring out of the window at nothing. The Grand-Baie summer sun beat down on the pane and licked at his skin, burning him, but he paid the physical sensations no heed. All his focus lay on his memories, especially his earlier encounter with Lara.

How did meeting her again make him feel? He didn't know, and this uncertainty rattled him. A part of him didn't dare browse his feelings.

He'd made such great progress only a week earlier, when he'd gone on a date with Annabelle de Castelban. At his sister's engagement party, his mother had invited every eligible young woman in their circle, it had seemed, and there'd been a spark with the pretty brunette. A lot of people brushed her off, her reputation as a wild party animal during her university days still sticking to her years later, but he'd seen something in her smile. Guileless. Not someone trying to stick to him to finagle a connection to the illustrious Marivaux and Armont names.

And now, Lara had landed in his life again, after fourteen years ... Was Fate really such a cruel bitch?

He didn't want her back. Not in his proximity, not in the same place, not on the same soil. The more distance between them, the better. He'd had to work so hard to finally accept such a reality, so why had the universe chosen that moment to put her back onto his path?

He ran a hand in his hair, letting his fingers work at untangling the knots. He should cut the long locks, but damn if he found the time.

Why now? He'd just started to get over the idea none of his relationships would work out because she was the only woman he'd ever loved. If he hoped to settle down someday, he'd do so for convenience and companionship, but never for love. Annabelle had let on she wasn't looking for roses and romance, either. They would be perfect together.

But just one face-to-face meeting with Lara and his certitude spun away like a crazy top.

No, she shouldn't be here. He'd wanted to run when he'd recognized her earlier. Run as fast as his legs could carry him. Run from the hurt and anger that inevitably crept into his whole being and consumed him completely whenever he thought of her.

Yet, he hadn't been able to resist. One glance at her, and he'd been a goner. Again. So, he'd given in, not fighting the joy of being around her again. He'd revelled in those short but sweet moments they'd shared. She'd felt so good in his arms.

He sighed and ran his hand over his face again in a gesture fraught with weariness and frustration. Lara. He'd stumbled aback when he recognized her. She'd changed in the past decade and a half since the last time he'd seen her.

She was a woman and not a skinny eighteen-year-old anymore, though she still boasted a very slim figure. The long hair had also tricked him. The straight brown locks with the chestnut highlights framed the sides of her face now and covered her forehead in a thick fringe. In the past, she drew it back into a high ponytail that bounced with every step. He'd loved to tug on her long hair, which would annoy her so much, and when she'd frown and narrow her gaze at him, he would swoop in and steal a kiss. After which, she would smile. Reluctantly, but she'd smile, nevertheless.

Why was she back? He had returned to Mauritius because she wouldn't be there. Her life was in London. What was she doing here? Though she had said she was on vacation.

He closed his eyes and let his head touch the surface of the window. The glass was hot against his forehead. As drained as he felt, he couldn't bother with a possible burn to his sun-sensitive skin. Meeting her again had shaken him up. More so because he couldn't bear to see her and know she belonged to another man now. To that tall, dark, and handsome husband of hers, who, he'd been loath to admit, resembled a Bollywood movie star. The guy also had brains since he was some hotshot actuary or something, working in investment. And Lara had seemed happy with him. He remembered the joyous expression on her face when he'd seen them once at Piccadilly Circus in London.

That day, he'd known for good she was lost to him, stupid fool that he was. He'd been an idiot for leaving abruptly for France years before while his relationship with her had been unfinished business.

But it had all been a long time ago. A different lifetime, even.

He forced his eyes open and rubbed his nape as he peeled himself from the window and stepped closer to his desk. No use pondering the past. He actually had a future to look forward to now.

Eric steeled himself with resolve. In a swift move, he pulled his executive chair and settled behind his desk, eyeing the pile of letters on the table with weariness. The time spent in South Africa meant he still dealt with a backlog. With a resigned sigh, he attacked the stack of envelopes. The sooner he got the task out of the way, the better.

The last letter was an invitation to a medical conference at *Le Sirius Hotel and Conventions Centre*. He disliked such events, preferring the hands-on side of medicine, where he could take care of his patients.

However, one of the seminars was about microsurgery techniques, which would prove efficient in paediatric care and benefit his patients.

He reached for the phone and spoke to his secretary via the intercom. "Claire, book me a place for day five of that conference, will you?"

Chapter Four

Will that bloody phone stop ringing?

Lara was tired of picking it up. However, since she was stuck alone during Doris' lunch hour, she couldn't rely on anyone else. She hated fielding calls. It didn't help when the clients wanted to interact with her rather than the staff. And she'd already dealt with a nightmare barely thirty minutes ago, when that guy she hardly knew, Vishal, had called to ask her out on a date. She didn't have it in her to field another crisis today.

She ruffled through a sheaf of papers with exasperation, exhaled a calming breath as she punched the button with a steady hand and laid her elbows on her desk to answer the call. "Lara Reddy."

"Hey, babe. How you doing?"

Sam. Bless her. Relieved, she let out the breath she hadn't known she'd been holding. She'd expected to hear her mother at the other end or some nagging client. Her best friend couldn't have chosen a better time to call, and she was grateful for the respite a short conversation with her would provide.

"Hey, babe. What a pleasant surprise. How's it going in Casablanca?"

Sam chuckled. "Oh, I wouldn't know ... seeing

how I was in Dubai last night … and am now heading to my beachfront property in Grand-Baie for a much-needed break."

"Oh my God! You're back!" Lara squealed.

"Finally. That hotel room had even started to look like home, know what I mean?"

She nodded. "That's the worst."

Sam sighed. "Okay, you sound rattled. What's up?"

Lara laughed. Sam knew how to lighten up her mood.

"You'll never believe this. I'm here just a month, and my sister is already trying to fix me up with someone." Diya needed a stern talking-to!

Sam burst into laughter, her voice bubbly with amusement. "Well, good for you. Finally, the family's out with it. I wondered how long it would take them to start arranging potential matches."

"Very funny," Lara said, her tone dripping with sarcasm. Nothing funny there—only more problems created by her entourage.

"Yes, it is," Sam replied as her voice lowered to the normal, slightly breathless tone. "Anyway, I need to drop by the office before heading to the bungalow. Let's meet up at six?"

"Of course. Should I order sushi?"

"Perfect. After a month of rich Arabian spices, I so need soothing Asian flavours for my palate."

"Great. See you any time after six."

She cut the call with a smile. Finally, something to look forward to. She'd have to run by the store on the way home to nab some Haagen-Dazs tubs. Only then would the evening with Sam be a hit.

***

Sam arrived at her place at precisely six-thirty and flopped down on the sofa as soon as she reached the living room. Lara took a minute to study her, then shook her head in disbelief.

In her dark-burgundy tailored suit, Sam could pass for a model. Actually, Sam would resemble a model in a potato sack. The A-line skirt touched her knees, but even what lay exposed could be contenders for the longest legs on earth. With her pale skin and reddish hair, most people mistook her for Caucasian rather than Indian.

Bloody cow. Sam didn't pay attention to her appearance other than to seem put together. Yet, it eluded Lara how a woman could look sexy and beautiful without any conscious effort. Her own five-foot-eight figure could rival any model's, but Sam had a special something that turned heads everywhere she went. "You look like such a bitch, you know?"

Sam stretched wine-coloured lips into a very bitchy smile. "Thank you, darling. It's the exact effect I wanted to achieve."

The corporate world expected nothing less from the women who dared to 'infringe' into its circle. More the case in Sam's cutthroat strategic business development world.

The atmosphere lay still for a minute before they burst into laughter.

"So, what are you doing around this area in the middle of the week?" Lara asked as she bumped the freezer door closed with her hip, tubs of ice cream in her hands. She'd called for the sushi delivery, which was supposed to come around seven.

In the living room, she handed Sam a carton and a spoon while she hogged the other. Flopping onto a seat across from her best friend, she popped the lid and dunked her spoon into what she called orgasm in a tub.

Sam sighed. "Long overdue for a break, sweets. I'm starting my weekend already here."

The words hid something, and the feeling deepened when she noticed Sam hadn't opened her ice cream. There was definitely something wrong because Sam was more of an ice cream fiend than she was.

Narrowing her eyes, she studied her friend.

Hollow cheeks, high cheekbones, and the shadowed circles camouflaged by skilful concealer application under the tired eyes.

Sam was an expert at hiding her feelings, but Lara knew her. Something was bothering her friend.

"Babe, what's the matter?" She then gasped and sat up straighter. "Something happened between you and Salim?"

Goodness, no. Her two best friends in the whole world couldn't be breaking up! She hadn't seen him at all next door in all the time she'd been here, come to think of it. Was Sam getting the bungalow in their divorce settlement?

No, that couldn't be. No couple was as glued to each other as this one. Or, actually, no husband was glued to his wife as Salim was to Sam.

Sam closed her eyes, and a veil of sadness settled on her face as she let the corners of her mouth droop. "I got my period. Again."

A flood of relief coursed through her. So they weren't breaking up.

Then, the implications of Sam's words filtered in.

"Oh, babe. I'm sorry." She reached out and clasped the perfectly manicured hand resting in Sam's lap.

"This is a curse. I just can't get pregnant. And all the travelling isn't helping. I swear I am just about ready to take a full year off and park myself next door doing absolutely nothing in hopes it will make me relax."

The vehemence in the tone hit her hard. She'd never known Sam to be so down and angry. And Sam, relax? Those two words did not go together in any situation. Still, she had to try to calm her friend.

"All hope isn't lost. You've only been trying for a few months—"

"A year!"

"Twelve months, then. It's not something you can just wish for and have it fall into your lap."

Sam managed a faint smile. "I know that, silly. I thought the injections the last doctor prescribed would do the trick, but I've got this thing again."

Lara threw her hands up. *And here we go again.* "Sam, if you keep changing doctors every other month, you're bound to be on a hectic road with all their different treatments. How can you expect anything to work, then?"

Silence greeted her words before Sam burst into tears.

Great. She'd bumped herself off the list of nominations for *Best Friend of the Year* with her comment. But she and Sam had vowed to be perfectly honest with each other, come what may. At least she wasn't faltering in her role. Yet, she wanted to kick herself. She'd never been good with words, and she'd probably made it worse. Sam would take a hug as pity, so she remained where she sat, lost about how to change the gloomy mood.

An idea popped up.

"You'll never guess who I met the other day," she said.

Sam stopped crying and dried her tears with a delicate stroke of her finger.

Lara couldn't resist a frown at how the perfect face was not marred by crying. Trust her perfectionist BFF to use only waterproof makeup.

Blinking, she remembered the topic. Her throat closed for a second, refusing to allow her vocal cords to utter the sound of his name because saying it aloud would change everything.

But she was doing this for Sam. So, she leaned forward and dropped her voice to a low, conspiratorial tone. "I saw Eric."

Sam's eyes grew wide as she bolted upright in her seat. "Get out of here! You met him? And is it the same person I'm thinking of?"

Lara smiled, happy to see the mood back to friendly chatter. She nodded. Sam was one of the few people who knew of her past with Eric.

"Well, are you just gonna sport such a dumb smile? Come on, out with it. I want all the details." Sam's voice thrummed with excitement.

Lara laughed and recounted the meeting at the clinic.

"Okay, the real question I want you to answer. Was he wearing a wedding ring?" Sam asked as Lara finished her tale.

The elation of sharing the confidence crashed, the shards wrapping around her like tendrils of choking agony. "He had a ring on his right hand."

"So he's not married."

"You've forgotten how European, especially French, men wear wedding rings on the right hand."

"No, but this convention means squat in Mauritius. If it's not on the left hand, the ring means nothing."

Could there be hope? Could Eric be unattached after everything that had happened?

And where on Earth would such confirmation get her? Eric was out of her league, always had been.

"Come on, Lara. So this means he could be free, and what you saw could've been a misunderstanding—"

She shot to her feet. "I know what I saw, Sam. The photo didn't lie, and the paper said he and his French floozy named Sophie de-whatever-bollocks were expecting their first child."

"Still, it doesn't sound like Eric," Sam said in a soft tone.

Lara whirled around to stare at her friend. "Excuse me? I remember thinking you're the one who wanted to lead a mob to rip the skin off his spine when you found out."

Sam rolled her eyes. "Don't I recall that."

"Then what the heck are you talking about today, giving him the benefit of the doubt?"

"Because life is short, you idiot. And we're all

Chapter Five

"Seen today's papers yet?" Doris asked as she popped into the office.

Lara smiled without lifting her focus from the reports on her desk. "Yes, good reviews again."

"It's no mean feat, you know, especially since the conference is not yet over."

She glanced up at her PA. "As you say, it's not yet over. I'll bask in the glory tomorrow when everything's concluded, and I'll know nothing untoward happened."

"Oh, well. Suit yourself."

The words carried on a heavy sigh, and she caught the exaggerated shrug before the other woman walked out of the office.

She couldn't help but smile. Doris, and most of her staff, thought she was hard on herself. Somehow, she had broken through their reserve and established a positive team spirit on all the floors of the conventions centre. They'd dubbed her as "the MD's own slave driver," given how she never let up in her own perfectionism. She laughed them off, but she couldn't slacken the reins just because she'd been doing a good job until now. One moment of inattention and everything could crumble—the centre was too young to stand on its own feet. She'd been given a job and had vowed to do it to the best of her capabilities.

The clock on her desk read eleven-thirty. She'd promised to attend a talk, the last one of the morning, set to end at noon. She would then have to mingle with the guests during the one-hour lunch break.

She also had a few phone calls before leaving her office and attended to them before going down to the main conference floor. A quick pass through the main lobby assured her the catering manager had again pulled off a spectacular spread on the white-draped trestle tables. She'd been observing him since he'd seemed a bit out of it during the conference lead-up. She knew his wife had just had a baby. The poor bloke had to sleep over at his in-laws' place rather than his own home, as most young mothers on the island chose to spend the first forty days after birth at their own mothers' house. The tradition always gave her the heebie-jeebies. She'd cut the man some slack as he'd seemed to feel the same way. Still, he hadn't let her down, nor had the IT guy. Highlights of every talk played continuously over the many screens and interactive terminals dotting the area.

All seemed set. She prayed no mishap would happen today, and they'd all emerge from this maiden voyage unscathed and actually flying high.

Pausing at the closed door of a soundproof room, she hoped she would be able to slip in quietly without disrupting the exposé going on inside. Inconspicuous—that's how she should be around here. And so far, she had managed to be just that.

leading paediatricians."

If he hadn't been standing stock-still, he would've lost his footing.

Lara *worked* here?

His mind went into overdrive, scrambling for all the implications the statement carried for him. Surely, they wouldn't appoint a temp to such an important position.

Which meant she could be here permanently. And alone, too? Come to think of it, had she actually confirmed she was here on vacation back at the clinic?

He recovered in time to shake Prem Hemant's hand, forcing his mind to clear. "It's an honour to meet you, sir. I have studied a lot of your work at the faculty in France."

The cardiologist's face broke into a significant smile. "Really, young man? Where did you pursue your medical career?"

"The faculty is now known as Bordeaux Segalen," he replied before turning to Markus. "Thank you for introducing us. But I already know Lara. Our acquaintance goes back to our high school days."

"Good Lord, ain't that a surprise." Markus turned his startled face to Lara.

Prem Hemant also turned to her. "I thought I knew all your friends from your high school days. How come we never saw this young man at home?"

"It was a long time ago, Daddy," she said in a small voice, not lifting her gaze.

A movement caught his eye. She clutched her hands so hard, knuckles white. Yet, she refused to acknowledge him with a glance.

She's searching for an escape.

Why did Lara want to run? He meant her no harm. In fact, he wanted only the best for her. He wouldn't presume he was that, but he'd try to be, if she ever gave him a chance.

Their paths hadn't crossed again for no reason. He had to take his shot.

With a step, he moved to her side and dipped his head so he could speak in her ear.

"How about having a drink with me later, when you're finished here?"

She froze before she snapped her head up, fire blazing in the depths of her gaze. He'd bet she was about to open her mouth to give him a verbal lashing.

But after a second, she blinked and settled her features into a mask of calm, detached composure.

Her mouth betrayed her, though. Set in a tight line, the lips opened only to say, "No."

He wouldn't disrespect her consent. Ever. But a part of him wanted—needed—closure if a second chance wasn't on the cards. For that reason, he'd push.

The sound of a throat clearing cut through the tension-filled air, and they turned towards the two men who were still in their midst. Prem Hemant and Markus Hendrickson both wore quizzical expressions.

Eric bent his head slightly, his lips mere centimetres from her ear.

"Please," he said in a whisper. "And also, it would be rude of you to turn me down now."

She jerked her head away in a swift move, and he caught the smell of her perfume. Light and sweet, with headier notes of some flower, maybe ylang-ylang. He'd smelled the essence at a plantation on nearby Reunion Island once.

The delicate scent belied her ferocious nature, though. Anger flashed in her eyes, which she'd drawn to slits, and fury turned her mouth into a tight, white line.

He had her cornered. Far from him to be jubilant, but they needed to have that—possibly—last conversation.

He needed to say sorry, at the very least.

"Five-thirty, lounge bar," he added.

***

Through no mean feat on her part, the hours flew by. She'd wanted to lose herself in work, lose track of time, but she reckoned the precise moment when five o'clock struck on the clock. Her focus trained out the window onto the sprawling garden bathed in late afternoon sun, Lara bit her lip.

She should've said no. The thought had bugged her the whole afternoon, gnawing at her insides while she cursed her weak resolve. Eric had no right to affect her so much, not now, not after having dropped her out of his life like a hot potato he didn't want to handle. She should despise him, be on extreme alert in his presence, especially so she would notice when she turned into an idiot who fell under his spell after a mere four-five seconds of staring. How had she not realized he had all but compelled her into accepting the date at the lounge?

It's not a date!

She couldn't afford to go. It wasn't simply a matter of being in close proximity with him, but also pertinent to the little sanity she had left, snatches of equilibrium Roy had not robbed her of. Eric played havoc with her senses, and she hated the loss of control more than the treacherous feelings blooming inside her whenever she thought of him. As if a door had opened and everything that could overwhelm her was trying its damnedest best to squeeze in at the same time.

Yet, in not saying no, she'd agreed to meet him, so she couldn't go back on her word.

Damn him. He still knew her so well. Her demise had come from the penetrating, intense look he had sent her when she'd been about to decline his invitation.

That same long, pointed glance had been her downfall in the past, because it could conquer all her defences and lay her bare. Somehow, it had always spoken to her about the formidable, demanding man Eric could be beneath the easy-going attitude. Shivers used to course through her when he'd stared at her like that, when she'd imagined him undressing her with more than his gaze and setting his warm hands all over her body.

When Eric trained that kind of attention on her, she'd agree to whatever he'd ask of her.

Hence her inability to say no to his invitation.

Damn it. Why did he have to have that very effect on her? She still reeled from a painful divorce with a man she'd grown to love. So, she shouldn't be pining after another man, no matter if he happened to be her first love, the one that got away.

But she'd caught her breath and felt her heart go all pitter-patter when she'd taken full notice of Dr Eric Marivaux in the conference room. He wore a dark olive-green suit over a beige shirt, with a green and gold silk tie. The outfit had brought out his light golden tan and made his thick hair gleam with the rich colour of a wheat field basking under the sun. His deep-blue eyes had struck her as darker than she remembered, as if offset in contrast to the golden aura of him. Mind-boggling gorgeous would be an understatement, something she hadn't thought possible. How could he appear even more handsome than all those years before?

True, a nineteen-year-old teenager couldn't compare to a thirty-three-year-old man. Age had defined and sharpened his features, and those mesmerizing irises still holding so much laughter had acquired unfathomable depths brought on by life experience. From a lanky lad, he'd grown into a well-built man, and his shoulders had filled, thus giving him the breadth to carry his height of well over six feet.

Lara sighed and closed her eyes. Like a kaleidoscope of images and sensations, in her mind, she flashed back to the memory of her first kiss. Under the gentle heat of miraculous winter sun in Curepipe, feelings had wrapped around her, imprinting themselves into her whole being for a lifetime. The first time a man's warmth had wrapped around her, and she'd given in to the heady, intoxicating feel of being alive in the embrace of someone who pressed light, fleeting kisses onto her lips while she basked in the protective hold of his arms.

Of Eric's arms.

A tear trickled down her cheek, and she blinked hard, her gaze unfocused, to stop the moisture and return to the present.

Quarter past five. She should go down.

At the edge of the lounge, she stopped in the doorway to give the interior a quick scan.

There he was, seated near one of the windows facing west, towards the sunset. Rays of sunlight merrily danced in his hair, lighting them time and again with a soft, golden glow.

How handsome he is.

She pursed her lips and gave herself a mental slap. She was here to honour her word. Full stop.

Eric had deserted her and broken her heart. She wouldn't hand him a second chance to toy with her again.

***

Eric felt Lara's presence before he saw her. A sudden tension bristled along his spine.

He turned to face the doorway in case she thought of fleeing.

She met his gaze, distrust pinching her face. The beautiful, lush mouth was again in a thin, flat line.

Any sane person would duck for cover right away. He refused to give in to her formidable stance, though. If she thought he'd flinch from the accusation in her eyes, she'd be wrong.

She had every right to hold a grudge against him. But he would stand his ground because this was a new beginning.

She slowly made her way to his table, and he

stood while she seated herself. Manners drilled into him from childhood about etiquette and propriety might bring good dispositions. Not that Lara appeared ready to cut him any slack, though.

"Should I order a 7-Up for you?" he asked once he returned to his chair.

"I prefer Pepsi."

Since when? She used to hate any kind of cola. From the tight expression on her face, she might've contradicted him just for the fun of it. Seems she'd make him sweat.

He tensed and nodded, signalling the waiter. After he ordered, silence descended even after the server brought her drink and set the glass before her.

Eric watched her. *Merde,* but she was more beautiful than in his memories. Teenage Lara had nothing on the grown woman. She'd matured into an alluringly sophisticated creature.

However, beneath the façade, had she really changed? He still seemed capable of rattling her, same as long ago. She was not over him, possibly, just like he'd never gotten over her.

Where did that leave them?

Her left hand lay on the table, and he darted a quick glance at her fingers.

She pulled her arm back and placed it under the table as soon as she noticed his perusal.

Not enough time to spot if a paler band of skin rested on her third finger where her ring should've been.

The seconds ticked by, and she neither spoke nor did she reach for her drink. He'd been right. She'd ordered Pepsi to contradict him.

Lara. He wanted to sigh. *This is me you're trying to kid.*

"You know," he said. "When I asked you for a drink, I didn't mean it just literally. I planned on some conversation, as well."

She shrugged. "What do you want to talk about?"

"Everything and nothing." He paused. "How's life? And how's your husband?"

She lowered her eyelids at the mention of the other man. The silence stretched, and he wondered if she would answer him or tell him to get lost.

Lara took a deep, audible breath and brought her gaze up to meet his.

"He's doing okay, I guess," she said softly.

Trouble in paradise? A part of him wanted to jump with joy. Callous of him, but the only thing he registered was that she could be free. The urge to find out burned through him like wildfire, but he wouldn't press, at least not yet. So he raised an eyebrow.

She squirmed under his scrutiny before squaring her shoulders. "How's your wife?"

He clamped his jaw, and a muscle started ticking in his cheek after a few seconds.

So that's what happened. Lara thought he'd married Sophie. So much for Lara having faith in them.

But what was done was done, and they had to look forward, not back. Could they have a second chance today? Or in the future?

He wanted Lara. If there was a chance she wanted him, too, he would fight to make them happen.

So, he shook his head and gave her a slow, lazy smile. She'd never been able to resist that one back in the day.

"I'm not married, Lara. Never have been."

She widened those almond-shaped eyes, and her lower lip trembled when she opened her mouth. Different emotions played on her features. Surprise, doubt, insecurity, and finally, anger. She bit her lip as if to refrain from saying something aloud. A blank mask settled over her face in the second that followed. Yet, as before, she couldn't mask her gaze.

Her pupils were dilated by some strong emotion, and the dark irises darted back and forth.

"What happened with your husband?" he asked gently.

She stared back for what seemed like ages. Had he pushed her too far?

"We divorced three years ago. I'm back here now."

Words died on his lips at her whispered statement. He'd hoped to hear she was single and had prayed for it. Hurt crashed through him that she'd had to face something as terrible as a divorce. She'd had her share of struggles in the past, enough for a lifetime.

Lara must've suffered through her breakup. The agony on her face spelled the trauma all too well. She deserved careful, gentle handling. He'd have to go slow with her.

She shot to her feet. "I'm sorry. I have to go now."

No—he wouldn't let her run away. Not when

he'd found her again.

Eric caught her wrist as she passed by his chair. She slowly turned and faced him.

"Have dinner with me one night."

The words spilled from his lips before he could think them through. What happened to careful and gentle handling? If he spooked her, she'd run. Not good.

Training his gaze on her, he pleaded for her acceptance with his eyes.

She pursed her lips and withdrew her hand, running the tips of her fingers along his when she pulled back.

Don't do this, please.

"I have to go," she said softly before turning and leaving the room at a hurried pace.

Chapter Six

Lara slumped on the sofa in her living room when she returned to her house.

She had no clue how she'd gotten home. She remembered hyperventilating while walking to the car and then trying to regulate her breathing once inside the vehicle. She'd switched on the engine, and the next thing she knew, she sat on her sofa. How on earth had she survived driving back with no conscious thought? She hadn't even made it back into her office. Of course, it wasn't like her to cut and run like this, but there had been extenuating circumstances, right?

Thank goodness she was still in one piece and hadn't hurt anybody during the drive.

Why is everything getting so complicated? Why now?

She closed her eyes for a second and clutched her hand, which he'd grasped as she'd been leaving. Her skin still tingled where he'd grazed it.

No man had ever left such an impression on her. Not even Roy.

She threw her head back, staring at the ceiling. Why was she getting all worked up over Eric? She had no place in her life for a man. And he had betrayed her. Getting thrown once, shame on him. Getting thrown twice, shame on *her* for allowing such a thing to happen when she should've learned her lesson.

"Have dinner with me one night."

The words, spoken in a husky, seductive tone, had flowed over her like a caress. His deep blue irises had pierced through her heart to her soul in the way only he could.

Roy had dimmed memories of Eric when he'd walked into her life. Now her husband was gone, and her first love seemed hell-bent on stepping back in.

What should she do? Barricade the door, or open it wide?

Wanting an anchor, she had the good sense to ditch her clothes, wrap her knuckles, and put on the ankle supports. Then she started attacking the tethered punching bag in a room at the back of her house.

An hour later, she was half-naked, glistening with sweat, exhausted both physically and mentally. Still nowhere close to finding an answer, let alone a solution, to her dilemma.

She should be ashamed for wanting to welcome a man who had discarded her after stomping all over her heart.

The loud ring of her phone zapped her out of her thoughts. A quick glance at the screen, and she sighed. In the wake of the meeting with Eric, she'd completely forgotten she had to go out that evening.

"Hi, Sam." Would her friend pick up on the weariness in her tone?

"Where the hell are you? The function is about

to start, and you were supposed to be here ages ago."

Lara sighed again. No way out of the whole affair. Sam's sister-in-law, and incidentally Auntie Zubeida's daughter—one just couldn't escape neighbours who morphed into relatives of some sort here—was getting married. If she didn't go, she'd have the whole Majeed clan and her own mother all on her back. In other words, Hell would look like R&R.

"I'll be there shortly. Some unexpected stuff cropped up at the centre in the afternoon."

"All right, we're waiting for you. Hurry up."

The pain in Lara's heart came back. Another wedding, she sighed.

She remembered her wedding. She'd been radiant, according to Roy.

"If I wasn't already smitten with you, I would have lost my heart when I saw you walking towards me in your bridal outfit."

Until the moment before the ceremony, she'd thought she'd been dreaming, and reality would poke its head in soon dissolving the arranged marriage.

Lara had never thought she'd marry someone like Roy. A man like Eric had seemed more likely. Born and raised in England, where she'd spent her first sixteen years, a proper Indian husband hadn't fit into her plans. Instead, she would move out of the family house and become one of the many young, single and carefree of a new generation living in cosmopolitan London.

First, her father landed the once-in-a-lifetime position to manage Mauritius's newly established cardiac surgery hospital. Then, with patriotism as an excuse, her mother had utilised the perfect opportunity. She'd brought her daughters back into a culture-driven world where she could make them lead proper lives away from the loose morals of Western culture.

The marriage proposal from Roy Reddy, a British subject born to an Indian father and a Mauritian mother, had come one month after her eighteenth birthday. Roy's mother had been an acquaintance in London, and Gayatri Hemant had kept in touch with her. When it became time for Sarita Reddy to search for a bride for her son, she'd naturally thought of Lara.

Under normal circumstances, she would have refused the proposal, like the half dozen 'proper' matches her mother had pushed her way since she'd turned eighteen.

However, this proposal had come seven months after Eric's departure to France. And a few days after she'd stumbled upon a picture of him with a beautiful blonde socialite in the glossy pages of a French society rag.

With a heavy heart, she'd agreed to marry Roy, knowing she needed to confine Eric to her past. Her mother had ascribed her acceptance to her being homesick for London and Roy being a way for her to go back there.

In a sense, her mother had been correct. Lara had wanted to put distance between her and Mauritius, which had brought her nothing but shattered illusions and a broken heart.

Tears gathered in her eyes as she thought back to that harrowing episode of her life, and she quickly blinked them away when her phone rang again. Sam.

"You're thinking of your wedding, innit?" her friend said in greeting.

Spot on, but she couldn't admit to that. "I was thinking of your own wedding and how Salim crashed through the door to have a forbidden glimpse at you before the function."

Sam burst out laughing. "Yeah, and all the old biddies nearly had heart attacks."

After a pause, she added, "Lara, I know you must be thinking of Roy today. Don't lie. I know he's on your mind."

Lara remained silent and lowered her gaze to her lap. Was she so transparent? Did everyone know she was tortured by the memory of her failed marriage?

Sam sighed. "I have to go now. Try to forget him, and come over and enjoy yourself."

She nodded in reply, then added a small yes. What else could she do? Happiness seemed to thrive around her, but the feeling didn't appear like it wanted to knock on her door.

Are you sure? What about Eric?

Where had *that* come from? She was alone but not unhappy. Twice, she'd made the mistake of putting all her trust in a man, and twice, it had been thrown back into her face. First with Eric himself, then with Roy.

A third time would be one time too many.

What if he's thinking of you?

She shook herself inwardly. *Get a grip, Lara.*

Eric had his life, probably filled with his work and a woman who hung on to his every word. Gorgeous, rich, and eligible men like him didn't remain single for more than a day. So why would he pine for Lara, the one he'd dumped?

She should heed Sam's words and try to enjoy herself tonight. Granted, it would be no mean feat, but she could definitely try.

Well, at least if she stopped thinking of Eric.

***

"Penny for your thoughts," a soft, throaty voice said.

Eric forced his wandering mind back to the present and focused on the woman who sat opposite him at the restaurant table. The slight smile on her beautiful face took the edge off the sharp question.

"I'm not lost in my thoughts," he replied with a chuckle.

"You haven't listened to a word I've said all through dinner," Annabelle said with a pout.

He closed his eyes for a second. She spoke the truth. He'd been miles away, thinking of Lara and how she'd run from him earlier.

He sighed. He'd go after her. But would she allow him back into her life? By the look of things, he had his work cut out.

"Eric." Annabelle sighed. "You're zoning out on me again."

He blinked out of his worries. "Sorry. I have a lot on my mind today."

She skewered him with a narrowed gaze over the flicker of the candles lighting the table. In the soft glow, she was stunning and elegant in her navy blue dress. However, her piercing grey eyes drew his attention, the silver irises fixed on him.

The waiter arrived, cleared the dishes and left.

Eric leaned across the table and gave her his full attention.

"I know I haven't been good company tonight, and I'm really sorry."

Truth be told, he didn't want to be here.

Annabelle watched him over the rim of her coffee cup. Then she shook her head, put the cup down, and trained that frank gaze once more onto him.

"This is not going to work," she stated.

He agreed, but he wouldn't be a *connard* and say so aloud.

"I'm sorry," he simply said.

She shook her head again, sending long dark tresses flying every way. The waiter had a very narrow escape from the lashing locks.

"We both know why we're here. We both thought we were having dinner with your mother."

His turn to sigh. The woman had set them up, something he hated.

"And when your mother calls," Annabelle continued. "You drop everything and say yes. Trust me, she might not have a job title, but everyone on the island knows of her. Her formidable reputation precedes her, and her influence makes things happen."

Yes, something like that. As if by magic, too. He'd never underestimated his mother, and he wouldn't start now. Still, he'd fallen into that trap, as well. Easier to acquiesce than fight back, though he would where it really mattered.

Like Lara.

He took in a sharp breath at the thought of her.

He shouldn't have her on his mind, not while he was here with Annabelle. Not fair on his dinner partner, even if they had been coerced into this date. They'd reported to the maître d' pulpit of this French restaurant in Pamplemousses, a small village twenty minutes from either Grand-Baie or Port-Louis, the capital city where Annabelle worked … only to find that Agnes Armont-Marivaux had had to excuse herself, but her booking still standing, the two of them could have dinner together.

"Okay, something's really on your mind. Dish," she said. "I'm a good listener."

Really? She wanted him to talk to her of the woman who held his heart in her grip?

"Fine, I'll go first," she stated. "I have a confession to make."

He raised an eyebrow at this.

She rolled her eyes before fixing them on him again. "Remember how I told you I didn't want romance and love and all that hoopla?"

He nodded.

Her turn to raise her eyebrows. "Well, I lied. I do want all of it." She paused to take a deep breath. "And I know that's not going to happen with you."

Her words made him reel. Here she was giving him the perfect out—he should jump on it.

But he couldn't. She was too much a precious, beautiful soul for him to hurt her that way. "I'm sorry."

She shrugged. "It's okay. I like to tell myself I can do that, marry for convenience and not love, but I can't. I just have to take one look at—"

Was she going to confess her secret crush?

Silence settled between them, making him yearn to know.

"Who?" he couldn't resist asking.

Annabelle sighed. "My cousin, Simmi, and her fiancé."

The name rang a bell. "Your cousin? Do I know her?"

She nodded. "Of course you do. Simmi Moyer. Bernard Moyer's daughter."

He remembered now, mainly because Simmi's mother had been of Indian origin. That wedding had created rifts and havoc in their French-Mauritian community when it had taken place so many decades earlier. It had been held over all their heads as something to *not* do ...

And sadly enough, Simmi, being the product of that frowned-upon union, had borne the brunt of the social exclusion directed her mother's way.

He'd thought of that when wanting to pursue Lara. A part of him had hoped things would be different in their time for their children ...

"How is she?" he asked. He'd lost touch with Simmi. They'd been around the same age, friends when they'd been kids. Maybe he should reach out to her once more.

Annabelle gave a long-suffering sigh. "Like I said, engaged. To this guy, Lars."

Something wasn't adding up here. "And you ... like him, too?"

She blinked. "Wait, what? No! Actually, I'm the one who set them up on a blind date. I didn't know him back then. He is a friend of Magnus, my ex. No, they're just so ... mushy and in love! It's a pain to watch. I just wish I could find someone like that, too, you know," she finished.

He hesitated to reach out and grab her hand. Not that he thought it would be misconstrued, but he didn't want to rub salt in her wounds.

"You deserve someone who worships the ground you walk on, too," he said.

At this, she laughed. Then, as she sobered and peered at him again, she grew serious. "You have someone like that, don't you?"

He frowned. He'd never said anything to her.

She rolled her eyes once more. "Come on, it's written all over you. Not to mention that you are who you are—son of Agnes Armont-Marivaux, successful paediatrician also with a reputation that precedes him all over the island. You've got height and good looks, and you're still unattached in your thirties? Hello? I'm not that much of an idiot to not be able to put two and two together."

He debated whether to tell her anything. In the end, she made the decision for him.

"Tell me. What's her name?"

What point was there in fighting? He wouldn't be hurting Annabelle by telling her about the woman he loved.

"Her name is Lara."

"Hmm. Full name?"

"Reddy."

She squinted, then her eyes grew wide. "Wait a second. Isn't that the new MD of the conference centre at *Le Sirius*?"

Surprised, he stared at her. "How do you know that?"

"*Mon chou*, I work in PR. I know everything there is to know about anything or anyone worth their salt on this island."

Okay, she'd firmly put him in the friend zone with that chummy endearment. His shoulders relaxed, though his spine still bristled. If she really knew that much, could he glean some info about Lara through her?

"Okay, I get it. You're too much of a gentleman to ask. I'll tell you what I know."

"I didn't say anything!"

"You didn't have to. PR, remember? I also know how to read people." She leaned forward and propped her cheek onto one palm. "Your girl is the buzz of the place. They say Markus Hendrickson personally recruited her after he had top headhunters find her and pinch her from the corporate business hotel she worked for in London. Her first conference was a stellar hit, and there are rumours that, with her expertise and drive behind the centre, they are going to bid to host the next Commonwealth Nations' conference should Mauritius be hosting it.

"Now, her personal life. It's all a bit hush-hush. Reports say she is divorced. Already was when she rose up the ranks in the English capital. Comes from a very well-known family from Curepipe, her father almost a celebrity thanks to being renowned for his pioneering of cardiac treatments locally. Personality-wise, they say she's a bit of an ice queen, but I'm reserving judgement on that until I meet her myself. They also call Simmi an ice queen, yet I know her as one of the warmest human beings to have ever existed." She finally paused for breath. "Question is, now—where do *you* fit in amidst all that?"

Should he tell her? Strangely, a part of him told him he could trust her. And *merde*, he so wanted—no, needed—to finally get his thoughts and feeling about Lara out in the open.

"She spent about two years here as a teen, for her A-Levels. We ..." he paused. "We dated back then."

Annabelle's eyes grew even wider. "No way!"

"Way," he said with a chuckle. Being with her felt like being young and carefree again. He'd missed that kind of lightness in his life.

"So now ..." She tilted her head as she studied him. "She is single, from what I've heard, and so are you. What next?"

He sighed and ran a hand in his hair as he leaned back in his chair. "Next? I have no clue."

"It was serious between you, wasn't it?" she asked softly.

He nodded.

"Then you just have to win her back."

"As if it's that simple."

She made a grimace. "That's true. Especially considering who you are and all that."

He grimaced, too. She didn't need to spell it out—they were speaking of his mother now. Formidable Agnes Armont-Marivaux was one obstacle he would totally crash into in his quest to get Lara accepted as his partner. Lara would never fit the bill. She was of Indian origin, divorced, and not from a 'good society' family.

But this was his life, and no one could or would choose for him. One way or the other, he would have her.

Even if Lara didn't appear to want him back, he'd win her over in the end.

"Any help you need, I'm here," Annabelle told him.

Eric smiled at her as he did reach out to clasp her hand this time.

"Thank you."

Chapter Seven

Emerging from deep sleep, Lara turned onto her side.

How come the edge of the pillow felt cold and wet? She frowned without opening her eyes. She wasn't at home, so where had she slept? Sliding farther, she bumped her cheek against something soft and slightly threadbare. When she opened her eyes, the sight of Sarah, her childhood rag doll, greeted her from the edge of the mattress. Across the room, she found Ronan Keating front and centre on the Boyzone poster staring at her from the life-size image tacked onto the wall.

She was home. Well, no longer 'home' for her. Her parents' place and her former bedroom.

The function had lasted until the wee hours of the morning, and her father had refused to let her drive without getting some shut-eye first. Hence, she'd crashed in this room which looked like she had stepped out as an eighteen-year-old yesterday. Her mother hadn't altered a single detail. Wistfully, Lara recalled the many mornings she had awoken in this same squishy bed that never remained warm enough in the cold temperatures of Curepipe. Interior heating had been an alien concept in Mauritius back in the day and still was today.

This morning felt no different than the ones she'd experienced over a decade before. The birds sang outside the window, heralding the promise of a sunny day, even if the temps wouldn't hit much above twenty-seven degrees Celsius—a veritable heatwave for Curepipe natives—in the thick of summer. The sound of her mother exuberantly chatting on the phone drifted upstairs, along with the clutter of breakfast dishes. And she lay snuggled in her single bed, wrapped in the too-thin, faded blue quilt, the sight of Eric's handsome face floating before her eyes.

Lara sat up with a start. Cold air washed over her where she'd dropped the quilt, but she dismissed the shivery sensation.

Eric's face didn't belong to the here and now. He should be firmly confined to her past, to the two secondary school years she'd spent in Mauritius. He had no place in her life anymore.

Wait, it must be the poster playing tricks on her mind. Strange how she'd never reckoned how much Eric had ended up resembling Ronan Keating. Especially with the long hair now, they could be doppelgangers.

She blew at the strand of hair that had fallen across her face and tucked it behind her ear. She'd undone the braid before going to sleep. Her hair had still been damp, an invitation to catch a cold or worse if she'd kept the not-dry hair tied up in the cold weather.

A grimace tugged at her lips when she saw the kinks in her locks. Great. When she actively wanted waves, her hair never complied. Disgusted, she glanced at the display on the Minnie Mouse clock on the bedside table. Ten past seven.

Damn. She had to be in her office at nine. If she was lucky enough to evade any traffic jam while going through Port Louis, the trip alone would take an hour. And no, she would not be testing the very steep slopes of the new mountain motorway, not when she had a tendency to lose track of speed in her brand-newMercedes. She didn't have a death wish, thank you very much. Still, how the hell had she not thought to set on an alarm to wake up at five-thirty?

She scrambled out of bed and dashed into the bathroom. She'd slept in an old T-shirt of her dad's, and on her way out after a quick shower, she searched for her discarded *kurta* suit. She groaned when the realization struck. Her mother had already spirited the outfit away for laundry. What would she wear?

Still clad in her towel, she dashed into her sister's room adjoining hers. "Dee, I need some clothes. Can I borrow your stuff?"

A muffled response came from the mound obliterated by a fluffy pink quilt.

Teenagers, she thought with a shake of her head. How come she'd never been plagued by the sleep bug when she'd been of Diya's age? She'd always gotten up with the sun, trusting the muezzin's call from a nearby mosque for the Muslim Morning Prayer as her wake up alarm.

Piles of discarded clothing dotted the carpet, and she rummaged through in hopes of finding something wearable. Petite Diya hardly topped five feet, whereas Lara had a tall, lean body. All the clothes resembled dolls' outfits.

Finally, she grabbed a stretch top and a wraparound skirt and quickly dressed. The top clung to her like a second skin and squashed her chest like a sports bra, and the skirt barely covered her arse, but she could manage in them. She'd do without underwear for a few hours, though. Diya's stuff would be like children's clothing, and though her mother and she wore pretty much the same size, she wasn't about to ask *her* for underwear. Oh, what shame. She'd have to hope she wouldn't flash anyone before she managed to get home to grab a change.

On her way down, she passed her mother, who stood on the landing with her ear glued to the phone receiver. Probably a very interesting gossip session, never mind that it was still so early in the day. Gossip knew no social schedule in Mauritius. Her mother appeared transfixed as she bobbed her head in agreement with whatever the other person was saying and didn't notice her.

With a shrug, Lara ignored her and went into the kitchen. She paused only long enough to hug her father, who sat at the kitchen table with the morning paper and a huge pot of tea in front of him, then dashed to the stove to grab hot water for a cup of coffee.

Diya stomped into the room as she was grabbing her first sip. How anyone could stomp with their feet in fluffy Minnie Mouse booties eluded her, but trust Diya to be ever the drama queen.

"Lara!" the girl whined. "Did you really have to make so much noise in my room? I can't go back to sleep now."

"It'll do you good to wake up like normal people sometimes." Their father chuckled before exchanging a conspiratorial wink with his eldest daughter.

Just like old times. She smiled back and settled down at the table with her cup of coffee. She loved to take the time to savour her wake-me-up drink, the only time in the day when she didn't feel bombarded from all sides by issues she had to resolve. So, she took her time. The minute she emptied the mug, she'd be out of there.

She'd hardly taken another mouthful when her mother stalked into the room. A cold, disturbing feeling swept over her as she took in the older woman's jubilant expression and wide smile. Trouble brewed as certainly as the witches turned the cauldron to bubbling in the opening scene of *Macbeth*.

As soon as her mother stepped into the room, both her father and her sister made a go for the door. Lara belatedly realised they'd both had the wisdom to leave before being snapped up by Gayatri Hemant's overflowing tongue. The caffeine hadn't hit her bloodstream yet. Otherwise, she'd never have been caught out. Alone with her mother in the deserted kitchen? Not good. How would she escape? She'd burn her mouth and throat if she tipped back the remaining scalding coffee.

She forced down a sip and another. Half the mug to go. She could finish the contents on the way to the sink. So, she stood and started away from the table before something in her mother's diatribe stopped her in her tracks.

"Excuse me?" She turned to face the woman who'd given birth to her and blinked. She had to have heard wrong.

"You silly girl. I knew you wouldn't realize what good fortune has befallen us. Nirmala just called. She has got such a good proposal for you. You'll never believe it."

"Proposal? As in 'marriage'?" Her voice came out in a croak.

"Pfft. But of course. What else could it be?"

Her mother added some derogatory Indian word calling her an airhead somewhere in the statement, but she let the remark pass. More life-threatening matters to tackle first.

A bloody proposal? For an arranged marriage? Never again, not on her life. While a part of her had always known her mother would try to fix up another marriage for her, she'd never taken the threat seriously. Or fathomed that the relatives would get in on it, as well. Stupid of her not to have anticipated such a coup. She was the talk of the island, wasn't she? The only way to wipe off her divorce scandal would be to shack her up with someone else ASAP.

Still, she couldn't blow her top and scream as she wanted to. A tantrum would only be ammunition for her mother's plough-Lara-down campaign. So, she settled for cool logic and detachment.

"Mum, what are you talking about?"

"Nirmala has this wonderful relative. The woman is so concerned about the plight of unmarried girls. Anyway, she has found someone for you, and like I said, you couldn't think of a better offer."

Her mother yapped like a happy puppy, unable to keep to one spot in her excitement. "He's a very good prospect. Rich, of course. Apparently, he has three houses, four cars, and a beachfront villa in Pereybère. Works in a very good position in the Ministry of Foreign Affairs. Must have some good contacts there. Probably even knows the Prime Minister."

Lara sighed. She could at least try to get her opinion forward, but knowing her mother, her words would only fall through. She should simply ride the tide out, except she didn't have time. The sooner she hit the road, the better her chances to make it to the office at nine. And by the look of things, she would be late because she absolutely had to get changed beforehand.

She had to put a stop to this drivel once and for all.

"Mum, I don't plan on getting married again."

Gayatri Hemant's eyes grew big. "What nonsense, Lara. Every woman needs a husband. You're getting such a good proposal. Don't be stupid and refuse this opportunity. You already let one good man go."

She blinked. "Excuse me? So now Roy is no longer a bastard but a *good man*? Since when?"

She should've known, though. This kind of reasoning coming from her mother? Nothing unusual or unexpected. Her mother twisted everything to suit her purposes all the time. Lara had no hope of emerging the victor in such a setup.

So, she blanked out the shrill voice and slurped

her coffee, getting closer to freedom as she emptied the mug.

Then her mother stopped talking.

Bad sign.

Lara lent half an ear to the ramblings when the talking started again.

"Only problem is he has two children. They're already into university, but they could fight you for the share of his wealth you'll be due."

Lara didn't know which part of the statement angered her the most. That they were shipping her off to a man old enough to have twenty-year-old kids. Or how they'd already distributed the poor man's wealth between his heirs and his potential new wife before he'd even gotten remarried?

The fury built, rising up right along with incredulity. The pounding throb in her head picked up again, and her lungs burned with the need to drag a full cigarette to ashes in one pull.

Try as she might to calm down, she couldn't, and the words bubbled out of her.

"You mean you are saddling me with a man old enough to be my father, and on top of it, you want me to turn into a gold digger?"

Her mother only shook her head and tsk-tsked reproachfully. "Look at you getting on your high horse." She snorted. "He's a widower. Perfect for you."

At that point, Lara wanted to know only one thing. "How old is he, Mum?"

"If you really have to know, he's in his prime. Nirmala said fifty-nine years old," her mother replied with a dismissive wave of her hand.

"Damn it, Mum. This makes him twenty-seven years older than me. I could be his daughter."

What could she possibly have in common with a man so much older than she? While perfectly possible to meet someone so much older and hit it off, such a relationship seldom happened in an arranged match.

"Would you consider this unfortunate situation you dug yourself into?" her mother asked. "How do you think you'll cope if we're not here to lend you a helping hand? If we'd been by your side, I'm sure none of those idiotic fights between you and your husband would've happened. I mean, look at you—"

"Oh, shut up, will you?" Lara screeched the command, unable to contain herself any longer. "Stop trying to control my life. You've always done this. Why can you never let go?"

Yes, she was screaming, but she needed to win her calm back. She felt entirely capable of murdering both her mother and that Nirmala.

"Lay off, Mother. I'm not getting married again. Full stop."

What had sounded more deadly? The screams or the cold calm in her last statement?

Better yet—had either of her tactics worked on her mother?

No such luck. The older woman stood with legs braced and her hands on her hips. Battle stance.

Alerted by the noise, her father and sister returned to the kitchen. Neither Lara nor her mother bothered with them. Engaged in fight mode, neither ready to be the first to give in.

But the fight wouldn't be bring anything other than making her blow her top. Throwing one last glare at her mother, she headed out and paused as she went past her parent.

Gayatri Hemant's stricken expression conveyed she hovered on the verge of a heart attack. She clenched her hand to her bosom and heaved in big gulps of air.

"What am I going to tell your aunt? She has managed to get you such a good match. How will I tell her you're refusing? Think about it, my girl. You'll be well provided for. You won't need to work another day of your life. And he's not going to bother if you cannot give him children—"

Those last words cut through her with the agony of a red-hot sword tip plunging into her back. So even her mother thought her to be barren? Her husband had kicked her out of his life. His family spoke of her as an evil witch. Society had a thousand and one theories about what failings she must possess for her marriage to have crumbled. But she'd clung to the belief she had her family on her side all along.

Turned out she'd been wrong.

The pain of this realisation flared to obliterate every other hurt inflicted on her in the past few years.

Lara grew aware of a heavy weight dragging her hand down. She still clutched her empty coffee mug. Under her tense, forceful grip containing all her anger and disappointment, her knuckles had gone white around the handle.

The reality of her situation dawned on her then. She was an ex-wife. Getting a divorce had made her cross onto the other side, where people were no longer considered living, breathing creatures with a heart and feelings. More than a pariah, she also had the label of 'discarded property' slapped onto her back like a scarlet letter she should be ashamed of.

Sounds blanked, sights blurred, and nothing but the whoosh of blood at her temples hit home in her perception. Anger shrouded her, wrapped its ice-cold yet burning tentacles around her, scorching her insides like the creeping sting of frostbite.

What had she been thinking when she'd returned to this God-awful place?

In an impulsive fit, she hurled the mug across the room. The ceramic hit the far wall and clattered in pieces onto the hard tiled floor.

Silence rang while all eyes turned onto her. Emotional displays were so not her thing usually. No wonder they were all stunned.

But she wasn't done, far from it. She might be neck-deep in the most bottomless bog of social hell, but damn if she'd give up the fight. High time she put a stop to the marriage bollocks. They weren't in the goddamn Regency era, for goodness' sake. She also had to hold on to the little sanity she still had left, which wouldn't be possible until she'd dotted the i's and crossed the t's with her mother.

She stalked towards the woman and stopped a few inches before their chests bumped.

Only five feet tall, her mother's diminutive stature allowed Lara to tower over her. Using the advantage to the best of her ability, she narrowed her gaze. Her mum took a step back, only to bump into the kitchen counter, nowhere to run.

"Let me clear a few things with you, Mother, and please go repeat it to all those old cronies of yours."

Ice dripped from her tone, and her mother flinched as if burned by acid.

"First, I don't want children, which is why I don't have any. Not because I'm barren. Second, Roy gave me a generous settlement to leave with the least fuss, so I am well provided for financially and don't *need* a job to take me from paycheck to paycheck. Third, my job is my life, and sod you all if you think it's a waste." She paused to inhale. "Fourth and last, tell that old cow to get lost with her proposal and mind her own business for a change."

Not a breath could be heard in the stillness. She bent to stare straight into her mother's eyes.

"Have I made myself clear?"

She turned around and marched out of the kitchen without waiting for an answer. However, with every step she took, her bravado failed, replaced by the dull, sawing cut of betrayal in every cell of her body.

As she passed her father, he placed a hand on her shoulder. She stopped only long enough to peer into his stricken, concerned face.

"I'm sorry," he mouthed.

A heavy lump formed in her throat as she clutched his hand and trained her gaze on her younger sister. Tears shimmered in Diya's eyes, wet stains on her soft cheeks.

She shouldn't have to suffer like this, Lara thought. She was still too young and innocent.

Carefree youth. Had any girl of Indian origin

ever experienced some? People directed every moment of their lives, and they lost even the prospect of hope.

Not anymore, though. At least, not for her.

She'd also give her damnedest best to ensure her little sister got a chance at living her life the way Diya wanted to.

She reached out and touched the girl's delicate jaw. "Don't cry, Dee. It's not worth it."

She brushed past them and made her way to the first floor so she could grab her things from the bedroom. Halfway down the stairs on her way out, her cell phone rang, and she wearily answered without glancing at the screen.

"Hi Lara, it's me, Vishal. I was wondering if you'd like to go out for a drink later today."

The pounding inside her skull increased. She didn't need this, of all things. Not now, and probably not ever, she reflected. How did she get rid of him without being rude, though?

But she was overwrought, unable to be gentle and courteous right then. At one point, she would have to deliver the message that she wasn't interested.

"Vishal, I'm sorry. Today's not a good day. I have to go. Bye."

Reaching the last step, she paused when her feet touched the floor. Lara forced in a deep breath and lifted her foot to move away when a vicious grip closed around her arm.

She whirled around to find her mother right behind her.

"That boy, he's been calling you often, hasn't

he?"

She peered into the eyes ablaze with reproach, eyes so like the ones she saw whenever she looked into a mirror. Except hers had never carried so much spite and misplaced righteousness. The recrimination in the tone washed over her. She bristled with the disgust and outrage welling up in response to the position her mother had made her take today.

Yet, she chose not to reply and reached up to loosen her mother's grip on her arm before stepping away on her way out.

Her mother followed her. "He's not very proper for you, you know."

And just when she'd thought nothing could get any worse ...

Lara stopped in her tracks and turned around to face the older woman. She was sure daggers of rage and loathing shot from the glare she directed at her mother. For a second or two, she revelled in the satisfying pleasure of watching her mum squirm. Fuelled by a wave of contempt, she wouldn't mince her words when she opened her mouth. Truth be told, she didn't wish to spare any hurt her comments could inflict.

"Now, what is this supposed to mean, Mother?" she asked in a cold, detached voice. She cocked her head to the side and crossed her arms in front of her. "I suppose you're saying I'm not virgin enough to attract a young man who's never been married? Never mind if a total trollop hooked up with a guy like him. As long as she still had her hymen intact or had never gotten divorced, she'd be a 'proper' girl, now, wouldn't she?"

Her mother paled and flinched. Lara gulped when tears threatened to blur her vision and a lump settled in her throat.

"Don't you think I know I'm tainted from my divorce?" she whispered. She forced a smile onto her face. "How could I not when every one of you people here have done more than her fair share to remind me?"

Spent with her final question, her shoulders threatened to sag. But she wouldn't give anyone the satisfaction of knowing their poisoned arrows had hit home.

Lara didn't bother to see what theatrical display her mother was bound to make.

She passed by her father, Diya, and Neha, who must've come in at some point, on the way to her car. No one tried to stop her.

Just as well.

No one would've managed to, anyway. She slid into her Mercedes and slammed the door shut. Switching the engine on, she jammed her foot onto the accelerator and sped out of the courtyard in a cloud of dust and spitting gravel.

She thought she smelled burned rubber, but the only thing she fully registered were the tears finally coursing down her cheeks.

Chapter Eight

Eric breathed in the salty sea air, letting it sting his nose and fill his lungs as he strolled along the edges of the Caudan Waterfront esplanade in Port-Louis. He'd had a tough morning at the practice, where he'd been called for an emergency after dealing with a premature birth at the clinic. He frowned and kicked a small rock into the harbour's murky green waters.

A little girl with a congenital heart malformation. Not yet two years old—what had she known of life already? He'd been unable to do anything other than put her on the waiting list for a transplant. *Merde.* As a physician, he was meant to care for his patients and make them better. Yet, sometimes, he had difficulty keeping his personal feelings aside and not taking on his patients' suffering and pain. Whatever had possessed him to go into medicine? A doctor couldn't save all sick people. He was only human, after all.

The helplessness had brewed in him all day long, not helped by the turmoil Lara had already stirred.

He'd come here to unwind. To witness healthy, lively children playing and enjoying carefree childhood. That's the way things should be. Children weren't meant to suffer.

He ran a heavy hand over his face as something in the distance caught his attention.

Lara. Did he have to think of her, and she'd appear out of thin air? First, at the conference yesterday and today, she was at the waterfront.

Would he bump into her every time he sought to escape her? Maybe he couldn't avoid her. Was it Fate's way of telling him to deal with the matter?

He slanted his gaze back towards her. She sat at a table in a far corner of a terrace, seemingly engrossed in conversation with an insipid-looking youth opposite her.

However, she'd clamped her arms to her chest. If he remembered correctly, she usually did that when she was cornered and wanted an escape. He studied her face, which grew more flustered with every passing minute.

Was she in some trouble with this man?

But she'd say it was none of his business. She lived her life. He lived his. She'd made that clear the day before when she'd run away from him.

She definitely seemed to be in some sort of trouble, though, as she shook her head while speaking.

Drawn by the furtive glances she sent around her, he couldn't help but venture nearer. She must not have seen him approach because she didn't acknowledge his presence. She pressed her spine in her chair and threw her head back, eyes closed, lips in a tight, white line.

Something was wrong. Something to do with the guy. But one glance at him, and Eric wasn't sure if he was so at fault here, for the youth looked on the brink of crying.

As he swerved around the table right behind them, he caught the sound of her voice.

"Vishal, I'm already seeing someone."

His step faltered, and his heart started to race as he reached out to grasp the back of a nearby chair to steady himself.

Is it true? Is she with some other man? Maybe back with her husband …

But then, he caught her peering up as if asking for divine help.

He chuckled softly as a smile spread across his face. He pretty much had an idea what she'd gotten herself into. Another poor hopeful needed to be driven away. She used to attract boys like moths to a flame. Seemed that hadn't changed. He'd run to her rescue on more than one occasion in such sticky situations.

And today, he couldn't possibly ignore her plea for help, could he? Granted, she hadn't addressed it to him, but maybe he was God's answer to her. He had no way out of any predicament in which she starred, so he might as well turn any scenario to his advantage.

The fun's about to start.

***

Lara cursed softly under her breath. What would she do with this kid? She'd called him to gently inform him no future existed for them. Yet, her strategy appeared to have fallen through because Vishal just sat there. She'd just resorted to inventing a boyfriend in a last-ditch effort to get him to back off. But he just gaped, and tears filled his eyes again.

Disgust at his overblown reaction churned her stomach. He reminded her of a spoiled child who'd been denied a ride on the merry-go-round. She hoped he wouldn't prove her right and throw a tantrum in front of everyone. How would she get him to leave, then?

Suddenly, a warm, strong hand settled on her shoulder as the brush of a fleeting kiss caressed her cheek.

What the heck?

She swivelled, paying little heed to the possibility of smacking her skull against the head of whoever had kissed her. But she shouldn't have worried since he'd drawn up to his full height, which left her to stare at the jeans waistband of a virile man with narrow hips and an absolutely flat stomach.

Her mouth grew dry at this snapshot of male perfection. *Who ...?* Her gaze travelled upwards. A close-fitting white T-shirt hugged a well-defined chest and broad shoulders. A face with clear-cut features and sparkling blue eyes that winked at her.

Her mouth grew drier, and she struggled to swallow the lump wedged in her throat.

Of all the people in the world ... Of course, Fate would choose only Eric. She closed her eyes, only to have her traitorous hormones urge her to glance up again and drink her fill of the beefcake goodness.

She didn't want to see him—didn't *need* to—and certainly not when he looked as delectable as now. She couldn't tear her attention from him as she finally understood the allure of blue jeans and a white T-shirt on a man. She'd constantly harped on the need for a suit and tie for any man to make it on her sweet dream list. Roy had been an elegant dresser and hadn't possessed the casual streak to wear jeans.

Yet, on Eric, the very simplicity was a compliment to his masculinity and virility. Who knew casual could be more lethal than classy?

Had she ordered a drink? She needed something, anything, to soothe her parched mouth and throat.

Damn. She hated losing control, especially over her emotions, and Eric made her lose it every time.

As if on cue, he smiled, and she was a goner again. Her little pep talk to get over him? Vanished in a lust-blazed smoke.

"Hello, sweetheart," he said in a husky tone. "Sorry, I'm a little early. I finished with my last patient earlier than planned, so I thought I'd come meet you."

He spoke the words to her as if she were the only living creature within a mile. His face drew level with hers, his bright gaze plunging into hers, into her soul, laying her bare.

I'm glad you're here.

Bewildered, she shook her head. What was wrong with her? She had other issues to deal with, too.

What is Eric doing here, and what game is he playing?

But all conscious thought evaporated as he trailed a hand along her nape, where he stopped to play with little tendrils of her hair. He touched the delicate spot along her hairline, sending shivers down her spine.

She fluttered her eyelids, and a soft moan

escaped her lips. Was it really so hot on the terrace? Her tension-filled body grew light under his touch, making her wonder if she'd end up floating up to the sky if he kept doing that to her.

A strangled yelp brought her back to the present.

She'd all but forgotten Vishal sat at her table.

She blinked as if coming out of a dream. Her eyelids were heavy, as were her lips. What was wrong with her? And worse, where was she stuck?

She allowed her gaze to take in the man—okay, the kid—opposite her, then she turned towards Eric at her side. His hand still lay tangled in her hair, and his face hovered near hers. She jumped involuntarily, which made her forearm brush against the soft fabric of his T-shirt to register the warmth from his skin permeating the garment.

Lara tried to speak, but no word could escape her lips. Not even a croak.

Her mind couldn't form a coherent thought. Like in slow motion, she watched as Eric tilted his head, and his lips grazed her temple in a fleeting butterfly kiss.

"Play the part," he said in her ear.

His low, rumbling voice washed over her like a caress. The smoothness of his tone, the huskiness in his whisper, wrapped around her. She slowly blinked up at him as she parted her lips. His eyes darkened.

Lara suddenly realised they made an intimate picture in this pose.

As intimate as two lovers.

The lovers we never got to become.

They'd never become lovers because Eric had

left. Had left her for someone else.

But she dismissed the hurt. She'd had enough time already to dwell on that particular betrayal. More pressing matters were at hand, like the wreck of a man—child—she needed to be rid of. So she'd go along with this farce for now.

She peered up at Eric and pasted an adoring smile on her face, hoping it lit her features with the glow of a woman in love. At least, Sam said a woman in love glowed. She had no way of knowing, never having seen that elusive radiance in the mirror.

"There you are, darling. I was just telling Vishal about us," she said. "Oh, how silly of me, you two haven't been introduced. Baby, this is Vishal, my cousin. Vishal, meet Eric, my boyfriend."

Her voice trickled as sweet as syrup when she addressed him with an equally sickening smile, and Vishal gulped a few times as if trying not to throw up.

Eric drew a chair up and sat beside her.

"I sure hope I'm not disturbing you," he said, staring straight at Vishal. He turned to her, then. "I didn't know I'd be barging in. Forgive me?"

Lara smiled back. "There's nothing to forgive, darling, and Vishal was leaving, anyway." She turned to face the other man. "Weren't you, Vishal?"

She dreaded a teary episode, but fortunately, Vishal seemed to have found his composure. With the appearance of a forlorn, beaten dog, he quickly said goodbye and left.

As soon as he was out of sight, she heaved a huge sigh of relief and let her body sag in her chair. She brought her hands to her pounding temples, hoping to avoid a migraine. A couple of paracetamol pills to kill the pain and the comfort of her bedroom with all the curtains closed would do the trick.

The sound of a throat clearing startled her from her reverie, and she blinked to find Eric still sitting next to her.

He'd draped his broad frame in his seat, one arm casually on the back of her chair. His eyes were on her, and a smile lifted the corners of his mouth.

Damn it, he really is gorgeous.

But he's not for you.

She had to keep reminding herself of this. Her life without a man in it was complicated enough. He'd also let her down in the past, and he would probably do it again if she gave him a chance.

But what if he doesn't?

She dismissed the thought as soon as it struck her mind. *Dead end.* She had sworn off men, hadn't she? Look what trouble she'd gotten into with Vishal, and she hadn't even done anything there.

Still, she owed Eric her thanks. Had it not been for him and his timely intervention, she'd still be stuck dealing with Vishal.

"Thanks for the help," she said, forcing the words out. "I really appreciate it."

Eric's smile widened. His eyes were still on her, though—deep, intense, making her squirm. He wouldn't let her off the hook.

"Care to tell me what all this was about?" he asked in a slow drawl.

He'd always spoken English with a lilting accent, only the edges of his words sounding slightly sharp. Probably something he carried over from his

Mauritian French native tongue.

His voice hit her as low and full of concern. The tone invited secrets and promised to offer support and caring.

Lara breathed in, filling her lungs. Unfortunately, the sea air didn't unscramble her mind or change her situation as an emotional wreck, a disadvantage when dealing with Eric and his concern and attention.

She fought the part of her wanting to confide and ease the load on her heart. However, the heavy burden threatened to crush her, considering what had happened earlier with her mother.

She needed a sympathetic ear, and Eric had played the role so many years ago. Did it matter if he paid attention to her woes now? She certainly had no intention of meeting him purposefully again, so she might as well make the most of this opportunity.

So, she straightened and stared at him. Then, with a shrug, she started her story.

"Vishal is a cousin of mine who's got a crush on me, and the family doesn't see it with a good eye. So I called him here to set things straight with him."

Eric certainly was a good audience. He didn't interrupt her, simply gave her all his attention.

Relieved that he allowed her to vent, Lara was drawn into the depths of his eyes, the gentleness of his gaze, the encouraging curve of his mouth when he smiled.

"Then, this morning, my mother butted in again, and I gotta say, she's only made things worse," she ended on a sigh.

Eric laughed at the mention of her mother—a

rich, deep bellow, full of insouciance and amusement. Its echo tingled its way into her, and she remembered the many laughs they'd shared in the past.

"How *is* your mother?" he asked, bringing her back to the here and now. "She used to be tough."

Don't go there—don't go thinking of the past.

"Well, let's just say she's not getting any better with time." She chuckled. "Probably the onset of menopause."

***

Eric watched as the smile broke upon her face.

How beautiful she is.

He was pretty sure she hadn't laughed in a long time, though. Her face appeared weary, her features drawn, with a greyish tinge to her skin. She used to glow with a golden light, like women in those advertisements for Arabian bronze blush beads his sister had been pestering him to buy for her for months.

He'd noticed the fatigue on Lara the day before, but today, the strain looked more pronounced. She'd also lost weight. She hadn't been so thin when he'd seen her at the clinic.

"I have a feeling you need a break," he said. "You're probably working too hard."

She glanced back at him for a while, seemingly lost in her thoughts.

There used to be a sparkle in her eyes. Now, I can't see it.

Had life really been so hard on her?

After a little while, she gave him a weary smile in reply, and she shrugged, like in the past.

Just like his girl used to.

That girl still lived in her. He'd glimpsed her, even if only for a fleeting second.

His girl. Eric vowed to bring her back. Come Hell or high water, he'd make her return and give her all the love and care she deserved.

All the love and care he hadn't been able to give her during those years they'd lost.

He had to tread carefully, though, especially with a control freak like her. He doubted the years had made her any mellower.

So only careful planning and organized steps to woo her again, bring her back to life as the cheerful, carefree young woman he'd known. He would take his time to court her because he would rest only when he and Lara became man and wife. He'd also put his desires aside for the moment and show her she could count on him. Hopefully, she would realise it soon, but he'd wait. He could be a patient man when the need arose.

Small steps, one at a time.

A light wind started to blow around them, signalling the approach of dusk. Lara peeked at her watch.

"Eric, I really have to go. There's this wedding I need to go to this evening, a friend of mine."

"It's okay. I'll walk you to your car."

She darted a quick glance over her shoulder as she bit her lip.

"Only if you don't mind," he said.

She smiled back after a few seconds, and they both made their way to the parking lot. Walking side by side, with less than a foot between them, negotiating the pressing crowds. But the distance could've been as vast as an ocean while she kept to herself during the five-minute trek to the marina parking area.

"Which one is yours?" he asked as he surveyed the overflowing lot.

"The blue one near the docks."

He caught a glimpse of the brand-new Mercedes coupé and whistled softly.

She laughed again—the soft, husky sound could drive him over the edge. At the car, he held the door while she got in. He shut the door, and she lowered the glass, turning towards him.

"Thanks for everything, Eric. I really appreciate what you did for me today."

Bending by the window, he brought his face level with hers. "At least if nothing else, we're friends, Lara. Don't forget it."

Her right hand lay on the steering wheel, and he reached out and clasped it with his own. He brought it to his lips and pressed a kiss onto the back.

"Bye, Lara."

"Bye," she whispered.

***

Lara sat in her car for a long moment. The warm imprint of Eric's lips still tingled on her hand.

His parting words had rubbed a soothing balm on her heart. They had undoubtedly been friends before being anything else. Could they build on that again?

Or was this very foundation too weak? The structure hadn't held in the past.

When his head had levelled with hers, she'd wanted to see his face and eyes for the truth. Yet, with the setting sun behind him, shadows had played upon his features, cloaking him with a thin mask of darkness, enough to conceal anything his expression might've revealed.

What she would have seen in his too-beautiful, haunting face? Hope? Love?

Would you have liked all this coming from him?

Silly notion. Her future had no place for a man. But a part of her was desperate for attention, consideration, love, and affection.

All of which she could get from Eric.

A jolt of adrenaline went through her, along with extreme unease and discomfited. Her first instinct was to search around for an escape.

Is there one?

Weariness rushed over her, making her slump like a limp noodle onto her seat. The high spirits Eric had put her in crashed like a thousand shards of crystal, leaving her spent.

She had to get over this, over him, because there was no future for them.

Shaking her head, she switched the engine, eased the car out of its parking space, and made her way back to her house.

Cut your losses and gear up for the most vital battle.

She still had a tough evening ahead of her, where she'd be facing her mother again.

Chapter Nine

The late afternoon sun filtered through Sam's lace curtains hanging in the house. Lara had sighed and simply let her best friend get her kicks out of decorating both sides of the semi-detached. Lord knew she'd never have time or the inclination to hang up frilly window accessories around any place she lived in.

She glanced at the sky before closing the front door. Sun rays pierced through the thick canopy of rain-laden grey clouds, making twilight hover over the island at five-thirty. The air hung thick and stifling, not a hint of breeze to alleviate the high humidity.

March in Mauritius. They'd be putting away their thickest coats in England in anticipation of spring. But on the tropical coast, only two weather conditions prevailed—humid and more humid.

She stepped out of her high-heeled stilettos in the hallway and welcomed the cool touch of the glossy marble under the heated soles of her feet. She then dropped her handbag on the sofa and headed upstairs to the bathroom. Thanks to the suffocating heaviness shrouding everything, her clothes stuck to her skin.

Once in the bathroom, she rid herself of the cotton blouse and linen skirt and removed the pins in her bun before turning the shower on to full spray. After stepping under the cool jet, she allowed the water needles to drum on her exhausted body, washing the remnants of the cloying heat from her skin and hair.

Ten minutes later, she stepped out of the cubicle, wrapped herself in a thick towel, and walked into her bedroom. Her wet hair loose, and in a pair of shorts and strappy cotton jersey top, she picked up her cell phone, intent on calling Sam's mobile as she went downstairs. Her friend hadn't visited her side of the house this weekend.

She'd barely woken the screen up when the phone rang in her hand.

"Hello, Mum," she said with a sigh.

"Is this the way to greet your mother? You haven't called me in a week, and that secretary of yours never puts me through to you."

"It's because I'm busy, Mum. I'd call you if anything happened."

"Never mind. When are you coming by Curepipe? It's been so long since we last saw you."

Lara sighed again and rolled her eyes.

"For God's sake, we met four days ago at the groom's reception for Yazmin's wedding." Trust her mother to turn a challenging day into an even harder time. She sorely lacked the energy or the patience to deal with her. "Mum, sorry, but I have to go now, okay? Bye."

She sure has guts.

Ever since the whole proposal incident, she'd

kept a low profile with her mother. But Gayatri Hemant was back to her overwhelming self again, as if nothing has happened between them, and Lara knew no respite from her.

The halfway landing was dark and gloomy when she reached it. Grappling for the light switch on the wall, she pressed the button to turn the wall sconces on.

A few steps from reaching the ground floor, the lights went out on her. At the same time, a brilliant flash lit up the house, followed seconds later by an ear-splitting, crunching sound that boomed over the whole area.

A thunderstorm.

Her mind froze, and she stood rooted to the spot, as it always happened when thunder raged. One of her first memories was two-year-old her waking up in a strange bed after hearing thunder during her first visit to Mauritius.

She'd been lucky so far not to have run into any thunderstorm on the island. With summer being nearly over, she'd believed herself spared the trauma of the sickening roar when it hit the island.

Some part of her brain that still functioned told her she had to get a grip and light some candles so she could see where she was going. But panic clamped down and anchored her solidly on the step as cold sweat broke on her back and the icy numbness wrapped around her.

A sound like a chime filtered through her consciousness. Startling, she glanced down. The phone was ringing in her palm and she forced herself to answer.

"Hello?"

"Lara, it's Eric. Where are you? Are you alone?"

Eric?

"Lara? Hello?"

"I'm … I'm here … at home … alone … it's dark … power out," she said, hanging on to the sound of his voice.

"Where do you live?"

A blinding streak of light and another horrendous growl resounded, and she nearly dropped the phone.

"Lara, where's your house?" he again asked.

She gulped in a deep breath and forced a coherent thought to form in her numb mind. "Number twenty-six, Seaview estate, near the hotel in Grand-Baie—" *Beep, beep, beep.*

The line went dead. The phone screen had also gone blank. Damn, the battery was out. No electricity meant she couldn't recharge it right away.

Bloody phone and her own lack of vigilance over the battery. No way was she going out to try the travel charger that plugged into the car.

The storm gathered momentum outside, winds picking up and lashing rain onto the windows. Every successive thunderbolt sounded louder than the previous one.

Lara sank into a motionless heap on the stairs. Her limbs had frozen solid, and her heart thrashed frantically rush in her chest. Cold sweat broke on her forehead and on the palms of her hands. The cell phone dropped onto the marble floor. Beyond caring about the damage, she didn't check if the device had exploded into pieces.

She couldn't recall how long she stayed thus, arms wrapped around knees she had brought up to her chest. Mere minutes could've been hours for all she knew in her fear-induced daze.

Loud pounding resonated in the still air between two claps of thunder.

At first, it seemed the storm had started to pelt hail outside, but this was Mauritius, not England. No hail here.

And when the noise didn't stop, she reckoned it had to come from the door.

But she didn't dare to move. She lay ensconced in her little world where the thunder couldn't get her, and no way would she break from it. Perhaps the visitor would leave if he didn't get any response.

When the pounding didn't stop, she forced herself to the door with a dragging step and opened the panel, blinking in surprise.

Eric stood on her front porch, and he pushed into the hall as soon as she opened the door wide enough for him to enter.

Eric is here, and everything will be fine.

A deep sense of relief washed over her as he shrugged out of his wet jacket. His solid presence filled the small space, and his aftershave's fresh, tangy fragrance soothed her ragged mind. Her heart stopped beating its frantic roll and settled at a somewhat normal pace.

Until another loud crack of thunder bolted, and she jumped in panic.

***

One minute she'd been standing before him, and the next, she'd pressed the length of her feminine perfection flush against his body.

For a split second, Eric didn't know how to react.

As she gripped his shirt in tight fists, she shivered, as much from the cold sheen of moisture on her skin as from the violent emotion.

She was scared.

He was here to make sure she had no reason to be scared.

So he placed his arms around her and pulled her to him. She sighed against his shirt, her breath warming the humid fabric and making it cling to his pecs. Then, wrapping her arms around his neck, she burrowed her face into his shoulder while pressing her whole body to his frame. The fruity fragrance of her damp hair made its way into his mind, and he once again noted how cold she was as the skin of her arm brushed the back of his neck.

A wave of tenderness and an irresistible urge to protect her overwhelmed him.

This was his girl, today his woman.

With his hand on her back, he cradled her softly. He caressed her hair with his other hand and murmured soothing words to calm her. If he paused long enough, he could make out the rapid beat of her heart slowing against his chest.

"It's okay. I'm here now. Nothing wrong's gonna happen to you," he whispered in her ear.

Little by little, the tension drained from her body, and she snuggled into his embrace. Lara felt firm, yet soft, against him. She had the luscious body of a woman, so different from the thin girl she'd been and yet so similar in the feelings she brought to his mind.

Tenderness, love, affection, and desire as hot and intense as raging flames. The latent fire burst from every fibre of his being. The heat gradually returning to her body seeped into his, and he grew rigid and tense, like a coiled spring.

Slow and easy. He had to remind himself of it. No point in frightening her away with the rash demands of his body. But *merde* if that wasn't hard when she fuelled the very blaze with her tantalizing presence.

And here she stood in his arms. With hardly a thing on to cover herself.

How long would he be able to keep himself in check before lust won over and he ravished her right there in her front hallway?

***

Had she been drugged? Or had she fallen and hit her head?

Everything inside her mind drifted in a hazy rhythm while her senses remained numb in contented inertia. Wherever she was, the place felt comfortable, oh so comfortable, with just enough warmth to blank out the chill, yet not hot enough to burn.

Peaceful.

Whatever she leaned against moved fleetingly under her, but she noticed the shift.

Where was she? She forced her mind into battle with her foggy consciousness. She remembered the lightning bolt and the subsequent thunder strike that had gone "ka-boom" while she'd had the door open... Why had she opened the door in the first place?

The 'thing' against her moved again. Finally, she forced her mind into focus. Little by little, messages started to travel up her synapses to form a picture in her head.

Her arms were wrapped tight around something deceptively hard because she could also feel a soft give under her grasp, like the sinuous play of muscles. Whatever she was pressed against stood firm and warm. Deliciously warm, but not scorching hot.

And it felt ... Lara shifted, which made her cheek brush against something resembling smooth cotton covering a shallow hollow. When she tried to tear herself away, a strong yet gentle grip kept her anchored. A light, gentle caress smoothed her hair, going down in long, calming movements.

A touch on her hair and firm muscle holding her in place? Bells rang. She was in a man's arms.

She gasped. *Eric.*

She stiffened and jerked her head up. True enough, there he stood. Or, she should state that as there *she* stood, wrapped all around him. *Shame on you.* She had her arms around his big shoulders and every inch of her front pressed against his body.

Shame, shame, shame. What a hussy.

How could she ever face him again? She hadn't ever let herself go with a man. Not even her husband. Theirs had never been a cuddly or affectionate marriage. Was that why she craved such hands-on contact? She'd been as limp as a rag doll against Eric, pliant and awaiting his next order so she could be ravished.

Embarrassment filled her and burned her cheeks.

As he gently released her, she disentangled herself from his grip with care. He opened his arms, allowing her to leave his embrace.

His embrace. Goodness, how long had it been since he'd last held her?

Don't. Go. There.

Breaking free from his hold, she took a step back and lowered her head. Wringing her hands, she lowered her gaze as her face, and her pride, burned with indignity. How could she have let herself go so much? The thunderstorm was not an excuse. She should've been made of sterner stuff.

His steady gaze burned onto her, and then he reached out and tucked a strand of hair behind her ear. The tips of his fingers brushed her cheek in a fleeting caress, and she closed her eyes for a second.

"Feeling better?" he asked.

Barefoot, she suddenly felt tiny in front of his mighty height of six-foot-three. Never before had she felt so delicate and vulnerable.

"I knew you'd be scared with the storm," he said. "That's why I came around to check on you."

He'd remembered she was afraid of thunder. What did it say about him, about their friendship? And possibly, about more between them?

The warmth in his tone and the caring in his words touched her heart, and gentle, soothing warmth flooded through her, radiating from where he'd touched her cheek only seconds before. The pleasant heat filled her with courage, and she lifted her eyes to stare into his.

His irises were an intense shade of turquoise, the shade deeper thanks to the twilight darkness in the hallway, and she lost herself in their depths. His warm smile mimicked sunshine and could melt ice.

And she smiled back, all notion of awkwardness brushed aside under the pull of his guileless grin. She stood rooted to the spot again, though from a different feeling this time.

When did he get so handsome? He'd always been a nice guy, too.

How had she managed to lose him?

Eric took her arm, snapping her out of her reflective musings, and drew her into the living room.

"I think we better light some candles. It's awfully dark here," he said. "Also, I love to stand, but right now, I could do with a seat."

He winked at her, and she smothered a giggle. Yes, she was pathetic, as pitiable as a fan in the throes of boy-band mania, but what could she do? No matter how idiotic it painted her, this feeling remained preferable to the distress caused by her family and their society. Eric was solid and reliable. He'd never shift and morph on her. If she allowed him, he'd become her anchor again, her safe harbour from all the storms. He'd give her the bubble she needed to thrive.

Nothing looked better right now. She needed him in her life.

So Lara gave in to the warmth in her chest as he tugged her to the living room. She leaned onto the doorway as he made his way around the ground floor, lighting the lavender-scented candles she'd placed all over only the day before. The soothing aroma drifted into the air. Perfect for her overwrought nerves, not helped by his presence.

He settled his broad, well-built body onto the sofa when he finished the task and patted the cushion next to him. "Come join me."

Don't tempt me. An open-ended invitation like that, and she'd jump all over him again. Jump his bones, literally.

Heat stung her cheeks, and she lowered her head to let her hair cover the flaming features.

She made her way into the room but sat at the far end of the three-place sofa. She didn't trust herself to be too close to him and thus left an enormous space between them as she huddled into her seat, drawing her legs under her.

She however couldn't escape his intent scrutiny and glanced at him. He smiled and then shook his head.

"You're still the same, especially where thunder is concerned."

She returned the grin. Amazing how she, a grown woman past thirty years of age, could still be afraid of thunder. Some things couldn't be explained. She chuckled softly.

The atmosphere around her shifted, and tension filled the room, making the hairs on her nape stand up and sending her heart into a frantic beat. She met his eyes. There burned a different emotion in them. The blue depths were dark, hooded, and fire smouldered in them.

Lara swallowed hard. Eric used to look at her like that whenever they'd been alone ...

"Some things don't change," she said in a hushed tone.

She didn't know how the comment came out of

her mouth. Speaking of the past was dangerous, because those memories constituted uncharted territory, a minefield of unfulfilled dreams and longings.

He studied her for a long moment. "Yes, it's true."

Silence settled between them as she pondered his reply. It sounded like a confession. Was it wishful thinking, though? Was she reading unspoken things into his every word? She didn't know.

She only knew that the soft, candlelit atmosphere drifted around them conducive to exchanging secrets and confessions. And she craved to know his secrets, to hear his confessions. Anything to fortify her certitude that she hadn't made a hasty decision fourteen years earlier, that she'd been right in taking a new direction.

"Didn't you get married in the past decade?" she asked.

He didn't answer her immediately. Instead, his eyes took a faraway glint, and a veil of sadness settled over his face.

He shook his head in reply a few seconds later.

A tug nipped at her heart when she took in his forlorn expression. She'd better drop the subject, yet, irrepressible curiosity grappled for hold all through her. "Why not?"

Eric remained silent for ages, his deep, sad gaze on her face.

"I didn't find the woman I wanted. The right one was already taken."

She drew in a sharp breath. Could he be talking about her?

"You got married shortly after I left," he said.

She nodded, and the words, heavy with meaning, hung in mid-air between them. A sizzling tension bristled in the confines of the living room, and she wanted to beat herself. Her mouth had won over again, and once more, she'd stuck her foot in it. Why had she ventured onto that path? She'd never wanted to bring up that particular subject between them. Then, she'd have to face the truth—maybe she'd been hasty in deciding Eric no longer had a place in her life.

"My marriage was arranged," she said.

But you've always had the choice to refuse.

Where did *that* come from? Her conscience had it in for her lately.

"Were you happy?" he asked.

She blinked. She'd expected recriminations after her last comment. Not concern, or caring.

He asked about Roy. She'd read between his every word in the past, and right now, she flashed back over a decade. "Does it matter?"

"If you were happy, then no."

A dilemma raged inside her. Tell Eric the truth, or pretend things were all right?

Sam's words rang in her mind. How long could she continue to exist in denial?

On a deep breath, she started her very own confession. "I thought I was happy. I thought Roy was happy. I thought ours was a happy marriage."

Eric didn't say a word. But his raised eyebrows queried her.

To say so little already hurt so much, and she wasn't sure she had it in her to face more truths and half-truths tonight. Better leave it there, and let him construe what he wanted from her words.

She shrugged and gave him a small, sad smile. "In the end, we found out we didn't want the same things in life."

He didn't prompt her for further explanation. She'd assumed he would, though. But he was just being his caring and attentive self. Tears unexpectedly stung her eyes, and she swallowed the lump forming in her throat.

No more of this melodrama. She needed to get herself back on track again. She couldn't allow herself to break down even more in front of Eric, of all people.

"Anyway, to cut it short, Roy wanted children, but I wasn't ready. So we divorced, and now he's remarried, and his new wife was expecting their first, last I'd heard."

***

The play of emotion on Lara's face gave her away. She'd started to let her hair down with him. But minutes later, the impersonal façade of the strong career woman had shuttered back down.

She still hadn't lost her knack for control.

As stubborn and uncompromising as ever. Granted, that Roy fellow must've been a swine to treat her thus, but was the man really so much at fault here? Lara drove a hard bargain. Always had, and probably always would.

So, was it foolish of him to believe he could make this whole business bear fruit? Or would he be trampled again? Patience was his virtue, but he didn't have a never-ending supply of it.

136

He heaved in a long breath.

No, he wouldn't falter this time. Everything would work out fine because he'd see to it personally. He loved Lara, and she still felt something for him. Today was of proof enough she wasn't immune to him. She could still have feelings for him buried under that hard shell of hers. But he'd bring down the walls of her fortress and conquer her every defence one by one.

He trained his gaze on her, and she returned a bold stare. Their eyes remained locked for a long moment, and spoke their own language. Neither would give in nor bow out first.

Where would such pig-headed tenacity leave them?

Brilliant light flooded the room, making them both blink in surprise. The power had returned. He should tell Lara to have a word with her estate manager since the emergency generators had failed to kick in when the electricity had gone out earlier.

Eric glanced at his watch. Two hours had elapsed in the time they'd been together. How could it have been two hours already? They'd talked for only a few moments.

Lara bolted from the sofa and stood in the middle of the living room, wringing her hands together, hopping from foot to foot.

Et puis, merde, alors. Those short shorts and her skimpy top did *not* constitute clothing. He'd never seen her look so sexy, so tantalising. The late hour meant dinnertime. But he grew hungry for another kind of sustenance, which could earn him a kick in the groin if he pressed his intention.

He better leave quickly. He didn't trust himself to behave in a gentlemanly fashion when she appeared so delicious.

So, he stood and faced her. "The power is back, and the storm is over. You're safe now, so I'll leave."

He didn't hope she'd ask him to stay back. Knowing Lara, he still had a long way to go before winning her trust again. He made his way into the hall, and she followed in his footsteps.

On the threshold, he stopped.

"I live not far from here, in Cap Malheureux. Call me if you ever need anything."

She had his number since he'd called her from his cell earlier, and the call log must've recorded the contact info. Thank goodness he'd snagged one of her business cards from Markus back at the conference. She wouldn't have given him her contact information so freely.

Lara nodded but didn't say a word.

She made this hard on him. He snickered softly. When had he ever had anything easy with her?

"Come around one day and take a look at my house," he said, unable to resist the temptation to throw the invite out.

"I ... I'll think about it," she replied after a few seconds.

"Okay." He should be content with that. At least, she hadn't given a flat-out no. "Take care of yourself, Lara."

She nodded. "Look after yourself, too," she said, barely above a whisper.

***

Lara closed the door softly behind Eric. Shaken

to the core, she leant onto the hall wall for support. Her eyes drifted closed as weariness crashed over her.

Damn if she hadn't crossed a line in her relationship with Eric, whatever this *relationship* happened to be at the moment. Their friendship, or what had remained of it, had taken a turn into deeper territories. However, she didn't know if that was for the better. Or for the worse.

She only knew she felt torn. On the one hand, she had the security of her single status, her independence, and a fulfilling and successful career. Mistress of her destiny, captain of the path she charted for her life's path.

On the other hand, she'd been asking herself more often if being at the boat's helm gave back enough. She longed for a relationship and the warmth and comfort such a connection brought. Her heart constantly asked for love to fill its emptiness. She lived a lonely existence, with no one to share her joys, sorrows, or pain. Not to mention that an empty bed consisted of everything except a woman's fulfilment. Even when Roy had ditched her and she'd been smarting with indignation, she'd sometimes yearned for companionship and love.

Today, was Eric the answer for her? Had he been the answer all along?

Lara winced as the questions slammed into her like a haywire tennis ball machine.

Did she have the guts and determination to go after a relationship that had once seemed impossible?

How did anyone make the impossible possible? In Mauritius, of all places?

Chapter Ten

Back from the weekly directorial meeting, Lara stopped by her PA's desk. "The directors approved all pending decisions. You can send the newsletter around and update all the staff."

Fifteen minutes later, Doris popped into the office. "Just been on the coffee break. You've worked a coup. They're all talking of the upcoming film shoot."

She smiled. "So you'd say the mood is good among the staff?"

Doris rolled her eyes. "Good? They're ecstatic. They're all wondering how you've managed to get such an important film crew to shoot on our premises."

"I didn't do much, Doris. They contacted me first."

"You've sure worked wonders. They all revere you now," the older woman said with a wink before she walked out of the office.

A soft laugh escaped Lara's throat. She leaned back in her chair and gazed out the windowed wall of her office. The view opened to a lushly vibrant garden. Huge, colourful hibiscus blooms dotted the intense green of thick bushes and the lawn, and strategically placed palm trees offered shade from the burning tropical sun.

No wonder a Bollywood film crew wanted to shoot here. The very architecture of the centre made it stand apart from any other building on the island. Its modern design of steel and glass tended toward futuristic in some places. Under the Mauritian sun, the dome sparkled like a jewel. She'd been told the production team consisted of one of the biggest names in the Mumbai cinema industry. Not that she'd know, being clueless about Indian movies. Still, given the hype around the project, she'd been convinced the shooting would be for a blockbuster-type project.

The ringing of her cell phone broke through the silence. Her mind still lost on the garden's beauty, she picked it up.

"Lara Reddy."

"*Bonjour*, Lara. How's it going?"

Butterflies took flight in her stomach when she recognized the rich voice. "Fine, Eric. You?"

Damn, if she could form more than one-word responses suddenly. The sound of his lilting accent was enough to turn her brain to mush.

You're pathetic.

And frankly, I don't care anymore.

"Not too bad." He chuckled. "What's up?"

Her heart missed a beat. She didn't know what to say or do, so she threw out the first thing that popped into her head. "I just heard all my staff now revere me."

Stupid fool. Now he'll take you for an egomaniac. She closed her eyes in despair and cursed under her breath.

Eric laughed, and the rich, throaty sound wreaked more havoc among the butterflies in her stomach.

"How did you manage such a feat?" he asked.

Lara's eyes flew open, and she gave an inward sigh of relief. At least he wasn't taking her for an idiot. "Turns out part of the biggest Bollywood project for the year will be shot on the centre's premises."

"That explains it, then."

His laid-back tone prompted her to relax, and she rolled her shoulders as she slouched a little in her seat.

He'd always been easy to talk to. How could she have forgotten?

"Well, I figure they're more interested in rubbing shoulders with the actors, but still, I'm happy they like it. And the centre will get a lot of publicity as a result, so it's really killing two birds with one stone."

He chuckled again. "I'm glad for you."

Had his voice always been so husky, or was her mind playing tricks on her today?

She then realised he'd been talking. "Uh, sorry. Could you repeat that, please?"

"I said, how about going out with me tonight to celebrate?"

Her mind scrambled. Eric was asking her out on a date?

"Lara? Hello?"

"Oh, uh, I'm still there," she said, blurting the words. "I was just wondering—"

"About what?" he cut in with a gentle tone.

She had to stop this whole matter now before it got out of control. She had no time or energy for the complications of a relationship. She certainly didn't need to have her heart trampled again. She had to say no to Eric. No matter how much she hated being alone at times, better to be alone than unhappy.

So she took in a deep breath.

"What sort of celebration?" she heard herself asking.

What? That wasn't what was supposed to come out of her mouth!

"How about a movie? You still like popcorn action flicks?"

A soft gasp of surprise escaped her. He still remembered? How many little things about her *did* he recall? Roy hadn't even bothered to find out about her tastes, always assuming she'd go along with whatever he chose.

Eric cared.

"Um, what's showing?"

"They started projection of the latest Marvel at the waterfront. How does that sound?"

Back out, Lara, while there's still time.

"Sounds good."

"Great. I'll pick you up at seven."

***

Over two hours of non-stop, adrenaline-filled thrills—Lara adored the film. The plot had been hilarious, and though she'd figured out what would happen right from the start, she'd been reeled in by the rest of the story. There'd been no time for self-consciousness about being with Eric and the physical proximity between them as they sat side by side and shared a tub of caramel popcorn.

Earlier, she'd been high-strung, but the movie relaxed her. When the credits appeared on the screen, it all returned to her with a vengeance. Eric's very presence, the smell of his aftershave, his warmth so close to her.

She was in deep trouble because she teetered on the verge of giving in to him. She needed to get out of there, fast. She was losing what little control she had over her life. Come to think of it, did she *have* any control over her emotions where Eric was concerned?

"How about getting something to eat?" he asked.

Eat? As in spending more time with him? Definitely not a good idea, her mind screamed. However, her stomach answered for her, as it gave a protesting grumble.

Eric stopped in his tracks, right in the middle of the esplanade, and turned around to face her. A severe expression marred his handsome face.

"Have you eaten anything today?"

"Of course," she replied quickly.

Maybe a little too quickly, she reckoned when he narrowed his eyes to slits as he fixed them on her. Not a good sign because he could make her quake in her shoes when he stared at her this way.

"Okay, I forgot to have lunch because I was busy," she said with a shrug.

Totally not a big deal. Why did he have to make an issue of it?

He sighed and shook his head. "Lara, it won't do

you any good to starve yourself."

Oh, no, he wouldn't start with her. If he didn't want a fight, he'd drop that hot topic right this instant. Food and starving—not a path she wanted to venture upon. They reminded her of when she had failed miserably at everything, including living. She'd always hated having to confront her failings.

"Eric, let it go, will you?"

She started to turn in the opposite direction, towards the parking lot. This night was officially over, the comment about food throwing a dampener on her mood.

But he grabbed her shoulders with his strong hands and didn't allow her to move any farther.

"Lara, look at me. This is a serious matter."

She tried hard to blank out the concern in his voice. If she paid it any heed, she'd crumble. Neither the time nor the place to let *that* happen.

"Eric—"

"Don't you remember what happened the last time you said this to me?"

Anger permeated every word in his question.

Damn him for treating her like a child. How could she ever forget what had happened?

She tried to shrug out of his grip, but he wouldn't let go. All her fighting was in vain. He stood like a dog with a bone, one he wouldn't release.

Oh, but he could be stubborn, too, when he wanted. She'd conveniently forgotten that.

"Lara, stop acting like a kid. This can be dangerous."

She tried another attempt to shrug free from his hold without success.

Then, he relaxed his grasp, clenching her shoulders in a gentle embrace while he peered down into her face.

"I care for you," he said in a softened tone. "And I don't want to see you go through all that pain again."

Tears filled her eyes. Eric had been the only one who'd noticed her distress all those years back. He'd been the only one to care. Had it not been for him and his help, she would've probably succumbed to the eating disorders that had punctuated her late adolescence.

He still cares, while no one else does. Not her parents, not her sisters, not even Roy. No one had ever noticed her aversion to food had nothing to do with dieting.

Eric's soft voice interrupted her thoughts.

"How about some pizza? You used to love that."

She could only nod.

They settled at a table for two at the food court terrace on the edge of the Caudan esplanade. Still shaken by her emotions, she couldn't trust herself to sit in a booth with him. She didn't know what the proximity would entail, and she didn't feel emotionally fit enough to test those uncertain waters. Not when he'd brought up the ugliest episode from her past, which she tried to forget every day and had convinced herself she'd gotten over. The first time she'd picked up a cigarette had been to curb the urge to eat before throwing it all up. That's how she'd gotten hooked on the cigs. She'd found a less dangerous way to cope. Win-win, right? Her husband had thought it stress relief or some other manner to fit in socially.

No one had noticed except for Eric.

His presence threw a reassuring blanket over her, cutting out the chilling loneliness of being an island in the immensity of an empty ocean. Eric brought comfort, something she hadn't experienced in a long, long time.

He'd had the same effect on her in the past, and she hadn't found the same feeling elsewhere. Not even with Roy.

Could it be she was falling under Eric's spell all over again?

Or had she never fallen out of love?

Her self-induced psychotherapy drew to a slamming close when the café owner slid their food on the table. The tantalizing aroma of the tomato sauce and basil on the Margherita pizza and the sight of rich melted cheese had her forgetting all her inner dilemmas. The knot usually twisting her stomach had disappeared, and a screaming appetite had settled in its place.

She grabbed a slice and couldn't keep a moan from escaping once she took a bite of the deep-dish pizza. Eric laughed softly, and she grew aware of his gaze on her.

Lara dared glance up. He was smiling at her. All her movements froze solid, yet she could feel her insides melting like the mozzarella cheese she'd just bitten.

"It's good to see you eat," he said.

"Like a normal person, you mean?" The teasing question rolled from her lips out of the blue. She hadn't thought she'd have in her to strike for light and funny right then.

Another one of Eric's miracles—how he brought out the best in her.

He threw his head back and laughed heartily. The sound melted her insides even more, and she giggled. Then, the laughter died, and he peered at her with so much tenderness on his face, her heart pinched.

"You should laugh more often, Lara. It really suits you."

She wanted to agree, tell him she hadn't had many opportunities to laugh, tell him he made her laugh as no other person could.

But she couldn't. Not only because emotion choked her throat and moistened her eyes, but because she'd be in too deep if she confessed.

"I think it's time to go now," she said in a whisper.

He graciously acquiesced to her request they leave. Probably satisfied she'd eaten at least one slice of the pizza, he had the rest of the food packed for take-away.

They walked companionably to the parking lot in silence that felt comfortable and intimate. They didn't need empty words between them because a touch, a glance, could spell out so much. Walking side by side, with their hands close enough to touch but not touching, struck her as being in the place where she was meant to be all along.

Could the secret be to let go and live for the moment?

Once at his massive, silver Toyota Prado, he held the door open while she climbed into the SUV.

A little more chivalry and she'd believe he would've held her hand daintily like a gentleman helped a lady into a high carriage. She stifled a giggle at the thought. Eric sure behaved like a gentleman, though. Somehow, she'd thought men were no longer gallant, and she'd been pleasurably surprised when he'd been so courteous ever since he'd picked her up at her place.

The drive back to Grand-Baie took place in hushed quiet. A comfortable silence again, but she grew aware of the tension mounting between them.

Soft music played in the car. She could make out Ronan Keating's distinctive voice crooning the lyrics to the *Notting Hill* soundtrack "When You Say Nothing At All." How fitting, because her and Eric's best communications happened when they spoke with their eyes and hands and let the silence around them develop full of meaning.

Where was she heading with him? It seemed apparent *he* wanted a relationship.

Or was she mistaking friendship for something else? Eric hadn't clearly stated his intentions, had he?

So lost in her thoughts, it took her a few seconds to grasp that the car had stopped. They were in front of her house, the light on the front porch sending a soft, faint glow into the interior of the SUV.

The night draws to a close, Cinderella. At least your ride didn't turn back into a pumpkin.

And what about her Prince Charming? Did he sit right there beside her in the vehicle?

Silly notions best suited to a teenager, not a grown woman. She shrugged them off. Yet, she couldn't discard the magic as easily as she wanted.

She'd spent a pleasant evening, and now, she reckoned the trip could turn into 'drab' as quickly as it could morph into 'fantastic.'

The moment of truth ... She turned to her right to face him.

"Thanks for a lovely evening."

"Pleasure's all mine," he said with a smile.

Silence fell heavy between them again, the chirp of crickets piping up from outside. But inside the car, their eyes locked as emotions and feelings wound up in turmoil.

The soft click of a seat belt unbuckling echoed in the stillness. Blood rushed in her ears.

She sat still as Eric drew nearer until his warm breath brushed her skin. Anticipation rocketed inside her, making the blood pound heavily along her temples.

She closed her eyes, and his lips touched hers in the next second. Softly, gently. His kiss lingered as he coaxed her into replying in kind, flooding her with sensations.

Past, present, future—the lines blurred. She gave in to the pull of this kiss, to the enchantment of this touch.

How could a single touch like this one make her feel so much? In a heartbeat, her mind transported her to another time when Eric had kissed her the same way. When things had been perfect. Before doom had befallen them ...

A part of her heart yelled at her to break the spell, but she was beyond hearing its call.

She couldn't draw away, *wouldn't* draw away.

Parting her lips, she returned his kiss and tilted her head so he'd get closer. The gentle touch deepened and roughened, and he grazed her lips with his tongue in a light, tentative, inviting caress.

This whole experienced carried her onto another plane. She gave up the consciousness of everything except the sensations triggered by Eric's kiss. Into some dark, pulsing, bottomless void where she willingly lost herself.

And then, the palm of his hand—smooth, warm, but strongly male—pressed against her cheek, all while he sought her mouth with his in a hungry frenzy.

As suddenly as it had started, the kiss ended.

Blood pounded and whooshed in her head, sounds morphing louder with a dull echo as she returned to Earth, back to the interior of the Prado.

Lara forced her eyes to remain shut. She couldn't take opening them to find out nothing was as she'd experienced. Who'd broken the kiss first? Surely not her because she wasn't so much of an idiot. Her senses reeled, figuring out why Eric's mouth no longer drank from hers.

Her lips tingled, and she could still feel his hand on her cheek. She opened her eyes, only to lose herself in his orbs that carried midnight in their depths. Darkness from the night or from something else? Some other, debilitating feeling ... like the lust singeing through her still.

Hopefully, she wasn't the only one who'd had the world tilt on its axis in the past few seconds.

He should say something. But what if he'd only open his mouth to tell her they were making a huge mistake? She gasped. Yes, they *were* making a terrible blunder, but not giving in would be equally stupid. Either way, they'd burn.

Might as well go down in flames.

Did she dare say it aloud? She pulled in a deep breath.

"Eric," she said but paused when he cradled her jaw and rubbed the pad of his thumb along her cheekbone.

"The offer for dinner at my place still stands, you know," he said in a raspy voice.

No, not a mistake. If it was, it wouldn't be one-sided. She could live with that, surely. They were both responsible, consenting adults. If they met the end somewhere down the road, so be it. But this was Eric. Her rock. The one solid thing in her life. What he gave, he'd never take away.

And though she couldn't think straight, as his kiss and his touch had messed her up in a jumble, she couldn't get past how right this moment felt.

A part of her knew she shouldn't, and couldn't, trust herself to answer him. Slowly, she reached for the door latch.

But try as she wanted, she couldn't tear her eyes from his face.

"How does Saturday sound?" she heard herself asking.

Chapter Eleven

The rest of the week passed in a blur. Lara had no idea how she functioned, let alone got anything done. The centre hadn't sunk, so she'd done a good job even while phoning it in, it seemed. Thoughts of the date, and the subsequent kiss, with Eric kept drawing her to La-la-land, and Sam, that cow, hadn't been any help—amid a flurry of giggles unbecoming her, her bestie had told her to seek the sexual healing she so clearly craved. Lara had cursed her out before shaking her head. Sam had still been laughing when she'd cut the call.

Back at her house that fateful Saturday, Sam's words kept ringing in her head. *Sexual healing*. She did need it, but with Eric?

The eruption of a swarm of butterflies in her stomach gave her the answer. She had to admit she wanted him. And what about him? What did *he* expect of her visit?

With a sigh, she resigned herself to face the situation ahead of her. She'd take things as they came and would deal with them when, and *if*, certain things actually happened.

The decision anchored in her mind, she faced the daunting prospect of choosing her dress for the evening. She'd need to wear something light and comfortable, as summer still raged on the coasts. Yet, she also had to choose an outfit that wouldn't make Eric think she was coming on to him. At the same time, the clothes should convey she'd be interested in 'it' if ever the occasion arose.

Goodness, was *she* really thinking in those terms?

Lara giggled. The last time she'd been so nervous for a date had been ... Actually, she couldn't remember. It'd been way more than a decade since she'd prepared for a date with a new man, and she had to admit the thrill of attempted seduction got to her in a powerful, elated rush.

Her feet grew heavier with every successive trip she made between the wardrobe and the full-length mirror. Nothing looked appropriate. Most of her clothes were formal business suits or traditional Indian attires.

Half a dozen unfruitful trips later, she stood nowhere near a compromise. The soles of her feet grew hot as she paced the rug between the wardrobe and the bed. Exasperation won and she pulled all the clothes from the racks and threw them in a messy pile on the floor.

A peek of a tie-and-dye design caught her attention, and she pulled it from the mountain of fabric. The sleeveless cotton sundress hung light and breezy, perfect for a summer evening, with the knee-length skirt not too short and the non-plunging neckline. The deep, bottle-green colour made the same kind of statement as a bold red, but without the apparent seductive undertone.

Thirty minutes later, during which she'd ironed the dress without burning it and after having taken a shower, she was ready. Lara checked the image the mirror sent her. The dress draped over her figure and hinted at her curves. All right, at the bones of her hips, since she didn't have fleshy curves. But still, the illusion of femininity helped bolster her confidence. Lightweight, strappy wedge sandals encased her feet. She wore no jewellery or accessories since the humid heat would only make them cling to her skin and make her uncomfortable. A dab of tinted moisturizer had evened her skin tone. A touch of lip-gloss emphasised her full lips, and a few vigorous brush strokes in her thick hair left it shiny and full of bounce.

She looked exactly like she wanted—fresh, casual, with a hint of sophistication. She smiled at her reflection and couldn't help imagine Eric being bowled over when he saw her.

The elation remained with her as she left the house and got in her car. But once on the road, Lara realised she had no idea of the precise location of Eric's house. The only indication she had pointed towards Cap Malheureux, located a fifteen-minute drive northeast from Grand-Baie.

She pulled over to the side of the road and reached for her phone.

"Hi, Eric," she said when he picked up. "I'm on my way to your place, but I don't know exactly where to go."

"Hey, Lara. So you're not gonna stand me up, after all." He chuckled.

A hot blush crept onto her face, for the idea *had*

crossed her mind a few times. She shrugged the mortification off, though. "I don't know the area very much, so I'd need concise directions. The roads seem to have changed since I was last here."

"You're right. They *have* changed, but Royal Road is still in place once you leave Grand-Baie," he said. "Do you know the red church on the beach in Cap Malheureux?"

"Yes." The church was a tourist landmark, and everyone knew its location.

"As soon as it leaves your rearview mirror, you'll notice a rocky wall on the left, about two hundred yards down the road. That's the property. The gate is at the far end, in dark wood. The code is five-seven-six-zero. Punch it in, and it'll open by itself."

"Fine, that should do. Thanks."

"Anytime."

A little while later, she eased her car along the driveway leading to Eric's property. She'd had no trouble finding the house, his directions perfect.

Tall bamboo hedges grew on both sides of the lane, giving it the feel of a narrow tunnel. The exterior setting already impressive, she lost her breath and braked a little stiffly when she emerged into the courtyard.

The house sprawled low in a Mexican hacienda style, with a single floor, whitewashed walls, and terracotta tiles on the roof. A profusion of colourful bougainvillaea grew on one side of the villa and shaded a large patio from prying eyes. A rolling, lushly green lawn occupied half of the property, and the sea appeared within reach beneath the sloping landscape.

She spotted an empty space in the garage at the side of the house. The setup was designed to accommodate three cars, but Eric's massive silver Prado occupied nearly two spots. She managed to fit her Mercedes in and walked to the front door.

With every step she took, anticipation grew in her, making her jittery and excited. She stopped before the heavy oak door and rang the real, old-fashioned bell.

A minute later, Eric answered the door.

"Hey."

"Hi."

The awkwardness melted the moment she took in his smile, which competed for attention with the big smiley face on the apron he wore, *Kiss the Cook* scribbled under the smiling circle.

Laughter bubbled in her throat, and she threw her head back and gave in to it. She'd also forgotten his quirky sense of humour. He could always brighten her day with a well-placed quip.

"So, are you gonna invite me in?" she asked.

"Sure." He winked.

"Well, move out of the way. You're blocking the path."

His smile widened, and he motioned towards the front of the apron before giving her a sly grin.

"Oh, heavens." She gave an exaggerated shake of her head yet drew closer and dropped a kiss on his cheek.

He sighed. "I'd been hoping for a real kiss to let you in, but this should do, for now."

He let the words hang between them, and the butterflies woke up in her stomach. A real kiss that could—*would*—lead to more?

Apparently oblivious to the turmoil he'd created, he took her arm and drew her into the hall before closing the door.

"I'm still busy in the kitchen," he said. "Get something to drink, then you can take a look around."

He led her into the kitchen, in a far corner of the house. Lara poured herself a glass of chilled white wine while she took in the spacious kitchen.

The golden glow of the afternoon sun bathed the room, the light filtered through wispy lace curtains at the windows and bouncing off the light yellow walls and pine wood furniture.

Eric stood at the centre island, busy arranging a platter of food.

She settled her gaze on him. The sun highlighted his thick, blond locks and paled the fine dusting of hairs on his bare forearms. Unabashedly checking him out all over, she wet her lips at how broad and well-defined his shoulders appeared under the casual, white cotton shirt. His long legs were encased in grey denim. The fabric shifted with every move he made, reminding her of the play of those solid and sinuous muscles under the clothing.

Heat started low in her belly and flamed through her within seconds. She craved to touch him, yearned to feel his bare skin, and find out if it was still as warm as she remembered. She about died with the urge to run her hands in his hair, let her fingers tangle in their thickness when all she'd known before with him had been short, buzz-cut locks.

She averted her face, so Eric wouldn't see the

rush of colour stinging her cheeks from the debilitating, lustful thoughts she had of him. She had to get herself in check, or she could jump him right there and then.

"I'll take a peek around," she said. "It's quite hot here."

He smiled, and she turned on her heel, almost spilling the contents of her near-full glass in her rapid move. She ventured out a few steps into the corridor and, after a few deep breaths, turned into the living room.

Large, sliding glass doors occupied a whole wall, and the tangy, salty sea air wafted in on a warm breeze. Lara stopped at the view from the opened doors, which knocked the breath out of her.

The room opened onto the large patio she'd seen from outside. Beyond it, the endless horizon of sea and sky met in a stunning clash of cobalt and turquoise. The spectacular, peaked outline of the Coin De Mire Island cut through with its majestic, black stone solidity. The late sun played upon the jutting rock, mingling shadows and contrasts into its landscape and sending blinding flashes of light where its rays hit the water.

What an impressive house. To think he came home to this sight every day—she shook her head. Goodness, people would kill for such a view. All that had to be proof enough he'd made it, and made it big, on the island.

Which, in turn, made him more daunting. More inaccessible. More impossible for any 'them' to rise from the ashes.

So where the hell did it leave her?

***

Eric watched the woman standing in front of the opened doors.

Lara's here. In his house.

He'd tortured himself with the idea of this date since their outing to the cinema, dreading she'd work her way out of it. He couldn't bear the thought of losing her again, not when he had her so close and the level playing field so wide open between them. Crazy as it might drive him to find all his efforts seemed to have had no effect on her, the kiss they'd shared *had* been amazing.

Yet, he also knew her, and she wasn't easy to convince.

She turned and met his stare. Her eyes held his, and he was certain she'd sensed his presence the minute he'd walked in. They'd been so finely attuned to each other before, too.

One more certainty he'd relied upon back in the day. When two people had such a connection, they could weather any storm.

Or not. Look at them about to head into the same tornado again. Would Lara grant them a happy ending?

Across from him, her lips parted, but no sound escaped.

She blinked and took a sip from her glass.

"You like it?" he asked.

"The view is magnificent."

"I agree."

The flustered expression came back on her face. Colour stung her golden cheeks with a delicious, crimson stain, and she lowered those thick, long lashes that had never needed makeup to lure any man.

She must know he hadn't been speaking of the view outside. How would she react to his unspoken message?

She stared up at him with steely resolve darkening the narrowed eyes. Everything in her glare, in the coiled stance of her body, stated she wouldn't allow herself to be caught off guard.

We'll see about that.

The duel lasted for a long moment before she broke the silence with a calm, detached question.

"Where's the pool?" she asked, lifting her eyebrows.

"Around the corner." He gave a slight nod. "You can't see it from here."

The discomfited guise came back.

"You must be making a lot of money to afford such a place."

"I get along okay."

Tension bristled in the air, and their eyes never left each other.

Pig-headed tenacity—he'd always known such stubbornness bristled between them. None would bow down first.

Except, she surprised him when she lowered her head a few seconds later.

"I'm sorry, Eric. I had no right to pry."

He smiled. She wasn't as harsh and rigid as she wanted him to believe. He could fly the flag of hope high, after all.

"It's okay. No offence taken." He stepped towards her. "Actually, I bought the place with the inheritance my grandfather left me. The house used to belong to a friend of mine. I fell in love with the property the first time I saw it and bought it before he even put it on the market."

She gave him a small smile in return.

"How about a tour of the place?" he said softly. "Dinner won't be ready for another twenty minutes."

***

Lara couldn't keep her awe from deepening the more she toured Eric's residence. The house was every bit as beautiful inside as its front suggested. The rooms sprawled, large, airy, and filled with natural light. The various shades of vivid orange and crisp white on the walls, and the dark wood furniture, mingled to create an inviting ambience, bathing the whole place in a warm, cosy feel.

This had to be the most beautiful house she'd ever seen. And more surprising, she felt entirely at ease within its walls, letting the tension go as the setting worked its soothing atmosphere over her.

"Did you do the decoration?" she asked.

"No," Eric replied with a laugh. "I'm not good with it at all. You remember my little sister, Angélique? She's the one who designed all this."

"Of course, I remember her. She's about the same age as my baby sister, Diya. What's she doing nowadays?"

"She just left for Florence, actually, to get her diploma in interior decoration."

The sun had set by the time they returned to the living room.

"Dinner's gonna be out there," he said as he led

her to the patio, which occupied most of one side of the vast house. A comfortable-looking set of wicker sofas occupied two-thirds of the area, and a large, freeform pool rounded out the far end. In between, a candlelit dinner table set for two glowed.

She sighed softly and turned to face him. "You've gone for the whole works."

"The occasion was worth it."

A knot settled in her throat, and she had trouble swallowing. The desire she'd felt for him lingered in her, and her breath came out in ragged puffs whenever she allowed the sizzling emotions to surface.

What was she doing, getting involved so deeply with this man? Her mind screamed at her, but she chose to ignore its call. She'd see this through, if only for once in her life. Today, she'd listen to her heart for a change.

She allowed Eric to take her hand and lead her to the table, where he pulled out her chair. Once she was comfortably settled, he made his way into the house. The soft, romantic rhythms of Kenny G's sax filled the air, adding a seductive feel to the twilight atmosphere.

Lara let herself drift to a hazy mood as the music lulled her senses.

He came back a few minutes later and slid a plate in front of her. Her mouth watered at the sight of the appetising, picture-perfect lasagne portion. Once he settled himself opposite her, she picked up her fork and took a bite of the rich pasta.

Damn, he's even a good cook. The taste of the meat and rich, cheesy béchamel lingered on her taste buds to bring forth a delightful feeling of well-being. And no hint of garlic. Had he remembered she hated the flavouring?

Over the flickering light of the candles, she met his eyes with hers. "The food is delicious."

"Glad you like it," he said. "I'd be happier if you actually ate all of it."

She smiled. "I intend to."

And she did polish her plate between the casual chatter he kept up throughout the meal.

"Second serving?" he asked with a smile and a raised eyebrow.

She settled back into her chair. "Now that would be pushing your luck."

He laughed as he stood and took her hand to lead her to the outdoor living room. They sat on the plush, comfortable cushions of the wicker sofas for dessert. Eric went into the house and came out with a decadent chocolate cake covered in thick cocoa and cream icing.

"This one, I bought because I'm not good at cake making."

"At least your food is edible, hardly what I can say about my cuisine," she said between pleasure-filled forkfuls of the delicious cake.

At a biting sting on her leg, she slapped her ankle.

"I see the mosquitoes have come out," he said. "We better head inside."

While he went to drop the dishes in the kitchen, she found herself alone in the living room a few minutes later. Lost in her thoughts, lulled by the romantic sound of the music, she stopped in front of the sliding doors.

A cool breeze wafted around her, the scent of citronella essential oil from the mosquito-repellent candles tingeing the air. She stood with her back to the interior doorway, but she could pinpoint the exact second when Eric stepped into the room. The nape of her neck started to tingle. All her senses picked up to rush forward in a kaleidoscope of stimuli to make sensual awareness shroud her like a fog. Her heart pounded in a frantic rhythm, and her pulse raced all through her body. At the chill running down her spine, every hair on her skin stood on end.

Even the air she dragged into her burning lungs struck her as still, heavier, denser.

Taking a deep breath, she forced her mind to focus. It wouldn't do her any good to lose all her marbles. To pass out before she even got to anything the least bit pleasurable? She'd make such a fool of herself then.

God, was this what sexual tension felt like?

She'd never before experienced such anticipation, such a rush of longing, or yearned for a man's touch, for him to take her body and do decadent, forbidden things to every part of her.

She made out when he started towards her because the fragrance of his aftershave intensified as he got closer. Her muscles tensed with every step he took as if anticipating the delivery of a much-longed-for promise.

Sam was right. Nearly fifteen years in the making, since their very first meeting, when the tension had sizzled between them from the very first glance across the room.

She could now smell the distinctive, heady musk of his skin. Her breath caught when he stopped inches behind her, her throat tight as his warmth radiated out to her. He remained motionless, so close they'd touch if she breathed in too deeply. She could only close her eyes as his warm breath brushed the nape of her neck. Shivers ran along her bare arms when he grazed her exposed shoulders with delicate strokes of his long fingers.

Lightly, he let his touch run along her skin. Teasing, tempting, making her want more, yet she begged him to stop the torture he made well up inside her.

He moved away, urging a moan of protest from her. The sound squelched into an incoherent plea when he splayed his hands flat on her waist, settling his fingers possessively over her.

Even through the fabric of her dress, her skin burned from the imprint of his heat. She'd have given anything to feel those strong, capable hands on her naked flesh.

His breath grew warmer on her neck, convincing her he'd dipped his head lower, closer. A strangled sigh escaped her when he dropped a fleeting kiss on the dip of her collarbone with his soft lips. And another. And another ...

She wanted him, no denying it. But, more than want, she *needed* him. The certainty thrummed in every cell of her body. She wouldn't fight this feeling. She was done fighting. Done with doing the right thing, with listening to what everyone deemed proper.

For once, she'd tune in to what *she* deemed

essential. *Eric.*

Slowly, she turned around, and he wrapped those strong arms around her to bring her closer to him. To crush her against the rugged expanse of his chest.

Her mouth went dry, and everything inside her melted in his embrace. If he hadn't held her, she would've pooled to the floor in a mass of liquid, lust-molten goo.

So all she could do was blink up into his eyes, where she encountered tenderness and the darkness of passion.

Just the two of them, alone, together, and about to do the one thing they'd never gotten to experience before.

"I haven't done this in a long time," she said in a low voice.

His eyes darkened even more, and his grip strengthened.

"We have to make it worth it, then."

Wild butterflies took wing in her stomach. Their momentum carried her up and made her stretch onto the tips of her toes to press her lips against his. He'd kissed her every other time before. This time, she would take the reins.

The illusion of her control lasted only a second before he slanted his mouth over hers and took over the kiss. He nipped at her lips, and when she opened for him, he teased her with his hot tongue. How could the edges of one's lips be so sensitive? With every stroke of his tongue, he awakened a tingling need in her that welled up fast into a raging inferno of desire.

His hand cradling her head, he bent lower,

deepening their kiss as she tilted to accommodate the ever-hungrier play of his mouth on hers.

Then, he bent his knees, and before she could shift her position, he'd swooped his free arm under her knees and had her in his hold. Lara yelped at the sudden sensation of losing the ground under her feet, but the sound lost itself in his mouth, as he hadn't stopped their kiss yet.

He tore his mouth from hers once he'd taken a few steps. The walls rushed past in a blur as he ate the distance with long strides towards the other end of the dwelling.

No one had ever carried her this way. Elated by the conquering display, a part of her couldn't stop thinking of the practicality of such a move.

"You should put me down. I'm not so light, you know," she said.

He chuckled. "You weigh hardly more than a feather."

They'd reached the bedroom, where he placed her back onto her feet.

He cradled her jaw in his warm palms. "A part of me is afraid of breaking you. *Merde*, Lara. When did you get so fragile?"

Not the time or place to talk about that.

I don't break easily.

She'd open a can of worms if she said the words aloud. Better she showed him and silenced his concern in the process. His lust, she craved. His prodding of her soul and way of life, she could do without.

So, she reached up and ran her hands over his shirt-covered chest. That, at least, had the intended effect, for he tightened his grip on her jaw and bent to place another scorching kiss on her mouth.

He released her face, pushed his hands into her hair, and she moaned. She'd always had a sensitive scalp—did he have any clue what his touch was doing to her? She had to do something, quick. With hands infused by desperate vigour, she pulled at the fastenings on the thin cotton of his shirt. Some buttons slipped through the buttonholes. Some pinged away somewhere onto the marble floor. Did she care? No. Not when the expanse of smooth, warm male skin revealed itself under the garment. Her palms flat on his pecs, she couldn't get enough of his warmth, of touching him.

He hissed in a breath. "*Merde*," he said against her mouth.

She smiled, only to have the elated feeling flare out in a blaze of fire as he pushed the straps of her dress down and divested her of the garment, her bra, and her knickers in one single stroke.

Damn him. How did he do it?

Did he have so much practice undressing women?

The stiff ridge of his jeans' waistband pressed into her belly. One more piece of clothing they didn't need between them. She attacked the metal button and the zipper, peeling the trousers and boxers from his hair-roughened legs.

Once he stepped out of the jeans, he grabbed hold of her shoulders and marched her towards the bed. When the back of her knees hit the mattress, she fell back in an undignified heap. She yelped again, only to have the cry stifled against his shoulder as he rolled her into his arms and cradled her close.

"I got you," he said into her ear.

Then, he made her peek up with his thumb under her chin, and he kissed her.

From that moment on, she surrendered. She only wanted to feel, to experience her first time with Eric and burn every nanosecond of their encounter into her memory.

She touched him where he touched her, kissed him where he kissed her, let her lips and tongue rove all over his delectable, hard-muscled body after he'd sampled every inch of her skin in the same way.

With his fingers first, then his mouth, he made her crash down into explosive release every single time he set his mind to the task of bringing her pleasure.

But Lara knew she waited for the ultimate prize, for the moment when he'd make her his ...

And then, finally, he hovered his big, manly body over her after rolling a condom onto his erection.

She parted her thighs, opened for him, and wrapped her arms around his shoulders before pulling him close to her.

Their mouths touched when he joined his body with hers, stretching her, taking her completely.

She moved when he moved, their rhythm instantly in sync as if they'd done this countless times before, yet still found something new and magical every time they came together.

Je t'aime.

She thought she heard the words, but right then, her orgasm soared and blanked out anything except

the feeling of completion she achieved ... for the first
time in her life.

Chapter Twelve

Eric awoke with a start and sat up in bed. The space next to him lay empty. Had he, again, only dreamed of Lara's presence?

He ran a hand over his face in weariness and confusion. If this had been a dream, how come everything, every touch and every kiss, had felt so vivid? He couldn't have imagined such an encounter.

Hadn't Lara spent the last evening with him?

His eyes adjusted to the dark, and he noticed the heap of clothes littering the bedroom floor. A soft breeze wafted in from the sliding doors, which were ajar. Turning in that direction, he made out the silhouette of a woman on the terrace.

Lara. She stood leaning on the railing of the balcony.

He heaved a deep sigh of relief as he closed his eyes and dropped onto the bed.

So she *had* spent the night with him. This time, his encounter with her hadn't been just another dream.

His whole body relaxed, and the tension left his stiff muscles as he swung his legs over the side of the bed. Sitting there, he contemplated her.

The wind lifted small strands from the hair she'd

tucked onto her shoulder, and the moon's cool glow lit the highlights in the shiny locks to make them glisten like spun gold. His shirt hid most of her, and he let his focus travel to her long, bare, exposed legs.

This woman was different from the one he'd left over a decade earlier. More grown-up, mature, and confident.

She appeared lost in her thoughts, her features slightly drawn, her gaze settled on a distant point in the sky. Longing filled his heart to bursting as he watched her, and, unbidden, his mind went back to the last time he'd seen her before this year. On the eve of his departure for France.

She'd cried without words or sobs as they'd parted. His heart had broken upon seeing her tears, yet, he hadn't had it in him back then to work something out for them. He also hadn't had it in him to reassure her things would be all right or ask her to wait for him.

That had been his worst mistake. When he'd next tried to get in touch with her, he'd learned she'd left the country. Desperation and extreme loss had overwhelmed him. The news of her marriage, relayed by Rahul Kiran, her neighbour, when he'd finally deigned to answer Eric's frantic calls, had driven the nail in the coffin shortly after. That's all Rahul had told him—that Lara was married, that Eric should leave her alone.

He'd messed up big time back then.

But not today. Not anymore.

This time would be right for them. She was back in his life again, and he was going to keep her this time around, make sure she stayed, that she wouldn't ever wish to leave him again.

He would allow nothing to come between them.

***

The sound of doors sliding farther open startled her out of her thoughts and made her jump. Lara turned to find Eric standing in the doorway.

She gasped, a hand clutched upon her heart. "Goodness, you nearly scared the life out of me."

He didn't reply and just kept watching her intently. In the dark, his face loomed sombre, his jaw clenched. She frowned.

"Is something wrong? I didn't want to wake you, so I snuck out."

His heated, narrowed scrutiny kept her rooted to where she stood, and she could only watch as he crossed the space between them with two mighty steps. He stopped his powerful shape inches before her as he peered down, letting his intense eyes bore into her own.

She swallowed with much difficulty. Why did he ogle her like a big cat about to pounce on its prey? Her heart picked up an accelerated beat, and blood started to whoosh in her head.

He drew closer and brought his hands up to frame her face. Her mouth went dry, and the heat from his touch flowed into her bloodstream, igniting the latent fire smouldering in her. He slowly brushed her lower lip with his thumb, and a shiver coursed through her at the silent, sensual invitation in that stroke.

How could he do this to her with a simple touch? And how could she have allowed a man to have such power over her?

The question tortured her, but she chose to ignore it. His lips were now on hers, and he kissed her with a hunger and a passion more powerful than anything she'd ever dreamed existed.

Soon, he wrapped her in his arms and crushed her to him. She'd never relished feeling as feminine and delicate as she did when he held her this way. His heat enveloped her, overwhelming all coherent thought, and she gave in. Stopped fighting. Stopped thinking. Only allowing her body, her every sense, to feel, to experience him.

He tore his mouth from hers to trail hot, hungry kisses along her jaw.

"I don't ever want to lose you," he said in her ear. "I'll wait forever for you, Lara. But don't make me wait so long. Please."

Though she heard him, the certainty in the statements, the shameless begging in that last word, didn't fully register. Instead, all her thoughts converged on the gorgeous, sexy man intent on devouring her.

This time, she'd take the lead.

So, she stepped back and took his hand when he frowned at her sudden departure from his embrace. *Not for long.* Threading her fingers with his, she tugged him into the bedroom. Along the way to the bed, she let go long enough to discard the shirt.

He hitched in an audible breath when she stood stark naked in front of him. Her breathing came out laboured as she perused the length of his frame, catching sight of how ready and willing he was for her.

She bit her lip. "Where do you keep the

condoms?"

He nodded at the bedside table. She reached for the drawer and retrieved a small foil packet. Removing the condom from the sealed envelope, she rolled the thin protection over his rigid length.

They exchanged no words during those moments. They didn't need to because their gestures, their need, spoke their own language.

She led him to the bed and gently pushed down on his shoulders. He fell back into a sitting position, and she straddled him before he could reach out for her. With her previously denied yearning for him flaring in engulfing flames, she didn't need any other touch or kiss to make her ready to welcome him. She sank her body onto his, holding him into her core with a drawn-out sigh carrying every hint of the rough, encompassing passion that engulfed her under his possession.

He snaked an arm against the small of her back to pull her flush to him. Her breasts flattened against his chest, and when she tipped her head back with pleasure, he placed his hot, wet mouth on her throat. He pushed his hips up, slammed into her, and she tightened the hold of her legs against his waist.

Over and over, they soared together. Then, somewhere in the moment, they kissed.

When she opened her eyes to stare into his passion-filled gaze, something inside her tilted. Suddenly, it no longer mattered who stayed in control. Chaos, when created together, held a devastating pull of attraction.

Wrapping her arms tightly around his neck, she threw herself back to land on the mattress with him on top of her.

His chuckle drowned in the kiss she stole from his lips.

He started moving against her, into her, and she gave herself to him.

***

Eric awoke shortly after dawn, the early morning sun streaming through the thin curtains stirring him out of deep slumber. He never bothered to close the heavy drapes in the bedroom, preferring to awaken naturally with the sunshine. That is, unless his screeching phone tore him out of sleep to go take care of an emergency.

This morning, he awoke with a languid, heavy inertia in his muscles. That's when he remembered the past night. He smiled at the brush of soft, rounded buttocks against his groin.

He propped himself on an elbow and watched the sleeping woman in his bed. She looked content, peaceful almost. Her face was relaxed and smooth, her beautiful features bereft of their usual frowns. The morning sunshine played upon her skin, lighting her matte complexion with a honeyed glow.

He'd come across many beautiful women in his life, yet none had ever struck him as more beautiful than Lara. He chuckled at the thought. He'd fallen in love with her at first glance. Her answering glare had shot daggers at him, though, as he'd been her most tenacious opponent on the high school debate circuit, the only one who had dared go head to head against her in order to land the top spot in the competition. Everyone had written off the contenders from the other schools, Lara's English-speaking academy clearly the most probable winner with her at the helm of its team. He'd taken his French-speaking school's team, perfect outsiders, all the way to the final battle her side had relentlessly won. Fire had lit her dark eyes every time they had met, and he'd wondered if she burnt with the same ardour inside.

From what he'd gathered the previous night, she certainly did. She'd responded to his every touch with a passion and an abandon he could only cherish. She didn't give herself easily, yet, she'd been totally his when he'd made love to her.

A small smile appeared on her face. Tenderness overwhelmed him, and love burst in his heart. He'd devote his whole life to make her happy, if only she'd let him.

He sighed. No good to venture *there*, his mind chided. He'd promised to take things easy with her. So be it.

She stirred in her sleep. But she didn't wake up, and merely turned onto her stomach.

His body grew tense, already craving her again as he took in the sight of her graceful back and the thick brown hair lying on her pillow like a shiny river. She'd dyed it sometime in the past decade— her hair had been midnight black when they'd been younger.

He wouldn't wake her. Not yet. She probably needed the sleep. He hadn't forgotten the tiredness she'd carried around like a draining cloak these past few weeks. The rest would do her good, as would some food once she woke up.

He got up and threw on a pair of shorts before

making his way into the kitchen. The clock on the wall showed six o'clock. He reviewed his plans for the day as he put croissants to heat in the oven.

Sunday. His parents surely wouldn't expect him for lunch, since he hadn't said anything about attending this week. Knowing his mother, though, she'd probably nag him into attending the family meal so he wouldn't be alone.

He chuckled. Little did Agnes Armont-Marivaux know her son wouldn't be on his own today, and hopefully, from now on.

Still, he'd give her a call and work his way out of the family commitment.

***

The air around her felt warm and snug, the strong sunshine bathing the place tickling her skin. The song of chirping birds, heralding a bright, beautiful summer day, filtered through her hazy, still-sleepy mind.

Lara emerged out of a soft, dreamy, cottony world as she opened her eyes. When she glanced at it, the room was unfamiliar, yet she felt at home in its surroundings. Could she be in a hotel on the coast? The sun's warm rays brushed her back, and the sheets wrapped around her provided delicate cool against her skin. She yawned and stretched out of slumber.

She couldn't remember when she had woken in such a peaceful way. Not for a very long time. She savoured the blissful feeling. Her body, limp and heavy, sank into the soft mattress.

Images of the previous night flashed into her mind, and she sat up with a start, drawing the sheet to her shoulders to cover herself. Her whole body grew tense, all notion of languor forgotten.

She was in Eric's house.

For God's sake, she was in Eric's *bed*.

After they'd made love all night long.

She closed her eyes and covered her face with her hands.

What had she been thinking? That was it, though. She *hadn't* been thinking. Her sex-starved body had shut her mind off and done as it pleased. She couldn't believe she'd given in to the heed of her body, and not once, but repeatedly. Thank God Eric wasn't here to witness the shame burning her cheeks as she remembered her lack of inhibition in the past twelve hours.

Eric. Where was he?

She sat up straighter and strained to pick up any sound in the house. After a few seconds, she made out his voice, talking to someone. Who, though?

It's none of your concern.

She needed to get out quickly. She didn't know how she'd face him. The only times she'd encountered a lover the morning after had been with her husband. The awkward feeling ate her alive.

Was that how people felt after the first time? If such was the case, then she totally wasn't cut out for a life of one-night stands.

She had no more time to ponder the question because Eric walked in, a heavy tray in front of him.

"*Bonjour, ma belle.* Slept well?" he said with a large smile.

The blush burned hotter on her face. How come she wasn't dead of embarrassment yet? And how could *he* be so casual and carefree? He simply took it in his stride unless he'd done this so many times.

Flames shot before her eyes as the heavy dagger of jealousy sliced her heart.

"Have you done this often?"

She wanted to bite her tongue the second the words were out. Too late. She'd let her motor mouth run once again.

He settled cross-legged on the bed and placed the tray between them before lifting his eyes to hers.

"You mean prepare breakfast for the woman I spent the night with? Let me think." He paused for a few seconds, his eyes never leaving hers. "No, I don't recall ever doing that."

She let out the breath she didn't know she'd been holding. Relief flooded through her, and she yearned to kick herself because his reply made her feel so good.

Then, another query slid in—he didn't make breakfast because he didn't bring women to his bed or because he always slunk away during the night?

Not something she should ponder. The women he'd taken to his bed before were none of her concern, and if he did a runaway act ...

"I figured you'd need some reinforcement after last night," he said with a wink.

Hot flames ate her cheeks again.

"Eric, don't tease, okay?"

She averted her eyes to stare down at her lap. Would she ever live through this? Highly unlikely. Shyness overwhelmed her, piling onto the embarrassment bubbling inside. Lara suddenly wished for the earth, or the bed, to open up and swallow her out of the situation.

His gentle fingers on her chin made her lift her face until her eyes peered into his.

"Last night was wonderful." His voice thrummed out low and husky. "I hope you don't feel bad about it."

She searched his eyes and her own heart. Did she regret last night?

No, she didn't.

"It was wonderful for me, too."

He drew closer and placed a gentle kiss on her lips.

"I'm glad you're happy," he said when he pulled away.

Happiness, warmth, and strange desperation wound up in turmoil inside her. The latter won the struggle, and her mind returned to the question that haunted her.

"Eric, what happens now?"

He remained silent for a few seconds, his face serious.

With a pang, she clamped down on the urge to touch him. How could he appear even more handsome, as if severity accentuated his features and brought out his virility with startling evidence?

Damn. What was she thinking? Her libido was getting the better of her again.

"I don't know, Lara." His low voice tore through her self-induced beating. "I guess we take things as they come. I don't want you to feel any pressure, but I want you with me."

She couldn't say anything in reply. He didn't ask, didn't order, didn't expect anything from her.

Her throat closed, and tears threatened to fall from her eyes. What was she to say? Eric didn't ask her for much. She could at least give him that, even if she didn't contemplate anything serious in the future. The two of them had no happy ending. She had to live for the moment. Seize the day, *carpe diem* or whatever other philosophy that would cushion her for a while before she slammed into the rocky wall of the cliff looming right ahead.

Nothing but the moment ...

So, she nodded and let a tremulous smile curve her lips.

He smiled back, and somehow, everything fell into place.

He nodded at the tray. "Eat your breakfast before it gets cold. There are croissants, and the coffee is as you like it. Black with two sugars."

She couldn't help but laugh. "How many more little things like this do you remember about me?"

He winked. "Just what's needed to win you over."

"You're a charmer, you know that?" She laughed as she picked up her coffee and took a sip.

A thought struck her, and she voiced it aloud. "Who were you talking to a few minutes ago?"

Great, Lara. Motor-mouth runs again.

"My mother," he said.

Something inside her froze. Family. She hadn't thought beyond the two of them. If their families got involved ...

"I needed to worm my way out of lunch today to be with you," he said.

At the mention of his family—the white people

who looked down on anyone without their colonist blood—dread filled her to chill her insides. Dare she find out?

"Eric, what would your family say if they knew about us?"

He took a sip of his coffee.

"There's nothing to say, Lara. It's my life, and I choose how to live it."

His words and the conviction in them sounded final. Could she believe him? Would it be as easy as him taking a stand for them against the world?

"What would *your* mother say about all this?" he asked, eyebrows lifted, bringing her back to the moment.

She rolled her eyes, and despite her churning thoughts and uncertainty, a hearty laugh escaped her.

"My mum would surely go ballistic. Probably have a heart attack." She chuckled. "Good thing my father is a cardiologist."

Eric laughed, too.

They never got around to eating the croissants or finishing their coffee. Because they were kissing, the world around them and all its considerations stopped spinning.

Chapter Thirteen

Damn. Lara blew out another sigh as she peeked at the clock on her desk. Still another three hours before she could meet Eric again. She'd come to hate Saturdays when his private practice overflowed with patients. And because she had a whole afternoon to kill before they could get together at six.

Work no longer appealed to her, as she now lived only for the weekends, especially the Sunday mornings, when she'd wake up with Eric by her side. She smiled as the thought crossed her mind. She hovered in an alternate reality lately, a place that made her want to get out of the office quickly so she could be with him.

For how much longer, she didn't know. She'd stopped asking herself the question. Why rock a boat that looked like it would never capsize on the calm waters of their relationship?

Live for every moment.

Her cell phone rang, and she fumbled with the screen in her attempt to answer, hoping to hear Eric's rich voice at the other end.

"Hi, Lara. It's Dee."

Diya? Why, ever, would her sister call her? Diya existed in her own little bubble, and she only came down to Earth when she needed to wrangle something out of one of the adults in her entourage.

"Hi to you, too. To what do I owe this honour?"

"Come on," her sister said. "I know it's been ages since we last talked, but you gotta admit it's not like you've been around lately, either."

True. Since she'd started to see Eric, she'd lost touch with other parts of her life. A flurry of guilt erupted inside her, scorching like acid. She'd also neglected a lot of things, a lot of people.

"So, what can I do for you?" she asked. "Knowing you, I'm sure you're gonna ask me for something."

"Shoot, am I getting so predictable?" Diya gave a startled gasp. "But yes, I do have something to ask. Actually, I was wondering if I could spend the night at your place."

Meaning she wouldn't be able to meet Eric? *Hell no!*

But then, another feeling took hold of her, rushing in the wake of the guilt. As the older sister, she had a duty to look after Diya. And she had to admit she hadn't been very present for the girl throughout the years.

Something niggled at her, though. Diya had a fleet of friends, and she was always crashing at their place. So why did she want to come to her house? "Dee, is something wrong?"

Her sibling laughed at the other end. "No. It's just Mum being a pain, and I badly need to get out of here for the night. I figure she'll let me go if I come to you."

Lara smiled. That did make sense. Come to think

of it, her mother hadn't nagged her for a long time. "So Mum's on your case, huh? Probably why I'm not her top priority right now."

"So, can I come?"

"Sure. What do you say to a chick night?"

"That'd be wicked. I'll get us some movies. Oh, and you do have a DVD player, right?"

"Yes, Dee." Her sister sometimes thought all adults lived in the Dark Ages.

"Wicked," Diya said. "See you later."

She pondered over what she'd say to Eric as she held the phone in her hand for a few minutes. She didn't want to cancel their evening, but she hadn't had the heart to refuse her sister. God knew their mother was tough to deal with, and she fully understood Diya's plight.

I'll owe him one now, and Eric'll never let me live through it.

She pressed the speed-dial for his number with a heavy heart.

***

"Couldn't you have picked something *not Magic Mike*-related?" she asked as she surveyed the pile of DVD cases her sister dumped on her bed.

"I did." Diya's eyes grew big as she defended herself. "There's *Love, Actually*. I am in *heaven* when I hear Hugh Grant's accent. Hugh Grant *and* Colin Firth in the same movie—what more can you ask for?"

"You're in heaven anytime a bloke opens his mouth and spins you some British accent."

"Hey, I'm much more discerning than that."

Lara raised her eyebrows.

Diya rolled her eyes. "Shoot. Fine. I admit it. Now, tell me you didn't let special things turn your head at eighteen?"

She'd already been married at eighteen. Grown up. Mature. A homeowner with a mortgage.

Had she had to grow up too fast?

Don't go there.

She shook her head as she surveyed her youngest sister. What a world of difference between them at this same age. Diya struck her as the typical teenage fashion victim, with well-cut jeans riding dangerously low on her hipbones, tighter-than-tight tank top baring her midriff, and pigtails. Innocence with growing sophistication.

"Are you trying to look like some anime character?" she asked with a dubious twist of her mouth.

Diya hit her with a cushion. "This is not your generation, and you won't get it. So drop the scrutiny."

"Thank God." She didn't want to appear scrambled together in what the youngsters considered 'cool' fashion. Whatever happened to notions like class and chic? A shiver ran through her as she contemplated being dressed like her sister. "Let's just hope you outgrow it when you're my age."

Diya poked her tongue at her in reply. "You got any food around? I'm starving."

Lara stared at the petite girl so unlike her elder siblings. Where she and Neha were tall, big-boned women, Diya looked like a strong breeze could break her in half. Deceptive, though, and she would be worried for the breeze in the confrontation, because her baby sister was nothing less than a phenomenon of Nature.

"You're always starving. God knows how you manage not to turn into an elephant with all the junk food you eat. Have you even heard of organic food?"

"I don't sit behind a desk all day, like *some* people."

"How dare you, you cheeky git?" Lara hit her with a pillow.

Diya burst out laughing. "You're just jealous that you look like a bag of bones while guys find me cute."

Immersed in the relaxed and carefree banter, she opened her mouth to retort how Eric found the bag of bones very satisfying. She caught herself before the words flew out. She had no intention of letting her family know about her and Eric. And to let Diya in on any secret meant the news would be plastered all over the place within the coming hour.

"I'll order some pizza. And don't you dare touch my cell phone," she said over her shoulder as she left the room. Diya was mad over the iPhone, the latest model that their parents had refused to get her. Knowing her sister, Lara was sure she'd be up to something forbidden, since the lure of danger always won Diya over.

She couldn't help but smile when she thought of her youngest sibling. Diya had been four years old when she'd married Roy, and the fourteen years apart in two different countries hadn't really helped their relationship, either. She was glad their friendship was picking up again. God knew the younger girl could do with some guidance.

They watched *Magic Mike* while eating their pizza. Halfway through *Dear John,* the doorbell rang. Lara made her way downstairs and opened the door.

She blinked, and surprise and astonishment battled inside her as she took in the sight on her doorstep.

"Eric? What are you doing here?"

What a sight, indeed. She gulped. Carefree and casual in jeans and a green linen shirt, he leaned against the opened doorway, smiling his gorgeous smile at her. Heavy golden locks fell over his forehead, and her knees went so weak with longing, she had to reach out and brace a hand onto the wall.

"I was missing you, so I thought I'd drop by for a minute," he said in a low, husky, and oh-so-sexy tone. "Aren't you gonna invite me in?"

He missed her? Her heart melted.

Then he reached out and wrapped his arms around her. With one big step, he entered the hallway, and the door closed with a tap from the heel of his shoe.

Fire ignited in her blood as he pulled her closer to him, and she eagerly returned his hungry kiss as she wrapped her arms around his neck, letting her fingers tangle in his thick hair.

"Laaaara? What's up?"

The call made its way into her heated mind, having the same effect as an icy shower.

She broke free from Eric's embrace just as Diya popped her head at the top of the stairs. The younger girl's eyes grew wide.

Diya grinned brightly, making Lara think of a shark about to sink its pointed teeth into some fleshy prey.

"Aren't you gonna introduce us?" the girl asked with a cheeky lift of her eyebrows.

No way out of introductions, not when these two had come face to face already.

Lara turned around. The heat of anger burnt her cheeks, and she narrowed her eyes to slits as she stared at her sister.

"Diya, this is Eric. Eric, meet my little sister, Diya."

"Hi, Diya. Pleasure to meet you," he said with a warm smile.

"Hi, Eric." Diya had all but drooled through the greeting. "Pleasure's all mine."

She needed the nosy git packing and leaving. A part of her was afraid Diya would really drool on Eric if she got any closer.

"Dee, aren't you missing the end of the movie, back in the bedroom?" she said through clenched teeth.

The message also implied, "stay there until further notice." Diya appeared to pick up the unspoken command because she turned around and headed upstairs.

For once, Diya had listened. Surprise, surprise.

Eric chuckled as soon as Diya went back up. Lara trained her eyes on him, and he seemed to choke back his laughter at the icy, pointed glare she sent him.

"She sounds sweet," he said.

"Don't let the appearance fool you. She's not the

little doll she looks like." In fact, Diya was a barracuda in sheep's clothing. No, she had not gotten her metaphors confused because that's exactly what her baby sister was.

A sly smile appeared on Eric's face.

"Seems like that's the case with the Hemant family. I know for sure you're not the ice queen you let people think you are."

He took a step with every word he spoke, and soon, she found herself jammed between him and the wall. Her heart rate picked up as he lowered his face closer to hers.

"I still haven't finished with you," he said before settling his mouth over hers.

All notions of little sisters and propriety flew out the window as her blood flared into flames at his touch. He snaked a hand under her skirt, letting his light touch graze her thigh. Before she could understand what she was doing, she braced her back against the wall and wrapped her legs around his hips. Somehow, she'd ditched her knickers, and he'd undone his jeans.

He'd gone commando under the trousers and thus had no trouble sinking the rigid length of his arousal into her waiting body. Goodness, how she loved the rush of letting him take her when and where he wanted. A couple of weeks ago, they'd had 'the talk' and decided on unprotected sex since they were going steady. She had pregnancy covered with the pill.

A milestone in their relationship, one she refused to contemplate whenever the notion popped into her head. Because she and Eric, in the long term, spelled—

Pleasure crashed through her. She bit her lip so hard to squelch the noise and blood registered on her taste buds.

"Now see what you've gone and done," he said against her ear before he kissed her and gently sucked on her lower lip.

Despite everything they'd done so far, this last kiss hit her as the most intimate thing Eric had done to her. Were she not holding on to his shoulders with tense arms, she would've melted to the floor at the wave of emotion.

With her forehead pressed into the hollow of his collarbone, she closed her eyes and let her senses stop swimming. Little by little, he released her so she could slide her feet back onto the floor. As she slowly returned to the moment, she smoothed her skirt and then reached for his jeans.

"Sending me away after doing the naughty with me?" He chuckled.

Heat seared her cheeks. "It's not that. It's just—"

"You're babysitting tonight. I get it." He reached out and tucked a lock of hair behind her ear. "I missed you tonight, Lara."

"Me, too," she admitted in a breathless whisper.

He released her and took backward steps. Then, with a wink, he opened the front door and stepped out, leaving her to stare at the wood panel.

What had happened here? Something inside her told her that a vital part of her being had shifted on its axis, but damn if she wanted to acknowledge it. Whatever *it* happened to be.

So, she did what she did best—put the concern away for the moment, and made her way up the stairs. She shouldn't forget, like she had just before, that she had an impressionable teenager in her home. After a quick dash in the bathroom to rearrange her clothing and her hair, she walked out and marched into her bedroom, only to stop in her tracks.

Diya sat in front of her vanity, the polished wood surface littered with all the makeup Lara possessed. Even the new, unopened ones.

"What do you think you're doing?"

A clutter resounded as Diya dropped a blusher box onto the table.

"Darn, Lara. You frightened me. Don't you know you shouldn't creep up on people like that, especially when they're wielding a mascara brush? I nearly poked my eye with the wand." She shrugged. "I'm having a look at your makeup, duh. What else?"

Lara stared at her, mouth agape and with her hands on her hips. "Who gave you permission?"

"The fact I'm your little sister," the girl said with a dismissive roll of her eyes.

Not for much longer. She should've drowned the brat a long time ago.

Diya threw her arms out and huffed. "All your stuff is Chanel and Dior, yet you've got only dreary neutrals. How the heck you landed such a hunk with such a palette, I wonder."

She didn't know how she should react. Be piqued by the barely-veiled insult or be aghast that Diya had sunk her teeth into the notion of Eric's presence in her life. She didn't want to talk of Eric, and certainly not with the nosy git in her house.

"It's none of your business, Dee."

Silence hung heavy in the next seconds, and Diya, looking nonplussed, continued with her experimenting in front of the mirror.

"So," she said. "I gather he's a good shot, as well. How was it?"

"How was what?" Lara asked as she leaned against the wall.

"The steamy quickie you had downstairs."

Lara scrambled to her feet. "We didn't—"

"Oh, don't give me that," her sister said. "You're smirking wider than Sylvester when he manages to eat Tweety."

Goodness. No point in denying it. As appalled as she was to discuss her 'quickie' with her sibling, she couldn't hide her head in the sand. Diya might be her baby sister, but the girl had grown up. What was she to do in such a situation?

Lara took a deep breath to try to calm her nerves. If news of this encounter leaked out ...

"Dee, give me your word you won't tell this to anyone, least of all to Mum."

Diya threw the eye shadow palette down and turned to stare at her.

"Hello? You think me *loco* or what?" She twirled her index finger at her temple to highlight her point. "Does any of us really need Mum working more drama than she usually does?"

At least she held some good sense in that airhead skull. Lara blew out a sigh of relief.

Diya grabbed her hand and pulled her onto the bed. Startling how the tiny girl could pack such strength in her delicate limbs.

"Out with the details, though." Diya grinned the shark smile again. "How long have you two been together?"

No way out, again. So Lara sighed once more. "Little more than a month now."

She didn't elaborate. However much she loved the budding girlfriend relationship with her sister, that's all she was prepared to share. She needed to change the subject.

"You never got round to telling me why Mum is now on your back."

"Oh," Diya said with a shrug. "She's found out about my boyfriend, who is totally unproper, apparently." She made quote marks with her hands when she said the word 'unproper.' "So Mum, with nothing better to do, as usual, is going bonkers and driving me mad in the process."

A boyfriend who did not fit the bill? Unless he'd been handpicked by their mother, no man would be considered 'proper.'

At the same time, though, Lara knew rules of propriety and the like existed as a framework for guidance. And it seemed to her that following rules and paying heed to advice were not part of Diya's genetic makeup. As a big sister, she had to look out for the girl.

"Dee, be careful, okay? I don't want you to get hurt. If this guy is not worth it, drop him."

Diya engulfed her in a big hug. "Aww, sis. That's too sweet." She squealed before growing calmer again. "I know what I'm doing. I'm careful. I just wish Mum would let me live, though."

Lara laughed. "The day Mum lets us do that, we'll know for sure she's gone mad."

***

Friday evening arrived, and Lara settled in her living room with a pile of documents in her lap. She spent more and more time away from the office and consequently brought a lot of work back home with her.

Tired of reading yet another report, with the graphs and figures of estimations and projections blurring before her vision, she closed her eyes and rested her head on the sofa. Home was *not* a favourable setting to dissect the financial reports of the different departments she had under her responsibility. Yet, she worked everything that way to share more time with Eric.

A smile lifted the corners of her mouth as she heard him puttering in her kitchen.

Intent on taking care of her, he usually prepared her dinner on the weekends. He stayed with her all the time he could, and they'd taken to arranging their schedules around each other. His presence brought the calm and comfort she'd longed for, and his attentive loving soothed her body, mind, and soul.

I could grow used to this life. She sighed. If only things could be so easy, with only Eric and her in their little world. But it was not possible. There existed a big, bad world out there, and she wasn't certain the society they lived in was ready for something like the two of them together.

And truth be told, she dared not find out, either. She refused to acknowledge anything that could burst the bubble she thrived in lately.

The telephone ringing cut through her thoughts, and she glanced around for the device. Fishing it from under a cushion of the sofa, she answered with a weary sigh.

"Good evening, darling."

"Good evening, Mum." Lara closed her eyes in despair. Just what she needed. "How are you?"

She heard a snort at the other end.

"As if you care. I haven't heard from you in so many days, yet you ask how I'm doing?"

"Sorry, Mum. I'm very busy lately."

The litany of excuses fell from her lips like a recorded, automated response. *For an excuse to ditch Mum, press one. For a plan to worm out of Saturday dinner, press two.* And so on ...

"Oh, never mind," her mother said.

This got Lara to pop her eyes open and sit up straighter. Since when did her mother let her off the hook that easily?

"Tell me, is that girl at your place yet again?"

She blinked. "What girl?"

"Diya, of course. She's never around anymore."

Lara sent out silent thanks. The radar had clocked in on her youngest sister, and for once, not on her. "She's not here, Mum. She's probably at some friend's place or still on campus. Isn't she doing exams right now? And why are you looking for her?"

"Oh, dear me. Didn't I tell you?" The tone dropped to a conspiratorial low at the other end. "She's gotten involved with some good-for-nothing, and she thinks she's in love with him. But that's not the worst, Lara. There are talks how that boy is a

Muslim. Can you imagine?"

Here we go again. Not only had she eluded her mother's ramblings lately, she'd also had a respite from the social mores and double standards. Perfect to consider a Muslim or Christian neighbour as closer than family, but let one of 'their own' try to fall for someone from a different religion or culture, and the sword fell.

Lara tuned out of the conversation as her mother continued her discourse on Diya and the 'unproper' boyfriend. She added a "yes" or a noncommittal "uh-huh" along the way, but she doubted her mother noticed.

Her boredom must have come off her in waves, because Eric came to stand behind her, and he bent to drop kisses along her neck.

What a tease. She had to get him to stop. None of *that* when she was on the phone with her mother, of all people.

However, she couldn't conceal the giggle welling up in her throat.

Deathly silence fell on the line, and she wondered if the call had been cut.

But her mother's voice came back on a second later.

"What are you giggling about?" *Long, very long, pause.* "Lara, I sure hope there's not some strange man with you."

Oh, no, her mother would really drive the nail in now. She needed to get out of the conversation, by any means. "No, Mum. There isn't some *strange man* with me, as you say."

And that was the truth. Eric wasn't 'some

strange man.'

Lara nearly laughed again, but she caught herself just in time. It wouldn't do to spill the beans after all her hard work.

"Sorry, Mum. I have to go now. I've still got loads of work to do. Talk to you soon. Bye."

She pressed the icon to end the call before her mother had any chance of following up on her question. If Gayatri Hemant came to know the whole truth about Eric ...

"What's the matter?" Eric asked as he settled in the seat opposite her.

She smiled at him and shook her head. As much as she reeled from the close encounter with her mother, she couldn't help but see the incongruity of the situation. "Nothing. Just my mother thinking I live a bad life because she suspects I have strange men in my house."

He chuckled. "I figure the strange man referred to is me."

She laughed along with him.

But moments later, the laughter died, and he grew serious.

Strong foreboding took hold of her, with an unexpected, biting chill. *Nothing good, that.* Her stomach churned, powering on empty. Bad sign, because an empty stomach and strong emotions did not go well together for her.

She tried to shake the feeling, but she couldn't. Somehow, the impossibility of breaking free from the disconcerting notion added to her discomfort.

"So your mum thinks you live a bad life."

He let the words hang between them. They

reached out at her, heavy, powerful, to grip her heart with iron hands.

Chills descended along her spine, and her hands grew cold and clammy. She couldn't utter a word, though, as the silence closed around her throat and paralyzed her vocal chords.

"It can be easily remedied, you know."

He spoke the words slowly, softly. Yet, they resounded in her mind. She didn't know what he was getting at, but suddenly, she grew scared, apprehension battening down her every defence.

Lara somehow raised her eyebrows in question, and the gesture seemed like all the prompt he needed.

"Marry me, Lara."

Chapter Fourteen

Obliterated by the irrational fear taking her hostage, Lara's head spun. Fear clogged her airways, and she couldn't breathe. This had to be a nightmare. When would she wake up? She *had* to wake up to take a breath, since her lungs threatened to burst in her chest.

The terror gripping her proved more debilitating than anything she'd experienced before. Her heart pounded, the only muscle able to move in her whole body. Cold sweat broke on her skin, and she wanted to hug herself tight to keep the warmth from leaving her. She wanted Eric to appear by her side, to hold her close to his chest and tell her she was imagining things.

She awaited deliverance, but none came. Her stomach started to heave, but she contained the nausea. Marriage and a future together had never been in her plans. She'd settled for carpe diem, and she could do nothing to stop the cold running icy in her veins.

This can't go on. She attempted to move, but her body felt frozen solid while her oversensitive mind amplified everything around her. The hiss of her shallow breathing. The drum roll of her heart in her ears. The numbness slowly creeping its way up her hands and feet. The overwhelming sensation reached her neck as darkness descended before her eyes, and she fell into the black void calling out to her.

Lara awoke as soft heat radiated from her limbs. She stretched her leg, and her foot rubbed against the warm and slightly rough surface of a woollen blanket. Her neck lay propped on something soft and lolled back with weakness when she attempted to lift it.

"Don't try to move."

Eric's soft, calm voice filtered through to her mind.

She opened her eyes. He huddled on his knees beside her, his face level with hers where she lay on the sofa.

Confusion filled her mind. "What happened?"

He touched her cold forehead with his warm fingers.

"You fainted."

"What?"

Disbelief flooded her, and she jerked up into a sitting position. Vivid colour erupted before her closed eyelids as her sense of gravity plummeted from the abrupt movement.

"I told you not to move," he snapped.

She popped her eyes open. Why did he look so strained? His lips were white with anger, but his touch was full of concern and precision as he held the back of her neck. With his other hand, he took her wrist and pressed two fingers upon her pulse.

Lara blinked. Here before her wasn't her lover, but the competent doctor in him. What on Earth had happened? She'd get no answers if she stayed this way, with no control over anything.

She tugged her wrist out of his hold with a gentle twist. "I'm okay now."

He snorted. "You were unconscious less than a minute ago, and you expect me to believe that?"

She frowned as she took in his words. "I never faint, Eric."

"You just did."

"But, how can that be? I feel fine."

He kept his eyes fixed on her. Was it her imagination, or did they turn to an icy, arctic blue? His jaw also appeared unusually clenched, a small nerve twitching along his cheek. Not a good sign.

"I guess you've had a shock."

That wasn't calm in his tone, but ice, and irony. She shook her head, which made her senses spin again. She blinked to let her balance settle once more.

Why was he so hard with her?

Cold, steely hands clutched her heart, and she gasped as the breath left her. The last words she'd heard before she'd lost it came back to her, and she clamped a hand to her mouth.

He'd asked her to marry him.

The scene played again in her memory as she stared at him, seeing the man she had spent the past two months with, yet, at the same time, a stranger.

He narrowed his eyes, eyebrows knit in a frown. Great—he'd probably seen the flash of recollection on her face.

"You don't think it's a good idea," he said, the words cutting the heavy silence like a knife.

She opened her mouth, but no sound escaped

with her tongue and throat dry as sandpaper.

His face grew more sombre, his lips drawn to a tight line.

The lick of apprehension tickled all over her spine. She'd never seen Eric angry. A formidable temper lurked in him, one that could cause mayhem when provoked, and the furore seemed to be coming out of its dormant state. Still waters did run deep, after all.

"Why?"

Only one word, yet, she felt the full blow he dealt her with it. Hurt, anger, and confusion battled for space in the three letters.

Lara turned her face the other way. She'd never wanted to hurt him. But she should've known they'd face this situation someday. Time to set things straight with him, to stare reality in its face and wake up from the dream. No more living for the moment, because the bubble had burst. No further evading any issue.

She turned around and focused on him. It broke her heart to see him so distraught, but she had to do what she had to do.

"There's no hope for us, Eric. Everything is against us. Society, our families. No one will accept us. It's next to impossible. Your life is here, as is mine, but this leaves the two of us nowhere," she said in a careful tone.

She'd heard of mixed origins couples emigrating to live their lives away from the prying tentacles of Mauritian society. No such possibility for them.

He remained silent for a few seconds. "Don't you think it's up to us to decide that?"

The calmness of his reply angered her. How could he imagine there wasn't anything, like a condemning society, their formidable families, to face for them to exist? No matter how much she disliked facing it, people *did* talk and make life difficult for others. She shook her head and bit her lip to keep all her justifications within her.

"Why don't you answer me, Lara?"

His voice slammed in cold, detached, and millions of miles from the man she held in her affection. The shift in him came as a total surprise, and suddenly, she could make out the stubborn determination in his eyes as she peered at him. He raised his eyebrows, and the confidence and smugness in the gesture sent her temper over the edge.

Two can play this game. If he was so intent on an answer, she'd give him a very good one. "There's the real world out there, in which we have to live. How long can we hope to exist in denial?"

The outburst echoed in the room. Locked in a clash of will, both knew none would give up the first. Animosity filled the air as their eyes bore into each other's.

"You don't trust me."

Spoken on a whisper, the words carried upon the silence to her and sliced through her insides. Pain welled up and choked her throat.

"Don't say that," she said softly.

"You never trusted me, even back then ... Or else, we'd have worked everything out a long time ago."

The hint of recrimination in his tone hit her like

a slap. How dare he accuse her? Fury erupted in her blood, and fire ignited her mind. "How could I, when you disappeared off the face of the Earth after leaving me stranded here?"

In a quick, lithe move, he stood up and faced her from his full height. From her position on the sofa, intimidating didn't start to describe how he appeared to her, repressed anger tensing his every muscle.

His eyes drew to slits, and hardened once more to pale, icy blue.

"Stranded? I left you *stranded*? Not the impression I got, since you were already in another man's arms barely a few months later."

This time, he'd crossed the line. As he'd thrown the first punch, she wouldn't sit around waiting for another blow. Oh, no. She'd reply, and in kind.

Lara threw the blanket off her and sprang up to face him with defiance.

But the movement had been too quick, and her head spun as all her blood drained down her body.

He reached out and clasped her arms as she fell. He held her up, and a previous similar situation flashed in her mind. When they'd met again at the clinic ...

He pulled her close, and she snuggled into his embrace.

How good it felt to be near him. She sighed and settled her hands on his broad back, where her fingers encountered the bunched muscles in his shoulders.

The reason for the tension grazed her thoughts, and she stiffened and shrugged out of his arms. After flattening her palms on his chest, she pushed him away.

"Our break-up was my entire fault, then? You don't mention the snob you got involved with. What was her name? Sophie? Your picture in that society magazine left no room for misunderstanding."

He remained where he stood, his arms limp by his sides.

"That's exactly what it was, a picture—"

"No, it sure wasn't. I saw you with her, and I read the caption, Eric. Like I said, no room for misunderstanding there."

His nostrils flared, and he crossed his arms in front of his chest. "Really? What did it say?"

She rolled her eyes. "We're really going to do this?"

"Yes, we are. Because you've got it all wrong."

He was convinced of that, wasn't he? She glared at him. "Fine. The caption read, and I quote, word for word, '*Éric Marivaux, étudiant en médecine et héritier de la famille Armont, accompagnant Sophie de Maivière, qui attend un heureux évènement.*'"

He remained silent, which doubled her anger. If he wouldn't defend himself, it only meant ... She bit her lip.

"How much did you score in French that year, Lara?"

She whipped her head up to glare at him. What did that have anything to do with their fight today? She quirked her eyebrows and crossed her arms.

He chuckled, but the sound came out devoid of any humour. "Lara, the way the caption was written, grammatically, meant Sophie was the one happily expecting." He paused. "Sophie alone."

What?

"But I saw you with her on there. There could be no doubt—"

"If you'd waited for me, I would've explained it all to you. Yes, Sophie wanted the world to believe she was expecting my baby, but this couldn't be the case as I'd never slept with her. *Merde*, I'd never even kissed her."

Oh, no. She'd had it all wrong all along?

"But you didn't wait, Lara, and you jumped on the first escape route that came your way."

Oh, the gall of the man. "How dare you—"

"Yes, I dare," he said through clenched teeth as he took two steps to stop right in front of her. "I dare because you always search for the easy way out. And, *ma belle*, I'm sorry to say there *is* no easy way out, not in a relationship where two people are equally involved."

His words hit her like a blow, and she stomached the implications hard.

Before she could comprehend what she was doing, she lashed out and slapped his cheek.

Her mouth dropped open when she realized what she'd done.

Horror, and disgust at herself, brought the foul taste of bile in her mouth.

"I'm sorry. I didn't mean to," she said in a whisper.

He closed his eyes and averted his face. When he opened them again, he peered down at her.

"My patience has limits, Lara. I told you that once. I better leave," he said as he turned on his heel and made his way to the front door.

Numb shock descended on her as she watched

him move away from her, powerless to stop him, or call him back.

On the threshold, he stopped, his back still to her.

"You don't even trust yourself. That's probably why it never worked."

Upon those words, he walked out of the house, closing the door softly behind him.

Yet, the gentle click echoed with the full force of a slamming door in her head. His departure became the drop to make her overflow, and her weak legs gave way under her.

He had left. The immovable anchor had freed itself and moved away, abandoning her to be carried away in a sea of choppy waves ...

Lara sagged onto the floor, where she gave in to the sobs wracking her body. Tears flowed down her cheeks, but she had no power, no strength, and no desire to stop them.

In a crumpled heap, she cried the tears of a woman who may have made a very big mistake, and now had to pay the price for the rest of her life.

***

The pounding on the door wouldn't stop, alternating between two chimes of the doorbell. Why could the caller not leave her alone? She'd been alone for the past ... come to think of it, she had no clue how long she'd been holed up in her house. How many times had she phoned the office to let them know she was calling in a sick leave? Doris thought she had a bad cold. Not hard to deduce, since all the crying had rendered her throat scratchier than when she'd smoked three packets of cigarettes a day.

She'd also started to screen her calls, if ignoring the ringing cell could be construed as call screening. She couldn't be bothered. There were matters to think upon ... or not. However much she knew she would have to face the truth—the one Eric had spelt out—she also knew she was a total chicken who would hide her head in the sand for as long as she could.

If only the bloody pounding at her door would stop.

With weary steps, she trudged to the front door and threw it open.

"What?" she snarled at whoever had the misfortune of standing on her doorstep.

The misfortune was hers, though, because in front of her stood her bratty little sister.

Diya pushed into the house and started towards the living room.

"Why the hell aren't you answering your calls? Is it to escape Mum's wrath? You won't, you know. She's coming for you right after she's done with me." Diya shivered. "And I have no plans to let her be done with me, so I suppose you're off the hook for now."

God, would that girl stop her incessant babbling? Her head already hurt, and she didn't need the chirpy little butterfly in her home. If Diya stood here, it meant she'd decided to spend the night at Lara's place.

Better to cut her losses while she could. So she slammed the door closed and brushed past her sister on the way to the kitchen. She still had half of a chocolate cream cake waiting for her.

"Good grief! What's happened to you?" Diya gasped. "When was the last time you brushed your hair? And you're wearing sweats and wool in this heat? Are you sick?"

Just had my heart ripped out and trampled on. Nothing major. *Second time, too. No. Third. Shame on me.*

She plonked herself on a stool at the counter and reached for a fork that she dug into the cake, then pushed a huge mound of Chantilly cream and chocolate *génoise* into her mouth.

Diya chattered around her. Her sister sounded hysterical. She shrugged. When was exuberant Diya *not* hysterical? She was the only child who'd had the misfortune of taking after their mother.

Lara reached the last forkful of cake. A pile of cream with glacé cherries lay inside the box. With a finger, she scooped up the buttery goodness and pushed it past her lips.

And all that butter on her tongue made her sick.

She blinked at the box, realising she'd put away a cake intended for twenty people.

Nausea burned up her throat. How could she have lost control so much?

But nothing was really lost, was it? She could still win over this lapse, recover the balance, wipe away her loss of discipline ...

She rushed into the bathroom and dropped to her knees in front of the toilet bowl. Reaching down her throat with two fingers, she made her gorge rise so she could throw up all the cake.

That would make things right. Erase the excess. Bring a semblance of order and control to things spinning out of her grip ...

Someone grabbed her shoulders and shook her. She blinked into her baby sister's face. Right. Diya had arrived a little while ago, hadn't she?

Why was the girl dragging her away? She wasn't done yet. She threw the strong grip off, and forced herself to throw up again.

Diya left her blissfully alone.

Lara didn't know how much time she remained there on her knees. Her throat burned, her eyes were all misty and blurred, her stomach churning on empty. She'd gotten rid of the cake. She should be feeling all right, shouldn't she? So why were tears coursing down her cheeks again, and the clang of despair grabbing hold of her heart?

"Oh, babe. Tell me you didn't do this."

She blinked. *Sam?* How had she gotten here?

Gentle hands settled on both her arms, and she glanced around as if coming out of a deep haze. Sam held one arm, Diya the other. The two of them led her away from the floor towards the sink, where Sam ran the tap and moistened a small towel. She then wiped Lara's face and softly pulled her into the living room.

She paused on the edge of the room. Greasy pizza boxes lay on the floor near the sofa. A stain like spilled cola darkened one of the cushions.

This couldn't be her place, surely. What had happened to her, to turn her into such a slob?

And then, she remembered, and the sobs rolled up.

She would've crumpled to the floor had the two women not been holding her.

"Eric," she said in a croak. "He's gone." She turned to her best friend. "He's gone, and I had it all wrong."

"Shh." Sam soothed her with a hug. "Come sit down, and tell me about it."

She shook her head. "I can't."

"Of course you can."

Sam made her sit on the sofa, at the opposite end of the cola stain, and took her hands as she squatted in front of her. "When did this happen, sweetie?"

She choked back a sob, and snorted loudly to stop her running nose. "Friday."

"Today is Tuesday," Diya said on a gasp.

"She's in bad shape, I'll grant you that," Sam replied.

Lara glanced up at them. "Hello? I'm still here, you know."

"Only just." Sam snorted. "Okay, Zombie Girl. Tell us everything, and then, we'll bring you back into the world of the living again."

***

Eric reached out from the halfway place between slumber and wakefulness. When his hand landed flat on the bed, onto the cold, empty space beside him, he tried to shake away the cloak of cold threatening to engulf him. The nightmare was back to plague him—he remained all alone, Lara no longer here with her warmth and softness.

Except this time, his brain triggered the memory. He wasn't in the throes of a nightmare.

One week, and the pain hadn't abated one whit.

Lara had really left.

Or, he'd left ... The succession of events blipped

hazy in his mind, blurred by the warped veil anger and disillusion had woven over his perception.

He sat up and let his head fall into his hands. Cold and strangely empty. That's how he existed now. All because Lara wasn't there with him.

And probably wouldn't be again.

He sighed and ran a hand in his hair.

What had possessed him to pop the question? He'd vowed to take his time, hadn't he? Never one to let his temper get the better of him, he hadn't been able to contain himself.

She'd rejected him, though. He'd given her all he had, yet, it hadn't been enough for her. It had never been enough.

He wanted to kick himself. Why couldn't he have been satisfied with what she gave? He'd have coaxed more out of her with time.

But when the opportunity had presented itself, he hadn't been able to resist. He wanted her, as his wife. Nothing less.

Her reaction had thrown him off, and he'd never experienced the total loss of his wits as when she'd blacked out in front of him. Sheer reflex and training had kicked in when he'd checked on her vitals and stretched her limp body onto the sofa.

The fear of losing her had wrecked through his soul and torn his insides, and he'd prayed to never have to experience that feeling again.

He hadn't known worse waited further down the line. Because his life would stretch empty, as he'd lost her.

He stifled a curse as he let his body fall back against the pillow.

He and Lara as a couple—they could've worked.

Maybe if he'd given more. Maybe with time, she'd have seen what the future could hold for them.

But his patience had run out the minute he'd figured out she didn't trust him. Anger had taken over, burning logic and coherent thought, any notion of rationality, and had spelt the end.

Distress like he'd never thought existed had erupted inside him. Daggers of hurt and betrayal had slashed through him, and the pain had taken hold of his whole being.

What could he hope to build out of a relationship where the fundamental of trust wasn't even present? He knew Lara well, and he'd surely been in denial over the fact that she wouldn't commit in a situation where certain things escaped her control.

Et puis, merde! He threw the sheet off him in a fit. Damn the day when Lara had walked into his life again.

But he couldn't shake off the images of her crowding his mind, making him relive all the wonderful weeks they'd spent together.

He should've known he'd be trampled again. He hadn't heeded the call, and it was too late.

The ringing of his phone cut through his reflections.

"Eric Marivaux," he answered.

"Doctor, I'm sorry to disturb you, but we have an emergency. The Jeffries boy. His parents just brought him in, severe asthma attack with heavy coughing and wheezing."

He sighed. Not an emergency at four in the morning. Yet, he should've expected it. The seasons were changing from summer to winter, and the autumn-type period during the change spelt viruses and asthma attacks all over the island.

Weariness dropped like a heavy weight onto his shoulders, anchoring him to where he sat on the bed. He didn't want to leave his home. He didn't feel fit for anything other than a pity party. But such were the hazards of his job, and he couldn't escape his duty.

"Start the nebulizer with the regular dose I prescribe for him every time," he said. "I'm on my way."

Maybe if he threw himself in his work, he'd forget about Lara.

Fat chance. But he could still try.

With a heavy sigh, he got up and walked into the bathroom.

Chapter Fourteen

"Doris, get me another coffee before you leave, please." Lara sighed as she lifted her finger from the intercom button on the phone. She needed to get herself in gear, and coffee would surely do the trick. Again.

Seconds later, her PA walked in with a steaming mug in her hand.

"There you go. It's your seventh of the day, if I may remind you," the older woman said in a tone full of reproach.

She dismissed the comment with a wave of her hand as she sipped the hot brew. "You may leave, Doris. It's already one o'clock. I'm sure your family needs you."

"I'm leaving as soon as I finish some filing in the office. What about you, though?"

"I have a lot of backlog I need to work through, so I'll stay here for the moment."

Doris crossed her arms in front of her chest. Her whole stance spelt, *don't kid me, girl.*

She sighed. "Really. I do have backlog I'm carrying forward from the week I took off."

It pained her to admit she'd needed the time off, but thank goodness her colleagues, PA, and her boss had no clue why she had needed to stay away from the office. They were also clueless to the three-times-a-week evening visits she'd been paying to a psychiatrist, the same one who had worked with her during her first brush with eating disorders as a teenager.

Doris huffed, but left, nevertheless. Once alone, Lara eased herself into her seat with her mug in one hand and turned towards the windowpane. Sipping her coffee, she waited for the caffeine to kick in as she gazed at the beautiful gardens.

Not as beautiful as the garden at Eric's house.

She shook her head as the thought hit. Lately, she'd been having increasing trouble to work Eric and his memory out of her mind. Time had not dulled the feeling of loss at all. In fact, she'd say that with each passing day, she hurt a little bit more. Deader than the previous day, yet having to power on. She had no escape, easy or not. She chuckled without humour. Little things about their time together came back to haunt her at every occasion, and anything could trigger them off. She'd hardly slept in the past weeks, and combined with the desperation she threw into her work, fatigue and burnout were taking their toll on her.

"Aha. I knew I'd find you here."

The sound of the Slavic accent cut through her thoughts, and she turned her chair around to see her boss walking into her office.

Markus pulled up a chair and settled himself in front of her desk.

She gave him a welcome smile. "The mere fact you've bothered to come here implies there's more work coming. Am I right?"

"Lara, I love to work with you," he said with a wink. "You understand everything so easily."

"What is it this time?" She set her mug down and rested her elbows on the desk, bending slightly forward to give him her full attention.

He remained in his casual stance, but the way he wrung his hands together betrayed his excitement.

"Remember the bid we made the week after your first convention, for the Commonwealth conference?" He paused. "I just heard we've been short-listed."

She blinked in surprise. She'd winged the proposal together in a couple of days. "That's wonderful news, Markus. I wasn't sure they'd love our offer, but if they do ..."

Silence greeted her reply, and she frowned with worry as she stared at him. "I'm sure there's a problem, so what is it?"

"You," he said with a straight, solemn face.

She blinked. "Excuse me? I don't get it. I thought you said I was doing a good job here."

He sighed and shook his head. "Lara, it's nothing to do with your job. Actually, I can't think of a better director than you. But you've got me worried lately."

Uh-oh. Would he get on her case, too?

"Why is that?"

"Listen, what I'll say to you is off the record, simply from me to you, not from boss to employee." He paused, as if carefully choosing his words. "These past weeks, you've practically lived out of here so much you don't leave your office."

She opened her mouth to protest, but he put his hand up and silenced her.

"Hear me out. Something is very wrong with you. I won't pry and ask what, it's none of my business. But you gotta know this contract will be tough to bag, and it'll ask a lot from you."

He drew his intense gaze onto her, making her squirm.

"Will you be able to take it all on?" he asked. "It's the first time we'll be handling something this big."

More work? That's exactly what she needed. "We're more than ready for this, and the challenge will only make it better. Imagine how we could place the centre on the map if we bag this contract."

"If this is what you say," he replied with a quirked eyebrow. "I wanted to run the news past you. I'll be off now."

On the threshold, he stopped and turned to face her.

"Lara, my dear, try not to turn into the phantom of this place," he said with a chuckle.

She found herself smiling at his comment, and she welcomed the lightness, for she didn't have reason enough to smile lately. All because of Eric.

She'd always known she'd be in for pain in a relationship with him. Yet, why hadn't she reasoned with herself before getting into the whole business?

She sighed. It would do no good to think of the past. Because what had happened had been inevitable. She shouldn't let it have so much hold on her.

Lara forced her mind to focus on the information

Markus had supplied. The Commonwealth Nations' Conference represented a very big affair. If they landed the deal, it would indeed mean dedication and hard work.

Maybe that'd take her mind off Eric.

She wanted to kick herself as the thought crossed her mind. Why did everything have to come back to him?

Her phone rang, and she lashed out to pick it up, the receiver nearly falling out her hand in her haste.

"Yes?"

"Whoa, babe. Easy does it." The feminine voice at the other end chuckled.

"Sam, hi." Weariness crashed over her, and she let her body sag, limp, in her chair. "What's up?"

"I knew I'd find you in your damn office yet again."

She closed her eyes in annoyance. Everyone was saying that to her, lately. Couldn't they find another topic to talk about?

"I've got work to do, as opposed to some people who are on leave."

Sam laughed at her rebuke. "Speaking of leave, I'm at Caudan right now. Why don't you come join me?"

"Thanks, but I still got loads to do. Some other time, maybe."

God only knew what would've happened that fateful Tuesday if Diya hadn't called in the cavalry through Sam. The two of them had put her back on her feet, and she'd be eternally grateful. Not that what they did had changed her predicament. She'd returned to the world of the living, but it didn't mean she enjoyed life as a living being. Surviving suited her fine right now. And maybe forever, because that's how she'd have to live the rest of her days ...

The psychiatrist was doing his darnedest best to have her work through that, to no avail, it seemed, though. What did he know about heartbreak? She'd lived through it twice already, and if this third time was breaking her, then so be it. Who had that much in them to weather so much failure in love and relationships?

"Lara, I'm worried about you. You don't go out anymore, and this is not good."

She sighed. As if she wanted to enjoy herself right then. "Sam, don't start. I'm really busy, I swear."

"Okay, but how about dinner tonight? Don't tell me you work in the evenings, too, now," Sam said on a small laugh. "Come on, don't say no. And I know you don't have an appointment with Dr Tristan tonight."

"Fine," Lara replied after giving it some thought. "Let's meet at the Chinese restaurant on La Salette road in Grand-Baie at seven."

She put the receiver down and got up to take a few steps. Her legs had gone stiff from too much sitting, and her back hurt. Pins and needles erupted along her feet, forcing her to shed her pumps.

Maybe she should take a walk outside. The lawn under her soles would ease the tingling feelings, and the fresh air could do her some good.

Like erase any thought of Eric.

Damn, why was she thinking of him again?

***

The pretty girl with him tightened her arm around his waist and snuggled up to his side as they strolled along the waterfront.

Bad sign. She wanted something, and she wanted it like, yesterday.

"Can we have popcorn? And candyfloss? *S'il-te-plait? S'il-te-plait? S'il-te-plait?*"

If she hopped one more time, she'd smash his toes with the heel of her platform shoes.

Eric shook his head. "Bad for your teeth. You know you shouldn't have this stuff with your braces."

She stopped dead in the middle of the Caudan esplanade and punched him in the arm.

Merde, but since when did his younger sister's punches start hurting? Could those jujitsu classes she'd started taking in Italy be making her so much stronger? Even lethal?

"The orthodontist removed my braces last week, Eric," she said with a shake of her head. A long strand of dark brown hair whipped him in the face.

Right. He winced, because he'd had his head in the clouds lately. That's why she had returned to Mauritius for the two-week break.

"Sorry, Angélique." He pulled her into his arms and pressed a kiss to her temple. "Still, sugar is bad for you, so no."

She wormed out of his arms and pouted. "You're no fun."

He stared at her with raised eyebrows before lifting the hefty array of shopping bags in his hands. "Remind me again who footed the bill for all these?"

Angélique smiled. "You're not a bad sort." She

grabbed his arm once more as they made their way to the food court. "So, tell me, am I still allowed to drink water?"

Cheeky little brat.

"I'll even let you have a milkshake," he said with a smile.

While he got up to go place their orders, he squirmed, registering the intense, pointed stare of someone watching him burn the nape of his neck. He turned around and blinked.

Strange.

The girl behind the counter handed over his order, and he took the drinks back to their table. All through the trek, he still felt the stare, but *merde* if he could place where the scrutiny was coming from.

Angélique fell on her milkshake as if she were starving. Anyone looking at them would think he hadn't fed her in the past twenty-four hours, the time she had spent at his house. His baby sister had picked up on his doldrums, but thankfully, hadn't asked outright what his problem was. Instead, she'd whisked him into endless games of Monopoly, reruns of *The Big Bang Theory*, and a whole day of shopping today. Trust young adults to have their priorities sorted in such simple ways.

Angélique squealed, and Eric winced. Only one person could turn the twenty-year-old girl into such a hysterical banshee, and he twisted around with a smile as his sister jumped up and threw her arms around the tall, sandy-haired man who approached their table.

Patrice nearly toppled over under the exuberant assault of his fiancée. The kiss Angélique planted on him would surely bring security in their surroundings, since such public displays of affection had to be illegal. In the nick of time, the girl released the poor man.

He stepped up and clasped his future brother-in-law's hand. Patrice had turned red—from embarrassment, or from the death grip Angélique still had on him with her arms around his neck?

"Ange, don't kill him just yet, will you?" Eric told her.

His sister huffed and slapped his arm.

Patrice laughed. "You don't mind if I take her off your hands?"

Eric smiled. "Be my guest."

As much as he loved his sibling, twenty-four hours with her would turn any sane man into a raving lunatic.

The lovebirds left, Patrice saddled with the bags Eric had been carrying until then. The two stopped in front of the popcorn stall, where Angélique got a carton of caramel popcorn and a big, fluffy mass of candyfloss.

Eric shook his head. Patrice was toast. Angélique could do whatever she wanted to the big man.

As he took a pull from his milkshake, the burning feeling on his nape returned. The scrutiny felt less intense, though. Sitting back casually in his chair, he threw a quick glance around the food court.

A woman sat a few tables from him, and he'd bet she'd been watching him ever since he'd settled there.

Remarkably beautiful, with the ethereal quality

of supermodels on her well-defined features and in the shiny, chin-length red hair, he was certain he didn't know her, though a flicker of recognition did prick him fleetingly every time he returned his focus to her face.

She seemed to know who he was, though, gauging by the intense way she stared back at him.

Without taking her gaze off him, she stood up and walked towards his table to stop inches from him.

From up close, she looked even more ravishing, yet, her identity still eluded him.

"Eric?" she asked in a husky, slightly breathless tone.

Who was she? He nodded in reply.

"I'm Sam, Lara's friend."

Sameera. Lara's shadow in secondary school, her best friend. The one who'd told him he better forget Lara when he'd called her soon after the society magazine debacle.

No wonder she had appeared familiar. And no wonder she had stared at him so intensely when he'd been with Angélique, because no one would peg them as siblings at first glance. Sam must've thought he'd already replaced Lara in his life. She'd been out for blood last time he had spoken to her. Was this the case today again?

He was no chicken, and he'd hear what she had to say to him.

"Have a seat." He indicated with a nod. "You've changed. I didn't recognise you."

"You still remember me from back then?" she asked as she pulled a chair and sat down.

"How could I forget?" He gave a soft laugh. "You used to cover for Lara whenever we met."

A chuckle escaped her. "Yes, these were the good old days. Too bad it's changed now."

She let the statement dangle, obviously a challenge for him to pick up.

Questions lay heavy in her words, and he heard every one of them. If he recalled properly, Lara had mentioned Sam had become a business strategy consultant, and a very good one.

And if she was still the determined girl she'd been fourteen years before, he was in for some explaining.

He had nothing to explain, though, but he was certain Sam acted that way for her friend's sake. For Lara's sake, he would answer her.

"Nothing's changed, Sam."

She remained silent, but raised a perfectly arched eyebrow sceptically.

"I still love her exactly the same way."

"I find that hard to believe."

Her voice came out soft, but the tone held concrete hardness. He wouldn't want to be across any negotiation table with her opposite him. But he was done providing excuses, covering for Lara. High time he'd started thinking of his own happiness in the whole matter. His sanity, too.

"What's so hard to believe? How I may still care for her, even after all I went through for her sake?"

"Lara's hurting, a lot," she said. "Because of you."

A sigh escaped him, and he passed a hand over his face in a weary gesture. "Don't you think I know that?"

A flicker of surprise crossed her face, but she quickly concealed it. "Why did you leave her, then?"

"Because I was sick and tired of living only on her terms. I didn't ask for much, Sam. I swear I didn't. But Lara never thought of giving back, not a little bit."

Her face softened as she took in his outburst.

"Why don't you make her understand, then?"

He snorted, and her eyes grew wide.

"You know Lara as well as I do. Can you make her see sense when she's stuck in pig-headed corner?"

A small smile appeared on her face. "True enough."

"Sometimes," he started. "You have to step back and let others work things out for themselves. I can't do any more for Lara. She's got to tread the rest of the way."

"Will you be there, though?"

He hesitated before replying. What could he say? He noticed her eyes narrowed as she watched the emotion pass over his face.

"Can Lara count on you?" she asked.

Time for the truth, and nothing but. "Sam, no other woman can take Lara's place. I only hope she realizes it before it's too late, for her own sake."

Silence hung heavy between them, before she sighed.

"She's lucky to have a man like you."

He gave a small, ironic laugh. Tell that to Lara, who'd never trusted him ...

"I better go now," she said. "I'm meeting Lara for dinner. It's been nice talking to you."

"Same here."

She got up and started to leave, and he called her back.

"Make sure she eats, okay?"

***

"Lara, drop the chopsticks. The linen is eating more than you are."

Lara glanced up at her friend, worried Sam might've seen through her ploy not to eat. She'd toyed with the lacquered duck pancakes and managed not to eat any. No such luck with the rice, though, as Sam asked the dreaded question.

"Since when do you, of all people, eat with chopsticks? And rice, too?"

Sam snatched the bamboo chopsticks and thrust a metal fork into her hand.

No escape. She'd have to take a bite or two. Sam would kick her into the ground if she confessed she had no appetite. How could she, when her life no longer had any purpose? Every day, she rehashed the mistakes she had made, and every time, she dug herself into her grave a little further.

Maybe if she kept Sam talking, she could work her way around the dishes. Why had the woman ordered enough food to feed a regiment? So she could get the leftovers packed and not have to cook any dinner for a week?

"My stomach's not feeling too good. I must have caught some bug or something." The sickness excuse should work.

Sam dropped her fork and stared back at her. "This is what happens when you live on black coffee alone."

Damn it. No way out. Sam had always seen through her game. Why would that have conveniently stopped today?

"Okay, I'll eat. Pleased?"

The redhead smiled back and pushed the plate of Cantonese fried rice her way. "Very."

"How come you're having dinner with me today?" Lara asked. "Where's that husband of yours?"

"On a business trip to Cape Town. Good thing he's not here. He wears me out when he's around." Sam winked. "It's fun trying for a baby."

Goodness, no. Not marital bliss and sexual contentment. Not when she was in dire craving of both. "Have some concern for my new celibate existence, will you?"

Sam pointed at her with her fork. "And whose fault would that be?"

"Don't you start with this."

She didn't need her BFF to get on her back, too. Her conscience was enough, thank you very much.

"Come on, Lara. You could have all of it today, but the stupid git you are chose to throw it all away."

As if everything was so simple. A headache started to throb behind her forehead. The anger melted, to be replaced by the rational bent she forced into her perception anytime the void of loss threatened to engulf her.

"Why do I feel I have to explain myself to all of you? This never would've worked. We're too different, worlds apart in birth and upbringing, and we don't think the same."

"You still haven't given a valid reason," Sam

said. "All that wasn't a problem when you were together."

Lara threw her fork down and pressed her back into her chair. "Come on, it was only a matter of time before our families got involved, and by then, the whole of society would be rubbing their salt in the gaping wound. We would never have weathered that."

Damn it. She'd agreed to this dinner to take her mind off all of these things, not to actually have to motivate her every action with a valid reason.

"How will you know if you never try?" Sam asked in a dead-serious tone.

She stared at her friend with her mouth gaping open. First Eric, then Sam. Why was everyone intent on pushing her beyond her limits?

"We'd only get hurt if we'd gone ahead with it," she replied coolly.

"As if you're not hurting now?"

What was the woman getting at? What more was there to consider?

"That's not the point. It wouldn't have worked, full stop."

Sam remained silent for a long moment, and Lara felt the full force of her friend's scrutiny on her, until the woman broke the silence.

"I think you're making the biggest mistake of your life."

She nearly choked on the sip of water she'd taken. Was she hearing right? Sam, resident relationship bliss killer whose motto had been 'love them, use them, leave them,' talking of abandoning a man as a mistake? When had such a one-eighty turn happened?

"Why are you being so insistent? It's not like you," she said.

Sam shook her head, and sadness played on her beautiful features. "You know why I fell for Salim?"

Lara shrugged. She'd stopped trying to figure out how, overnight while in Cape Town, Sam had agreed to marry Salim after he'd chased her for years without success.

"It's because I realized with utmost certainty that I'd never meet a man who'd love me like he does," Sam said.

She tried to swallow the lump suddenly forming in her throat. So love had happened.

"You and Salim have something special."

"I know. But I'd never have known if I hadn't given him a chance."

The lump grew bigger, and tears stung her eyes.

"What are you trying to say?"

"Just that, sometimes, you gotta give in a little to get a lot more in return."

She stared at her friend for a long time.

Had she been hasty in rejecting Eric? Somehow, she couldn't help but feel a nagging doubt take root inside her. Why did that notion have to come plague her now, when all hope was lost?

"You know, Sam," she said. "Sometimes, I wish Roy was back, and we'd pick up from where we left off. Life was so uncomplicated back then."

"You don't mean it. In your heart, you know there's only one man there."

"Still, I can't help it." She let the words trail off, and they dissolved into the air like thin wisps of smoke.

"Be careful what you wish for. You might get it."

Lara came back to present when she heard the longing and bitterness in Sam's voice.

Intent on her own problems, she hadn't noticed her friend might also need her. "Babe, is something wrong?"

"Not really," Sam replied with a tremulous smile. "Remember how I wished not to have kids when we were younger? Seems like my wish got fulfilled."

Her heart went out to Sam, and she clasped the other woman's hand in silent support.

"I'm sure you'll get pregnant. Didn't you tell me you went to a new doctor?"

"It's funny, you know. I desire the thing I can most certainly not get."

Don't we all.

The thought crossed her mind, and a sinking feeling of loss settled inside her.

Maybe she *had* made a mistake when she'd let Eric go.

But she'd never know for sure. Because Eric was done with her.

Chapter Sixteen

"As usual, your father is busy, Diya is God knows where, and Neha's baby is sick. So I have no one but you to take me shopping."

Lara had more than grown tired of her mother's gripes. As much as she wanted to not pick up the phone when she saw the Hemants' home number on the caller ID, she couldn't do that. As a daughter from an Indian-origin family, she had a duty to perform where her family was concerned. Still, said duty didn't mean she couldn't worm her way out of the incongruous situations as they happened.

She sighed. "Take a taxi, Mum. It's what they're here for."

Her mother had just crossed past fifty. Couldn't she learn how to drive? Her father could afford another car, if not more.

"I have a daughter who's single and has her own car, and you want me to take a taxi?"

Great. She'd forgotten 'single' meant 'at the family's disposal for every errands.' Truly, single people were not expected to have a life in Mauritius.

Her mother rambled on. "When I know my daughter is free to take me where I need to go? Shame on you, Lara."

The childish whining got on her nerves, and she had no idea how, by some feat, she managed to keep the lid down on her temper. No good would come from trying to fend off her mother, so she might as well give in.

Cut her losses—her new philosophy in life.

She snorted.

"Fine," she said. "I'll take you on your damn shopping."

"No need to swear, young lady." Her mother huffed the reprimand in a tone full of reproach.

Still, the lure of the trip must've obliterated the older woman's outrage. God, she switched through moods faster than a chameleon through its colours.

"I'll have your opinion on the curtains to choose. I'm so excited," Gayatri Hemant said. "Bye, darling."

She put the phone down with another sigh. Her mother could drive anyone to the asylum without realising the damage she could wreck on a person's sanity.

Four hours later, a splitting headache tore through her head as the two of them settled at the table of a café in a mall of the edges of the town of Quatre-Bornes, for the afternoon tea.

For the life her, she'd never, ever again, take her mother shopping for curtains. They'd spent ages in the stifling, cloying heat of the open-air Quatre-Bornes market to sort through hundreds of different fabric swatches.

Not one had been up to the mark, her mother always searching for something else, something more, whatever the heck that 'something' happened to be, since it seemed to Lara even her mother had no clue what she was looking for.

A thought nagged her. Had this whole trip been pretence for them to spend time together? Her mother defined 'shopaholic,' and the fact she hadn't spent a single rupee in more than an hour made Lara suspicious.

She glanced up at her mother, who was busy fanning herself with a napkin.

"Mum, why did you drag me along today?"

The older woman fluttered her hand in an evasive gesture. "You know, darling, two views are better than one when decorating. And you have such good taste, as well."

The voice dripped nice and sweet as syrup.

She frowned, feeling her eyebrows draw together as warning bells rang up a cacophony in her head.

"Mum, I've got awful taste for anything domestic, and you know it. Diya's the one with sound decorating taste."

Her mother sighed and dropped the napkin to the table. "Whatever," she said. "I need to talk to you."

A heavy weight sinking her heart, she closed her eyes. Only a matter of time before her family found out about Eric and her mother asked for the settlement of the gossip account. News travelled faster than the CIA's satellite information on the island. A miracle she'd escaped the radar for so long.

She'd have to face the facts today. Was she ready? Hell no. But did she have a choice?

"What about?"

She'd admit to the affair, tainting herself further

in her parent's eye, but she needn't dwell on the matter for too long. The admission itself would compromise her. No need for the salacious details to mar her tattered-beyond-repair image even more.

Her mother sighed again and dropped the napkin. "It's about Diya."

Diya? Lara blinked a few times as the information made its way into her mind.

Tension left her body, and she let herself relax in the seat. However, knowing her mother, she'd need to be on her guard.

"What's the matter with her now?" she asked.

"Well, it's this boy she's involved with. He's more unproper than the last one. And it's been confirmed this one, too, is a Muslim. Can't you talk some sense into her? She won't listen to me."

Her mother never let her live it down that she was the older sister, and thus, like a second mother to her sisters.

She rolled her eyes. "Mum, she's young—"

"No, no, no!" Her mother shook her head. "She's living a dissolute life, and it'll just affect all her future prospects when it's time for her to marry."

Lara closed her eyes and pinched the bridge of her nose. They were back to it again. Marriage as the end of the road for the Indian woman. She'd heard the line ever since she'd turned thirteen, and nearly two decades later, the words still grated on her mind like nails on a blackboard.

Revolt gripped her when she realised her sister would also have to go through all that. Unable to contain the disgust, she forced her eyes open to stare at her mother.

"For God's sake, Mother. It's her life, let her live it," she burst out. "You've been trying to run all our lives since the day we were born. And it seems all you care about is getting rid of us through marriage. You did it with me and Neha when we turned eighteen, and now, it's Diya's turn?

"Stop it, you hear me? Stop running *our* lives like *you* want. Bad enough you uprooted us from the only life we'd known in England to shove us into this snake pit of conventions and gossip which did nothing but stifle us. You've been lucky with Neha and me, but why on Earth do you think Diya rebels so much?"

The silence blanketing their surroundings echoed louder in her head as she took in the startled expression on her mother's face.

She hadn't screamed, because all around them, people kept to their businesses. Yet, she'd never expected to deliver such an outburst in front of her mother. In blowing a fuse, she'd set the stage up for some mighty lecture, and she braced herself for the recriminations surely to come.

However, the woman in front of her remained silent, and after what seemed an eternity, her voice took on a previously unheard softness when she broke the stillness.

"Haven't I let you live, Lara?"

Stunned by the subdued tone even more than by the words themselves, Lara blinked as she took in the question. Her mother asking for feedback? Since when did *that* happen?

And what the hell could she reply?

Yes, she hadn't let her pursue her personal

hopes, and had clad her in their sectarian, cultural life?

And what good would the accusation do?

"It's not the point, Mum, and you know it."

Guilt took hold of her, and her conscience started to impinge upon her thoughts.

Was that what she'd have done all those years before, given the choice? Would she have broken from the pack ... for Eric?

The sound of her mother's voice cut through her thoughts.

"You know, I've always just wanted the best for you. A proper marriage, a husband who'd understand you, who'd provide for all you'd need. For society to acknowledge you for your worth, and to give you the status you deserved."

Lara snorted, and her mother grew quiet.

"Hasn't exactly turned out that way, has it now, Mum?"

Opposite her, the eyes with the faint lines at their corners lowered.

But after a few seconds, her mother brought back up the sharp gaze that rarely missed a thing, and Lara couldn't recognise the emotion in the dark irises or on the features suddenly looking older.

"What's wrong, Lara?"

The voice that could soothe her biggest worry as well as rouse up her worst nightmare softened to a level she had never heard before, and she swallowed, hard.

"It's not like you to lash out like this," her mother said.

Annoyed at the guilty pricking in her, she

shrugged. "Forget it, Mum. It's nothing."

High time they got out of there, as the conversation taking a too-personal turn. She'd never been chummy with her mother. She wouldn't start today.

"Is it Roy?"

She shook her head in reply. Better leave it at that. She reached for her cup of now-cold coffee and drained the contents with one long gulp. Perfect, they could leave.

After a tense silence, her mother fidgeted in her seat and drew in a deep breath.

"Is it because of the man you're seeing?"

So her family did know about Eric.

Stunned, she didn't allow the emotion to show. Better to play it cool and detached. No one could get a hold on her, then.

"What do you know about him?"

"Nothing much, I admit." Her mother shrugged. "But look at you. You're miserable, and it shows. There's got to be a man behind it all."

A small smile tugged at her mouth at the despondent tone. For a second there, she'd wondered if the woman who had given birth to her wouldn't get up, pick a sword, and slay all the dragons that dared breathe fire onto her daughter's life.

Her heart swelled, because, for the first time in her life, she'd recognized genuine concern in her mother's tone, and the realization warmed her insides beyond what she'd expected. At the same time, the emotion prompted her to take stock of her own thoughts and beliefs, to face the truth.

Maybe she hadn't given her mother an

opportunity to befriend her, and that was why they felt so awkward around each other.

But then, sadness cloaked her when she thought of the 'man' in question.

"It *is* because of him," she said with halting words. "But this episode of my life is over now, and I don't see it working out."

"Why, darling? What's wrong?"

She chuckled with irony. Conspiratorial concern from her usually hysterical parent. Who'd have thought?

"He's very unproper, Mum. He's white, from a very rich and old family, and he descends from French nobility on his mother's side. Society will have a rave about it."

Her mother watched her with a contemplative expression on her face. "Society's not all there is, you know," she said in a little voice. "Does he love you?"

"Yes."

"And you?"

She thought back a long time before answering. "I don't know."

Lara shrugged. In all her reflections lately, she hadn't asked herself the question, afraid of the answer she'd find. Not to know that she loved him, but in case she found out she'd never felt any love for him.

She shook out of the thought. "He's also a doctor. You always told us to stay clear of them and their crazy schedules."

Her mother smiled back. "Is he like your father?"

"No, he's a paediatrician."

"They're actually the best of the lot, you know," the older woman said with a laugh. "Well, after dermatologists. These never get called for emergencies in the middle of the night."

She laughed along with her mum. Something she'd never thought she'd do outside a forced social context.

"You know," her mother continued. "I always told you to avoid doctors because I know what it's like to be one's wife. When we were first married, your father worked all the time, as we had a house to support. And you came along less than a year after our marriage, and I was alone in a foreign country. I just wanted you to have someone who'd be there for you, so you wouldn't be lonely."

At the wistful tone, her heart went out to her mother—God knew she'd had her share of a tough existence. And her father didn't make matters any better, always running to and fro between conferences and surgeries.

With a guilty heart, she reckoned she'd never given her mother her due.

"Neha and her family are coming to dinner tonight. You sure you don't want to come?"

Her mother hadn't said 'home,' but she'd heard the word, nevertheless.

She smiled. "Okay, I'll come home with you."

Her mother smiled back, and she knew she'd carry the image forever in her mind.

Once they were in the car, she gave in to a sudden impulse and reached out and hugged her tight. After a few seconds, her mother returned the hug, and a strange peace descended over her.

"Lara, is there really no hope?"

"I don't think so, Mum."

***

Dinner resembled an Indian feast fit for a royal. Her mother had outdone herself with the many different dishes she'd prepared. No wonder. Neha and her brood of kids had come, and so, their mother had cooked for an army.

Lara glanced around for a sighting of her younger sister as she settled on the sofa in the living room. She finally noticed her by the stairs. As usual, Neha appeared harried by her children. The baby in her arms cried without letting up, and her two eldest clung to her clothes while making a ruckus.

A smile grazed Lara's lips. She'd always thought her sister to be the worst-case scenario of post-marriage life, run over by domesticity and losing her identity in becoming nothing more than a mother.

Then, her smile died. Where was the children's father, Neha's husband? Was it a wonder Neha looked so harassed, reduced to being a single parent to three small kids?

She needed to have a word with Rahul, her brother-in-law. He'd been a good friend when they'd been younger. There'd even been talks of an arranged match between the two of them. But she'd seen him as a brother, exactly as she saw Salim—Auntie Zubeida's son who'd married Sam—and nothing but friendship had bloomed between them.

High time she clocked the so-called friend over the head, because he was being a total arse with his family. With her sister.

The cushion next to her gave as someone

plopped down onto the seat.

She smiled at her father. "It's a wonder we caught you for dinner tonight."

Prem Hemant gave a hearty laugh. "Ah, the hazards of the job, sweetheart. So, how's my little girl doing? Haven't heard from you in a long time."

She chuckled softly. "Daddy, I'm thirty-two years old. Hardly a girl any longer."

"Oh, my, that old already?"

He laughed louder when she hit him with a cushion.

"You'll always be my little girl, though," he said as he drew her into a hug.

She hugged him back and let the contact soothe her, like it had so many times in the past. Her father and his steadfast love had been the only constant in her life, something she knew she couldn't do without.

"Daddy ..." She pulled away. "Have I been a disappointment to you?"

He frowned as he held her at arm's length, his clear, light-brown gaze on her. "Never, sweetheart. Never."

"Even with the divorce?"

"Even then. So what if you've had some misfortune in life? It can happen to anyone. Is this why you look so sad?"

"A little," she lied.

"Oh, I thought it probably had to do with a man, but I was wrong." He smiled at her as if she were a small child.

Her cheeks burned, and she must have turned a bright shade of red. Was she so easy to read, that even her father had picked up on her turmoil?

Astonishment cut her vocal cords, and she couldn't answer.

"Not a man, huh?" he continued. "Certainly not Roy. Maybe Doctor Marivaux ..."

She jerked her head up at the mention of the name. "How—?"

He laughed again, a hearty chuckle.

"Sweetheart, I saw the way he looked at you at the conference." He reached out and tucked a lock of her hair behind her ear. "And more important, I saw how you watched him back. I put two and two together. Simple."

Goodness, had she been that transparent?

"But I gather things are not so right, huh?"

He punctuated the question with bushy eyebrows raised, and she laughed at the mock-stern picture he presented.

But the laughter died seconds later, sadness clattering in her chest.

"Things went awfully wrong. And it might've been all my fault."

"How wrong? Bad wrong, or wrong a sorry could erase?"

"Not bad wrong, but I doubt a simple sorry would work here. We both have issues we need to deal with."

"You sure it's not just you who's got the issues?"

What did she answer to that?

When she remained silent, he added, "Think about it, sweetheart. It might be worth everything to ask that question."

His phone rang, and he got up.

"Duty calls, again," he said with a sigh.

He dropped a kiss on the top of her head and left.

Lara pondered over his words as he walked out of the room. She didn't want to acknowledge the potential truth in his advice, but maybe he was right.

Then, another thought passed through her mind, and she shrugged the whole idea off.

Though her parents looked like they'd accept him, Eric's family wouldn't welcome her with open arms.

The sound of bickering caught her attention, and she turned in the direction of her nephew and niece. But they sat quietly, for once, watching an animated film on the living room TV.

She got up and went in search of the noise, in hopes of distracting her from her gloomy thoughts. The rapid outbursts drew her to the staircase, where her mother and Diya were arguing over who would get the phone like teenagers.

Well, Diya *was* a teenager, but her mother? Laughter bubbled inside her, and she watched the two with fondness. Both turned in her direction with eager faces. They'd want to drag her into the fight, so she escaped and went upstairs, to the comfort of her old bedroom.

To her surprise, she found Neha there, breastfeeding her baby.

Her sister turned around.

"Oh. It's you. I thought—" Neha shook her head. "Never mind."

Lara could feel when she wasn't welcome, and Neha's attitude screamed at her to keep her distance. Her sister had always kept an ocean of ice between her and anyone else, and lately, Lara in particular.

They'd always ascribed the somewhat antisocial behaviour to Neha's timid and reserved temperament.

On any other day, she would've turned tail and stormed away. But since she'd built a bridge with her mother earlier, she had to build a gateway of understanding with her sister.

So, she stepped into the room and went to sit down on the bed.

"Where's Rahul?" she asked.

Her younger sibling shrugged. "Madagascar. He was supposed to come home this morning, but there have been last-minute complications with an order or something, and he had to stay back."

Those few words from Neha could be construed as rambling, since the girl she'd been had never spelt out her thoughts or her concerns to those who should be close to her.

"Everything okay between you?"

"Of course. Why wouldn't it be?"

The answer sounded way too bright to hold water. Her sister's marriage was in trouble.

Yet, how could she go about helping them? High time she had a talk with Rahul, when she managed to get her hands on him.

Lara laughed softly. "You realize I've been here for nearly five months, and I haven't met him once? I swear we talked more when I was in England than now when we're on the same soil."

Her sister remained silent. Did she even get to talk to her husband any more than Lara did?

The baby started to wail, and Neha shushed him before she turned him around and gave him her other breast.

He latched on, and in the silence, his eyes grew increasingly heavy as sleep settled over him.

She glanced up at her sister. "Does it hurt?"

Neha frowned. "Breastfeeding? No, it doesn't. A little on the first few days, but then, you get used to it."

"On the third, you should know by now."

Neha gave her a rare smile, before she returned her attention to the now sleeping infant. In a gentle move, she slid her finger into the side of the baby's mouth and deftly unlatched him from her breast. Next, she settled him on her shoulder, where she slowly rubbed his back.

How could motherhood, and the ease of being around babies, come to some women and not others? To this day, she still hadn't held a baby in her arms, always afraid she'd let the bundle drop and hurt the kid beyond repair.

"Were you always this good at it?" Lara asked.

"Babies, you mean? No, but I learned."

"Neha, don't be offended, but didn't you ever want …" She remained unable to find the right word.

"More?" Neha gently suggested.

She nodded.

Her sister shrugged, before her eyes took on a faraway glint. "You know, from the first time I saw Rahul, I knew I wanted to be with him. Look after him, have his children. I never desired anything else."

"Don't you ever find it limiting?"

Neha laughed. Lara couldn't remember when she'd last heard her laugh.

"Limiting? No. It's a job like any other. Just, I don't get paid for it."

A job like any other. Right. To thrive in any career, a person had to have an affinity for the profession.

What if she'd never had any affinity for motherhood?

She squirmed, and her sibling seemed to pick up her discomfort.

"Listen, Lara, I envy you and Diya for going after life like you're out to grab the best of it. I never felt like I had it in me to do so, that's all."

So Neha had always been certain of what she wanted, and how to get it. Maybe she would share her insight, if Lara asked.

"How did you know for Rahul?"

"If I loved him?" Neha prompted.

"Yes."

She shrugged again. "I never thought of it, really. I knew he made me feel better than anyone else did, and I went on that."

Eric makes me feel that way.

She shouldn't think of him.

"Weren't you afraid you'd lose the two of you in marriage and children? It's no longer the same, is it, once a child comes along?"

Neha finally smiled a genuine, warm smile transforming her face from the pinched expression to one that made her delicate features blossom with feminine grace.

"Marriage, and any relationship, is a give and take. If you're comfortable with it, it'll all come to you. I know I'm no longer the only recipient of his love as when we courted. That love had been for his girlfriend. I share it with the children now. But Rahul also loves me in a deeper way, as his wife. As his partner. As the mother of his children. As a woman who's trying her best to make a good life for him."

"It all scares me, you know," she said so softly, she barely heard the words.

Neha reached out and held her hand. "All of it doesn't take anything from you, but instead, only gives more back."

Wasn't that what Sam had said? She and Neha seemed to have figured out the secret of a happy relationship.

Emotion choked Lara's throat. Would the emotional day take its toll on her and make her burst out crying in front of her sister? She squelched the tears threatening to fall and choked back the sobs.

"Look at me here. I'm the older sister. I should be advising all of you," she said in hopes of lightening up the heavy atmosphere.

"We all learn at our own pace, Lara. When you're ready for something, you'll know."

Chapter Seventeen

"Eric, will you tell me what the problem is?"

Eric sighed. Exactly what he didn't need, his mother asking questions. What had gotten into him to come to lunch today at the Marivaux household in Floréal? Angélique had asked, and he hadn't been able to say no. Then, his little sister had done a runner on him, when Patrice's mother invited her to their family home for the weekend.

Consequently, he had lunched alone with his mother, his father away on a business trip yet again.

He should've left as soon as he'd finished his food, but that would've been rude, and his parents had never tolerated any rudeness or slight to propriety.

As he sat in a wicker chair on the colonial dwelling's opened porch, he let his focus drift downhill to the houses on the slope. Rich-looking abodes and well-tended gardens populated this area, one of the wealthiest regions on the island, where most foreign dignitaries and ambassadors lived. The trappings of fortune and luxury were not lost on him, throwing his thoughts back on the notion of whether or not he belonged in this world. The people in it would not openly accept a mixed origins couple. He knew it. Didn't mean he had to choose to remain in such a universe, though.

"Eric?"

At the touch of a cool hand on his cheek, he glanced up at his mother and forced a smile. "Nothing's wrong. Nothing at all."

To say any more would open the floodgates, and he didn't need that to happen. Not right now. Not ever.

"Don't give me this."

Had she picked up on his lie?

"Something is very wrong," she said. "Yet, you refuse to talk about it."

He closed his eyes, and the weariness he'd been keeping at bay crashed over him. He ran a hand in his hair then peered at her once more.

Under the pointed stare, she gasped. Good. As long as she kept her distance.

"Work is hectic, *Maman*. I get called in almost every night for emergencies."

Only half the truth, and she probably knew he fibbed. So, he averted his gaze.

"Answer me." She cradled his face in her palms. "For weeks on end, we didn't hear from you unless we called. And now ..."

When he didn't reply her, she rubbed the pads of her thumbs against his cheekbones and knelt in front of him.

He frowned. She'd dirty the skirt of her white dress. His mother never allowed a speck of dust to touch her clothes. She must be really worried about him.

She sighed. "*Chéri*, what is it that's eating you

alive like this?"

Try as he wished, he couldn't tell her. Not if he wanted to hang on to the little peace of mind he still possessed.

"*Maman*, forget it. I don't want to talk about it." He settled a palm over her hand and gave her fingers a reassuring squeeze.

She reached out and brushed a lock of hair from his forehead, then took a deep breath.

"The only time I've seen you like this was shortly after you left for France."

He remained silent, but the way he clenched his jaw must've betrayed him, letting her know she'd hit the mark.

"The same thing is happening again, isn't it?" she asked.

Seconds ticked by, before he finally nodded. He dragged her hands away from his face and stood.

"A woman?" she asked softly.

He nodded again.

"Someone I know?"

He shook his head.

"Who, then?"

Silence descended on them, a cool breeze wafting on the terrace. Winter hadn't fully hit the upper plateaus, and the air stung a bit.

He forced in a deep breath. He'd have to tell her about Lara if he wanted her to lay off with the Inquisition. Now? Not the best time, but when would it ever be the perfect moment?

His phone beeped. Saved by the event of an emergency. He glanced at the number, noting the text message had come from the nearby clinic. He could make it in less than ten minutes.

"I have to go. Sorry."

He started out of the house. But he hadn't counted on her tenacity, since she dogged his steps all the way to the drive outside where he'd parked his Prado.

As he opened the SUV's door, she grabbed his arm, hard.

"Answer me, Eric. Tell me what's wrong. Who is this woman?"

Her grey eyes battled with his blue ones. She wouldn't bow down. He recognized the same stubbornness that thrived inside him. Who was he kidding? He'd gotten the trait from her. No way out of a confession.

"Her name is Lara Reddy. She's the director of the new conference centre in Grand-Baie."

She opened her mouth, then closed it without making a sound.

Exactly the reaction he had expected.

"Do you love her?" she finally asked.

"Yes," he said. "But that's all there is to it."

She blinked. "She's from India, *n'est-ce pas?*"

Eric snorted softly. Lara had been right, it appeared. If she'd been an expat from India, a foreigner, their alliance could've gone down with only a little fuss.

What double standards. He loved his mother, worshipped his parents, but where *his* life was concerned, *he* decided. Not anyone else.

He reached up to her hand on his sleeve and worked her grip off. "No, *Maman*. She is not from India. She's from a Mauritian household whose ancestors came to work on plantations owned by the likes of *Papa*'s family."

She paled at the naked truth he hadn't bothered to hide in his reply.

"But how—?"

He chuckled, without amusement. "How is because I fell in love with her."

"But she's ..."

"Brown? Yes, I know."

She paled further.

"Though, I suppose it won't make any difference that she is a wonderful woman with not one ounce of evil inside her. A beautiful person." He paused. "All of it doesn't matter, *n'est-ce pas, Maman*?"

"How can you say so?" Her lower lip trembled as she asked the question.

He shrugged. "I'm stating the truth."

A truth Lara had warned him they'd have to face, and one he hadn't wanted to acknowledge.

He still believed they could've made it if they'd stuck together. If Lara had trusted him.

"No need to work your wits over this," he said. "It's over between me and her."

He pulled the SUV's door open and climbed into the vehicle.

His mother didn't hold him back. Just as well, because he didn't feel fit to battle with her anymore. She knew the truth, knew where he stood, and that was enough.

If it wasn't, tough. He was done living with secrets.

***

"Doris, please hold incoming calls. I don't want

to be disturbed for the next hour."

Lara took a sip of her coffee before putting the mug down. Work kept creeping up on her, and she needed to delegate tasks on a daily basis. However, the bid for the Commonwealth conference rested solely on her shoulders—she didn't trust anyone with it before she'd ploughed through with a fine-toothed comb.

With a heavy sigh, she picked up the gigantic folder and opened it.

Soon, papers littered the desk, some strewn onto the floor. As she pulled back to survey the huge load before her, dull throbbing picked up along her temples. When had she last eaten? Taking paracetamol tablets on an empty stomach was a no-no, apparently. And the blister pack was empty— she'd forgotten to bring in a new one. Guess she'd have to power through. Story of her life.

The intercom buzzed, and she groaned.

"What now?"

"There's someone here to see you. She doesn't have an appointment, but she says you'll see her, anyway." Doris paused. "Her name is Agnes Armont-Marivaux."

Eric's mother?

Lara blinked, her heart sinking right along.

What was *she* doing there?

Blood pounded in her head, and the pain brought a film of black over her eyes. She wouldn't faint, she told herself as she gripped the sides of her chair to give herself an anchor into this spinning moment.

"What do I tell her?"

Her PA sounded awed. Was this woman really so formidable that tough Doris cowered before her? Intense fear settled in a lump, blocking her throat.

Somehow, she had to face the terror, if only to know why Agnes Armont-Marivaux had taken the trouble to come to her office unannounced. Which looked more petrifying—to face up to Eric's mother, or to find out why the woman had sought her out?

She licked her dry lips and took a deep breath. "Send her in."

With resolve seeping into her every muscle, she got up from the desk and made her way to the door. The wood panel opened silently before her, and Doris ushered a beautiful brunette in.

In her fifties, the woman could still pass for a model in an advert for *Vanity Fair*, everything about her, from her posture to her graceful walk, conveying elegance and high-class upbringing. The linen suit on her screamed understated class, and her perfectly styled dark mane brushed her shoulders in those sleek, flippant curls only a daily blow-dry from a professional could give.

Yet, her eyes were her most arresting feature. A deep grey, they held a piercing quality, and Lara squirmed under their cold, assessing scrutiny.

She however picked up her courage and put her hand out. "We haven't been introduced. I'm Lara Reddy."

The hand clasping hers felt soft and cool, and she couldn't mistake the iron strength in them.

"Agnes Armont-Marivaux," the woman said, her eyes never blinking once.

Eric's mother, the voice implied, and Lara heard

the message. The cultured voice carried a pronounced French accent, though her English sounded fluent. She frowned. Eric's mother came, after all, from a French *duché*. Nobility might exist only in titles in modern France, but history counted for something. Of course she'd be fluent in English and other tongues.

Fear churned Lara's stomach, yet she didn't allow it to take hold of her.

"Please have a seat." She indicated the black leather sofa set occupying a corner of the office. "Would you like some coffee, or something to drink?"

"No, thank you."

She swallowed hard as she settled across from the older woman. Her mind screamed at her to proceed with caution. "What can I do for you?"

Icy eyes fixed her, yet, she caught a flick of the fire that burnt beneath the cold. *Not a woman to cross.* She could easily imagine what it would be like to be in Agnes Armont-Marivaux's bad books. God, why on Earth did she ever get involved with Eric?

"Paul Decaen had only good things to say about you," the woman said.

Lara didn't allow her surprise to show. So Agnes had gone to the president of the tourism and hotels' association—and her fellow white French-Mauritian—to get the dish on her. Why wasn't that surprising?

"Did he now?" she asked coolly. "Far from me to be rude, Madame Marivaux, but why are you here?"

"I came for the truth." Agnes Armont-

Marivaux's words rang in the silence that followed.

Truth. *Right.*

"What truth do you want to hear?"

Courage fuelled her blood, and she vowed not to back down in front of this woman. She sat up straighter and accepted the challenge.

"About what is going on between you and my son."

"What has your son told you?"

Two perfect eyebrows drew together, and fine lines marred the smooth forehead. Agnes appeared to weigh her words in her head before she spoke.

"Apparently, he's in love with you," she said softly.

Lara gasped. He'd gone as far as telling his mother that? Not at all like him to expose his feelings. Unless push had come to shove. What else had he said?

Her heart told her the time had come to play all her cards. She didn't have anything more to lose.

"It's true," she said slowly.

"What are your intentions, though?"

"My intentions?" She gave a small laugh. "Madame Marivaux, I have no intentions at all. But I'm not surprised Eric didn't tell you we've broken up."

"He did mention it, in passing."

Surprise flooded her, and she frowned as she took the words in.

Curiosity grabbed her, and she couldn't quell it. "May I ask what you're doing here, then?"

The other woman lowered her gaze, and when she peeked back up, the ice had left the piercing irises.

"Far from me to pry into your personal life, but may I ask why things went wrong between you?"

"Eric asked me to marry him, and I refused," Lara said.

"Why?"

A sad smile lifted her mouth, as she recalled another similar question being asked to her.

"Why? We had no hope of existing, that's why."

"Enlighten me here." The frown on Agnes' forehead deepened. "How long have you been with Eric, for him to speak of marriage?"

"A few weeks, but our relationship goes back over a decade. We picked up from where we left off, I guess."

When only silence greeted her, she glanced across, and found herself being studied.

However, this time, the scrutiny didn't make her uncomfortable, just quizzical. "Is something wrong?"

Agnes took ages to reply. "The summer after Eric left for France, something happened, and you were involved. What took place back then?"

Lara couldn't brace herself for the shock. "I got married."

The whisper echoed in the stillness, turmoil brewing in her. The black veil returned in front of her eyes, and she drew in deep breaths, trying in vain to stop the room from spinning.

"*Vous vous sentez bien?*"

Concern lay heavy in the question asking her if she felt okay, but she couldn't acknowledge the worry as bile rose in her throat and made her nauseous.

A glass of water was thrust into her hand, and she gratefully took a few sips. When the room returned back to normal, she glanced around, astounded to find Agnes by her side.

"I'll be fine," she said.

Agnes returned to her seat, frowning.

Lara's turn now to know the truth.

"Did something happen to Eric back then?"

His mother gave a pained smile. "He threw all he had in his studies, became a shadow of his usual self. In short, he stopped living. It took a long time for him to regain some normalcy in his existence."

Pain welled up and gripped her heart as the image of a young, desolate Eric filled her mind. Tears threatened to spill from her eyes, and she tasted their bitter tang in her throat, where a huge lump had settled.

"How is he now?"

Agnes patted her hand before she got up and picked her handbag. "He's back to the same state, I'm afraid."

Lara closed her eyes, and a single tear rolled down her cheek. Through a hazy mist, she heard the words spoken to her.

"I'll leave now. I got what I came looking for."

She only listened as the footsteps retreated, stopping when they reached the door.

"You don't look any better, either," Agnes said. "And I just want you to know ... I only want the life back in my son's eyes."

***

For days, those parting words echoed in her

head. Lara replayed the scene countless times in her mind, and she always came to one conclusion.

Agnes Armont-Marivaux had given them her blessing.

However, she couldn't help but erase a doubt in her mind—that she wasn't being accepted for her worth, but only for what she brought Eric. Could she hope to be satisfied with so little? Her marriage to Roy had borne the complete approval of all involved, and that'd helped a lot in building their relationship, and their very existence.

The ringing of the phone interrupted her musings. She picked up and had to keep the receiver at a distance because of the outburst from the other end.

"Whoa, Sam, calm down. You're so delirious, I can't understand a word you're saying."

"I have great news. I went to the doctor today, and guess what?"

Lara gasped when she registered the happiness in her friend's voice. "You're pregnant?"

"Yes!"

"Oh, I'm so happy for you! I told you it would happen."

"I know. I couldn't believe it myself. You're the second person to know after Salim." She giggled with gleeful abandon.

"This is wonderful, Sam. I never once doubted it."

"Funny, you know. All those treatments I've had, yet, it's a simple thing that did the trick."

"What was it?"

"Well, this doctor gave me folic acid

supplements. Nothing else. She said lots of women fail to conceive because they don't get enough folic acid. Amazing, isn't it?"

"Yes, it is. I'm so happy for you. I wish you were here so I could give you a big hug."

Sam laughed at the other end, and the merry sound seemed to come from the depths of her soul. "I'll take it on the line. I have to be off now, gotta call my family. Bye, sweetie."

"Bye, Sam."

She put the phone down with a heavy heart. The words echoed in her head, and she couldn't help it that her friend's happiness tinged her own misery darker.

As guilt assailed her, she shook out of the sombre thoughts. Sam deserved all the good coming her way, and Lara's loss was no reason for others to feel the same pain, as well.

She forced her mind to focus on the impending arrival, and as Sam's best friend, she wanted to celebrate the good news. A baby shower down the line, definitely. But what of the most immediate celebration? She reached for her cell, about to call Eric, but pulled her hand back as soon as she touched the phone.

Pointless to call him. What could she say that could take them across the rift she'd allowed to grow between them?

She shook her head, intent on chasing the gloomy thoughts away. She'd go out, and that would do the trick. She needed to gift Sam with something, anyway, so she might as well distract herself by hitting the shops.

However, more than an hour later, she still roamed the shopping centre at the entrance of Grand-Baie aimlessly, with no clue what to buy. She'd never had a pregnant woman in her entourage, not someone as close as she and Sam were, anyway. When her sister had been expecting, thousands of miles had spread between their two countries, and congratulations had happened over the phone. This left her completely oblivious about mom-to-be gifts and baby stuff.

She stopped in front of the bookstore and stepped in—the least she could do was get a 'congratulations' card.

The clerk on duty ignored her greeting, busy fussing over a white woman who stood before a magazine stand looking, for all intents and purposes, harassed by the constant, unwanted attention.

Lara took in the scene, and though highly annoyed by the clerk's behaviour, she shrugged her disgust off as she made her way to the card display stand.

Her mind wandered as she browsed around for a suitable card.

What a mighty example of the different worlds Eric and she lived in. When faced with the choice between service to a white person and any other racial group, the former usually won the upper hand. Only foreigners could hope to compete with them. She should open her mouth and spew out her BBC accent—that would surely send the clerk rushing, taking Lara for a tourist. She chuckled quietly.

"Lara?"

Her thoughts cleared, her spine stiffening.

Though spoken in perfect English, the sound of her name still carried a slight tinge of a French accent, sharpening the 'r.' She slowly turned around and took a deep breath when her suspicions were confirmed.

Agnes stood a few feet from her and closed the gap shortly after.

"I thought it was you, but I wasn't sure," Eric's mother said. "How are you?"

"I'm fine," she blurted before catching herself. "I didn't expect to bump into you here."

"Neither did I, but it's a small world, *n'est-ce pas?*"

The accompanying smile beckoned warm and sincere, and the tension eased somewhat from her shoulders.

A flutter of activity materialized around them, the formerly busy clerk suddenly intent on helping them out.

Agnes turned her now cold stare upon the woman. "We'll call you if we need your help. I believe there are people waiting for you at the counter," she said with a slight flick of her chin.

Though spoken in French, Lara heard the full rebuttal the words carried, and she couldn't help but smile as the clerk hastily got back to her counter.

"Service is not exactly what it was," Agnes said with a sigh. "But forget it. What brings you here?"

"A friend of mine just found out she's pregnant, and I'm wracking my brain to find a proper gift for her."

"Have you tried a pregnancy book? They're very helpful."

"I hadn't thought of that, but it's a good idea."

A tall, bulky man entered the store, and Agnes asked to be excused.

As Lara reached the self-help-books aisle, the pair caught up with her.

"Lara, come here," Agnes said. "Let me introduce you. This is Mathieu Laroche, the owner of this bookstore, soon to be a family member. My daughter, Angélique, is betrothed to his son, Patrice."

Agnes turned towards the man as she added, "Mathieu, this is Lara Reddy, a friend of Eric's. She's the director of the new conference centre in Grand-Baie."

Mathieu Laroche put out a large paw and gripped her hand in his.

"I saw you and Eric a few times, and I wondered when I'd have the privilege of meeting you," he said with a large smile.

Lara couldn't help but smile back. "It's a pleasure to meet you, too. You have a very nice store here."

"Ah, we do what we can," he replied in heavily accented English. "Though I have to say, it isn't often I've seen Eric in such good company."

She felt herself blush, and Agnes came to the rescue.

"Mathieu, you're making her uncomfortable," she said with a small laugh. "I won't keep you any longer, though. I simply wanted you to meet this young woman here."

The man said his goodbyes, leaving the two women alone.

Awkwardness cloaked Lara, and she struggled to find the proper thing to say.

"Is something wrong?" Agnes asked.

She shook her head. "No, not really."

"Eric also says the same thing."

The woman let the words hang between them, and she heard the sadness in the voice.

"Madame Marivaux—"

"Please, call me Agnes."

She nodded. Was that an olive branch? She wouldn't know if she didn't ask, right?

"What do you think I should do?" she asked.

Agnes kept her eyes on her for what felt like ages. "I think you two should work your issues out."

Lara didn't reply her, and let her head hang to hide the pain flooding her. "How can I hope to do this?"

"Lara, it's your life, and Eric's, ultimately. He made me see that." Agnes reached for her hand. "It's you who'll have to live it." She paused, as if for emphasis. "I come from France, you know, and my husband spent all his life here on this island. It was very much a culture shock for me when I arrived here, and to think we'd both come from pretty much the same culture." Another pause ensued. "I didn't want my children to feel this kind of ... off ... for lack of a better word, when they decided to settle down."

Lara nodded. That made sense.

Agnes grabbed Lara's other hand and held on tight.

"But this I do know, my dear girl. If my son has singled you out for his love, it must mean you're worthy of it. I trust him, if that's what you need to know."

***

Lara made her way back home and dropped on the sofa, dumping her bags on the living room floor. The house lay in a state of chaos. Less than when she'd let herself go after Eric's departure, but filthy, nevertheless. Not that she cared.

All her focus congregated on the thoughts screaming around in her head. Her skull neared explosion, with hot, searing pain pounding all over her brain. She got up and wet a cloth in the sink. Once back on the sofa, she applied the cool compress on her forehead and breathed out with some relief when the heat receded from her skin.

How had Agnes Armont-Marivaux guessed her thoughts?

She couldn't imagine any other reason for the woman to add those last words at the bookstore. Confusion and understanding battled inside her, and every time she dared to work some comprehension out of it all, the pain increased double-fold to send piercing daggers along her cranium.

Food. The hurt must be amplified thanks to her empty stomach. She wouldn't be able to reason with herself unless she ate something.

With a heavy sigh, she recalled her freezer was empty, as she'd yet again delayed a much-needed trip to the supermarket.

An idea struck her. Blessed be home delivery. She fished around for the phone receiver, and five minutes later, threw it on the sofa after calling the nearby pizzeria.

She closed her eyes and let the cool cloth

continue to work its magic on her.

From a faraway, misty place, she made out the sound of the doorbell ringing. Startled awake, she wearily got up to answer the door.

Would the poor delivery boy get a scare when she greeted him? She hardly looked her best. A hefty tip would compensate any fright she might induce, though.

She threw the door open, and the smile she had forced out died on her face when she noted who stood on her front porch.

He smiled. "Hello, Lara."

This couldn't be ...

"Roy?"

Chapter Eighteen

Lara blinked a few times, trying to clear the image in front of her. But as much as she willed it, the sight didn't change.

Confusion boiled inside her, and shock dried her throat.

Roy stood there. Tall, dark, and handsome. In a tan-coloured Savile Row suit, even while on holiday in Mauritius, his broad shoulders and tall stature could easily be mistaken for that of a model. Rimless glasses framed his eyes, and small lines crinkled there when he smiled at her.

Smiled at her. The cheek of the man.

Still, as it always inevitably happened when she saw him, she lost her breath. Dashing didn't start to describe his allure. Any woman with blood coursing in her body would take a second peek at this man.

But she couldn't ignore the cocky lift of his mouth. She travelled her gaze over him and saw the slightly arrogant and overly confident man who'd turned her life upside down on a whim.

Sense returned, and she quelled her surprise.

"What are you doing here?" she asked.

"Won't you ask me in?"

He hadn't changed, still thinking everyone owed

him everything.

Her eyes narrowed as she glared, but he didn't seem to feel any of the displeasure she directed at him.

Cut your losses, again. Nothing to be won with her slamming the door in his face, no matter how much she yearned to do just that.

So, she slowly nodded and moved aside to let him enter the hall.

In a few steps, he reached the living room and turned around to face her.

"May I?" he asked with a glance at the sofa.

"You might as well, since you're already here."

She stood in the doorway as he eased himself comfortably on the sofa where she'd been only minutes before.

He appeared out of place in the room. Too broad, tense, unfitting.

So unlike Eric.

She pushed the thought aside and focused her attention on the man before her. The man with whom she'd shared ten years of her life.

"What are you doing here, Roy?"

A slight tinge of anxiety invaded her as she watched him take in the disorder that reigned. But she didn't allow the sensation to linger. She was in her house. Not his, not theirs.

He startled a bit when he glanced at the bag on the floor. Clearly visible through the clear plastic lay the cover of the book inside—*Your Pregnancy and You*. A small frown marred his forehead as he turned around to face her.

"Is this for you?"

His intense dark eyes pierced her, and a quiver thrummed in her voice when she opened her mouth to answer.

But she snapped her lips shut. She had nothing to justify. If anything, he was the one who had things to explain.

She sighed and leaned against the doorway. "Roy, why are you here? And how did you find me?"

"You left this address with the lawyers."

"Not very professional of them," she muttered. "You still haven't answered me."

She lifted her chin and crossed her arms in front of her. With her shoulder braced against the doorframe, she hitched in a breath when she realised the tension that usually sizzled in her whenever she'd faced her ex-husband had left her.

In the time away from him, she had grown and shrugged off any influence he might've had on her existence, on her psyche.

Calm descended over her. Roy no longer had any hold on her. Closure, finally?

"I'm waiting," she said, tapping her foot lightly.

That gesture used to drive him to distraction. With a small smile of gloating satisfaction, she relished the movement, for the first time free from the need to pacify him.

A severe, sombre face stared back at her, and his deep eyes wrestled with hers.

She kept up with the challenge, didn't allow herself to back down, and lifted her eyebrows in question.

And just like that, the careful façade before her crumbled. He took his glasses off, and with his thumb and forefinger, pinched the bridge of his nose. Then, on an exhaled curse, he ran a hand through his hair.

Bells rang in her head at these exterior signs of his turmoil. Roy very rarely took off his glasses and never allowed himself to show any vulnerable expression. She frowned. What he was getting at? Could all this be a ploy of his?

"What's wrong, damn it?" She stiffened her spine and drew to her full height. "For more than three years, I don't hear from you, other than through lawyers, and now, you drop out of the sky, coming all the way from London, to flash me that dazzling smile of yours?"

He glanced up. "I haven't treated you right, have I?"

Fuelled by resentment and anger, she continued with her outburst. "Damn right you haven't. One day, you decided you wanted a child, when you never mentioned you'd ever want one, and expected me to do your bidding at the drop of a hat. And when I refused, telling you we'd never even cared for a cat, you asked what sort of woman was I for not wanting babies and you stormed out, and the next thing I saw of you was a sheaf of divorce papers. Served to me by a legal clerk in the lobby of the hotel I worked for, just past the clocking of lunch hour. Damn right you didn't treat me properly, Roy!"

"I'm sorry, Lara."

The words hit her like a bullet, and she had to sit down to let them sink in. She reached the sofa opposite him and dropped her weight in it.

He was sorry? After all this time? This

confession had to be priceless.

Laughter bubbled inside her, and she gave in to the hysterical fit.

She laughed harder at his puzzled expression. However, she caught herself before the fit turned to tears.

"If I ever thought I'd see the day ..." But then, gloomy depression fell on her like a cloak, and she shook her head. "What do you expect this'll change now?"

He shrugged. "I don't know, Lara. I don't know anything any longer. I hoped, maybe if we talked again, we'd understand what happened to us."

A wave of surprise almost knocked her over at the uncertainty in his unusually soft tone. She'd always known him as a confident man whom certainty never eluded. This new side of him puzzled her, and intrigued her even more.

"Roy, what happened was that I wasn't ready for children, but you were. I'm afraid to say you didn't handle the situation in a very civilized way, but it's over and done with, and we have to live with the consequences now."

"Lara, I'm sorry."

She didn't want to smile, but she had to. She'd wanted—needed—to get those words out, and she suddenly realised that those facts, and to say them out loud, no longer hurt as much.

And here was Roy ...

"Roy, it's okay. It didn't work, that's all. *We* didn't work. I admit I was hurt, and angry, but these feelings won't do any of us good, so better for us to leave such things to the past."

A weight lifted from her shoulders, and she sighed.

The sensation filled her with peace, and calm finally soothed her ragged heart.

Sadness and a wistful affection gripped her heart at the uncertainty and confusion drawing his features, ageing him beyond his thirty-nine years.

He took a deep breath. "I know I hurt you, and I'm so sorry for having said all those things. They weren't true, you know."

She couldn't bear the sincerity in his hushed tone, and she averted her eyes. "Forget it. It's all in the past now."

"I can't, Lara." He threw his hands in the air. "I can't believe what a bastard I've been to tell you all those things."

And then, as suddenly as the outburst had caught hold of him, he hunched in his seat, and his voice came out all strangled when he next spoke. "You would've made a very good mother, you know that?"

The whispered words slammed into her stomach like an iron fist, knocking the breath out of her.

"What?"

Silence settled while they both simply stared across at each other, cocooned in another world. One where emotion ran rampant, and past deeds and actions vied for acknowledgement and a reason for their existence.

"You'll make a wonderful mum someday. I'm just sad it won't be for my children."

Lara didn't know if she needed to laugh, cry, or have her head checked for hallucinating tendencies.

This was Roy spewing such words to her?

A nervous giggle escaped, and she quelled the laughter by pressing her hand to her mouth. A rush of emotions clogged her throat and tripled the size of her tongue, so she couldn't form a word, let alone utter a sound.

He must've seen the disbelief in her eyes, because he reached out and clasped her hand.

"It's true, Lara. I know you have what it takes to be a great mother, but it's you who's got to feel it first. My mistake for not having given you the time."

"Why are you telling me all this?" she asked when she'd shaken the stupor away.

Without taking his eyes off her, he smiled.

"Preety, my wife, is the perfect Indian daughter-in-law. A domestic household goddess." A small chuckle escaped him, before his voice grew sober again. "But there are days when even she is at her wits end with dealing with the baby."

Lara shook her head. "It still doesn't explain how I'd make a good mother."

Roy smiled. "I've known what it's like to be loved by you. When you love someone, you give him everything you have." He squeezed her hand. "I didn't realise it when I had it. But I hope this won't keep you from loving someone again. To this man, you'd give everything, Lara, even children."

The lump in her throat grew bigger, and she could do nothing to stop her tears from flowing. How had Roy pinned her down so well?

The doorbell rang. She blinked out of her thoughts and got up while drying her cheeks. Taking deep breaths along the way, she tried to blank all thought from the turmoil in her mind as she exited the living room.

The pizza delivery boy stood on her porch—she'd completely forgotten about her order.

Back in the living room, she dropped the box on a table in the corner and sat back down.

But Roy didn't look up, his focus riveted on a picture he held in his hand.

She wondered what he was staring at, and was on the point of asking when he broke the silence.

"I've never seen you like this."

"Like what?"

"So radiant. Full of life, of laughter. So beautiful," he said as he glanced back at her.

Her cheeks flamed, not simply from the words he spoke, but also from the unconcealed longing in them.

She reached out and grabbed the picture from his hands.

After a quick glance, she tossed the glossy aside.

Past memories, better forgotten, her mind screamed.

"Oh, that," she said with a small laugh. "A one-off happening." Silence stretched between them. "My life isn't that way most of the time."

She could've kicked herself at the sadness in her voice. He must've also heard her dejection.

"What's been up in your life?" he asked.

"This and that. Nothing much. Terribly taken with work. We got short-listed for the next Commonwealth conference ..." A hot blush crept up her when she realised she was babbling. "Forget me, though. What's up with you?"

"Nothing, either." He shrugged. "My relatives here wanted to meet Preety and the baby, so we've come down to visit."

"Did you have a boy or a girl?"

Roy smiled, and fierce pride burned in his eyes. "A girl. We named her Rani."

Rani—*Queen*. Lara had no doubt the little girl would be the queen of Roy's life. She smiled, too, before tension bristled between them as they faced each other.

It suddenly dawned on her that, despite having shared each other's lives, neither of them had ever really been intimate in exchanging confidences. They'd merely lived next to the other, rather than with the other. This intimacy between them today seemed forced and too polite. She should lighten the atmosphere by any manner.

"You've put on weight," she said. "I gather your wife is a good cook."

Roy gave a small laugh. "She cooks very well. The house is also spick and span, and her laundry skills cannot be rivalled."

She couldn't stifle the small laugh that escaped her, and he glanced at her with surprise. But then he, too, joined in the laughter.

"It's what you wanted, after all," she said.

"True, but like the saying goes, be careful what you wish for."

"I'm sure she looks after you well." She paused. "Better than I did, certainly."

"Believe me, after knowing an independent and determined woman like you, she sometimes strikes me as so ... passive."

She frowned at him. "You don't really mean it."

"No, not really." He gave her a sheepish smile. "I love her, but it feels ... different."

Where had their *love gone?*

The question popped in her head, and from the intense expression on Roy's face, he must be asking himself the same thing.

"We were a good team, weren't we?" he asked.

"Yes. But we couldn't make it work."

"Yeah."

The word hung in the air.

He reached out and clasped her hand. "Please tell me I haven't ruined your existence."

Emotion choked her throat, and tears stung her eyes. "No, you haven't."

A link broke between them, but in the following second, another, deeper thread wove itself in the path—that of friendship.

As she squeezed his hand, he smiled. And she smiled back.

Roy stood, and she followed suit.

"I guess I'd better leave, then," he said.

"I guess you should."

He raised an eyebrow. "Are you throwing me out or what?"

She laughed at his teasing smile. "Far from me to do so. My door's always open to a friend."

He peered down, before training his eyes back upon her face. "Lara, don't get me wrong, okay?"

"What?"

"For what it's worth, I've never seen you look as happy as you do in that picture."

She swallowed hard as the lump returned in her

throat.

"Have I made you happy, Lara?"

"Yes, you have," she said softly, before she reached out and hugged him.

After the initial second or two of surprise, he hugged her back, and she settled her cheek on his chest.

"Can I ask you something?"

"Uh-uh," she said against the soft fabric of his jacket.

"That man, he makes you happy?"

She jerked her head up and stared at him, eyes wide. "What are you talking about?"

"The picture. A man made you happy when it was taken. You shouldn't waste it."

His last words left a burning imprint on her heart, and she winced. When Roy squinted at her with concern on his face, she reached out and hugged him again.

"Take care, Lara."

"You, too."

A minute later, he left and got in his rental car. She stood on the porch until the vehicle had disappeared from sight, then she entered the house, closing the door behind her.

Darkness cloaked her, and she went around switching on the lights as she traipsed back into the living room, where she plopped down on the sofa. The headache came back with a vengeance, and her stomach gave a dull groan.

As she glanced around, her gaze landed on the pizza box in the corner, and she reached for it. The movement dragged at the surface of the coffee table, sending some papers onto the floor. She couldn't stop herself from glancing at the picture that landed face-up at her feet.

She reached down and turned the image over, then picked up a piece of pizza.

As she nibbled at the cheese, her attention kept straying back to the picture. With a groan, she threw the food back into the box and bent to pick the photo.

A radiant, sun-kissed woman stared back at her. The wind blew in her hair, and the strands shone like diamonds where sunshine hit them. Her face carried a delicate flush, and the broad, dazzling smile on her features shone, spelling out her happiness. The yellow colour of the strappy sundress matched the radiance of the bright tropical sun.

As she closed her eyes, Lara remembered how the sun had felt on her bare shoulders that day. Soft and warm, its rays had caressed her skin gently. The gust of wind had lifted her hair from the nape of her neck, and she could still feel the sting of the salty spray as it had hit her face every time she'd turned towards the sea.

Upon one such moment, Eric had snapped the picture. A totally unplanned, spontaneous image he'd managed to catch on his camera. As soon as he'd clicked the photo, she had lost her footing in the sand and had fallen. He'd been there to catch her, though he'd fallen down, too. They'd laughed when they'd hit the sand, and she'd grown serious again when, against the dazzling sun, he'd brought his face down for a kiss.

Eric always said she'd been so beautiful in the

photo, he'd had to have it printed so he could carry it with him everywhere.

A tear rolled down her cheek as the memories replayed in her head, and she opened her eyes to blink away the flood menacing to unleash.

Her heart constricted, and every time she thought of him, she wished for the world to open up under her feet and swallow her whole. She'd never experienced the hurt that slashed through her when memories of him returned to plague her.

Memories of how good it had felt to be with him. Of how well they understood each other. Of how peaceful he made her feel when she lay in his arms, as if nothing in the world could ever reach her.

She longed for their world, and she longed for him.

The tears flowed down her face.

Images of their times together flashed in her head, and then other images, and words, took their place.

Words she'd heard all around her ...

Neha telling her she'd known Rahul was the man for her because he made her feel better than any other person did.

Agnes' voice telling her Eric cared for her.

Her father's voice, asking her to work her issues out.

And Roy's voice, telling her not to waste herself if love lay so near, saying she'd happily give the man she loved children ...

When Lara realised she could picture a blond miniature of Eric in her arms, she stood up with a start. With a hand on her mouth to stifle her gasp, her heart pounded so hard, the muscle threatened to break out of her ribcage.

Realisation had her rooted her to the spot.

She loved Eric. She'd always loved him.

How could she have been so stupid? Cold dread filled her when she realised she'd nearly thrown her life out of the window with her foolish issues and insecurities. Another thought jumped into her mind, and the blood ran icy in her veins.

Had she lost Eric? For good?

Her stupid behaviour could've ruined everything. She had to know.

Adrenaline fuelled her blood, and she glanced around for her car keys. Throwing herself on the sofa, she sent the cushions flying in trying to locate the keys. When she closed her fingers on the ring, she pulled out with all her might. As she turned towards the front door, the lights went out, and a blinding flash of lightning lit the room. The growl of thunder resounded seconds later.

A thunderstorm? In June, on the edge of winter? *You have to be joking!*

She stood petrified. Panic burst through her, the rapid beat of her heart echoing in her head, and she closed her eyes and clasped her hands against her ears.

Soon, another strike came in, and she again couldn't move. Cold sweat broke on her skin.

Eric.

His name flashed in her head, and a renewed surge of energy took hold of her.

With quickened steps, she forced her way out of the house and got into her car, hitting the road in a screech of tyres, her foot hard on the accelerator. Heavy rain fell in a downpour, and visibility neared zero with the lampposts barely emitting any light in the thunderstorm.

She ploughed on, grateful the road lay empty before her. Caution advised her to take her foot off the pedal, but a desperate need to reach the man she loved surged through her and urged her not to stop. She'd lose him if she did.

As she reached his property, she pulled the car up and rolled the window down. Twice, she punched in the wrong entry code. A voice warned her the alarm would go off if a wrong number were entered for the third time.

She forced herself to take a deep breath as she recalled the sequence of numbers she'd so often punched into that very keypad. With intense concentration, she entered the code, and the door opened in front of her. As soon as the Mercedes could pass though, she sped into the property and braked hard when she reached the house.

She got out in the torrential rain, and hope plummeted in her heart when she didn't see the Prado in the garage. Out of desperate hope, she made her way to the front door, where she rang the bell.

The sound of rainfall drowned the delicate tinkle. With the power out, the doorbell wouldn't ring, either.

Only one thing left to do. Lara threw all she had into pounding upon the massive wooden door.

***

Eric had been sitting on a stool in the kitchen when the lights went out. Almost immediately, the low growl of thunder had rumbled through the air.

Lara! She'd be panicked by the storm.

He quickly stood, but turned back when he reached the kitchen door.

She wouldn't want him barging in on her.

With a heavy heart, he made his way into the living room, where he lit a few candles. Candles she'd left here and there, he thought with a sad smile. Heavy rain beat against the roof and drowned all the sound in the empty house.

Did he still have the heart and desire to remain in this dwelling any longer? While the place had been flooded with joy and happiness whenever she'd been here, without her, the empty structure appeared desolate and neglected.

He closed his eyes as he imagined the sound of her voice when she called his name. The lovely trill bounced upon the walls and filled the house with merriness. He remembered her way of walking around barefoot, and how she carried sand back in whenever she returned from the beach. He chuckled when he recalled the sound of the fridge door opening and closing at any time of the day, when she'd rummage in for something to eat.

She probably didn't eat any longer. Sorrow cloaked his heart, and he shrugged the memories off as he pried his eyes open. No good to ponder over all that, because a part of his heart would always bleed, no matter how long he gave the organ to heal.

He had finished lighting the last candle when a sound came from the hall. Venturing closer, he could make out someone was pounding on the door. From the urgency of the drumming, it surely had to be an emergency.

Numb shock overcame him when he opened up.

Lara stood before him, drenched from head to toe, a strange light burning in her eyes.

"What are you doing here?"

She stared at him for a few seconds, her eyes intense and fiery.

"Do you want children?" she finally asked.

He blinked. "What?"

***

Lara wanted to shake herself like a rag doll. What had she asked him?

Her near-hysterical nerves made her jittery, and she threw her weight from one foot to the other. A dash of practicality caught her. She might as well get an answer to the question, since she was so intent on working her issues out.

"Do you want children?" she again asked.

Eric stared at her with eyebrows drawn together. From the pointed stare he gave her, she was sure he must be weighing up if she'd be a likely candidate for a mental institution.

"Just answer me, please."

A puzzled expression settled upon his face as lines creased his broad forehead.

"Lara, first come inside, and then we'll talk. Okay?"

No! She needed to tell him what a fool she'd been all along. The thoughts and emotions screamed in her head, and it seemed her brain had cut all her control over her limbs as she stood there rooted to the spot.

When it must've dawned on him that she couldn't move, he reached out and gently tugged on her arm. He had her take a few steps until she stood in the hall, and he closed the door behind her.

In the dark, with only the muted glow of the candles shedding a semblance of light, she couldn't make out the expression on his face.

"Eric, we need to talk."

He remained silent for a long moment.

"I think so, too. What's the matter, Lara?" he asked, his voice dropping low and tinged with concern.

She wanted to throw her arms around him and tell him to hold her tight, but they had their issues to deal with.

"You do want children, right?"

"Yes ..." His answer sounded tentative.

"Anytime soon?"

"I beg your pardon?" He gasped. "You're not ... pregnant ... are you?"

Lara knew she played her whole life on how she'd answer him, and in the balance lay any hope of a future with Eric.

"No. But I'd like to be ... Having *your* baby ..."

The frantic beating of her heart grew more rapid when instead of saying something, he took a sharp intake of breath.

"What happened, Lara?"

She'd prepared herself for the question. Her worst-case scenario, in fact.

But, in her nightmare, his voice had been filled with anger, not the hope and longing ringing clear in his breathless tone.

"Roy came, and we talked. I realised that what you said was true. I didn't trust myself enough. But now, I know that if I have your support, I can overcome everything, and I can then lay aside all the insecurities that have robbed me of living my life fully for all those years."

She paused for breath, before finally saying what she'd come all this way to tell him.

"I love you, Eric. And I know the trust you've always had in us will be enough for both of us. If I have you by my side, I can make it."

She stopped talking when her lungs threatened to burst. The sound of her shallow and ragged breathing echoed in the still of the dark lobby. With every second ticking by, her hopes plummeted, until she couldn't stand the wait any longer.

"Will you grant me a second chance?" she asked softly.

Eric sighed. Her mouth went dry when he came to stand right before her. The glow of a nearby candle lit his face, highlighting the tautness in his jaw, the small muscle twitching in his cheek.

"I have one condition, though."

His face didn't lose its sombre air, and she gulped back. "What is it?"

He stared at her for a long time, then a smile broke upon his handsome face.

"Only if you'll be my wife."

As the words sank in, Lara's smile grew, and her heart soared.

"The sooner, the better," she replied, before she tilted her face and allowed her lips to touch his.

They sealed the deal with a kiss.

Epilogue

One year later…

Breathe, Lara, breathe.

Could this be the longest two minutes in a woman's life? She glared at the small device in front of her, refusing to allow herself to think while watching the progress on the strip.

A second pink line slowly appeared, and her smile grew on her face along with it.

Elation filled her when the realisation sank in, and she jumped in her spot with joy. Reining her excitement, she opened the bathroom door and cast a glance over the room. The pale light of dawn slowly lit the bedroom up, chasing the gloom and the shadows.

Lara Marivaux gazed fondly at the man sleeping on the bed. Joy and love washed over her.

He'd chased the dark and the gloom from her life, leaving no stone unturned, and had given her the security and the peace she'd so long craved. His trust in her had made her overcome all her fears and the obstacles in their path, and she'd found a new lease on life by his side.

She went and sat down by his side. A part of her

knew he deserved the sleep, having come in late from an emergency last night, but another part wanted to wake him right away.

But she couldn't bear it anymore, and sank between the sheets, angling closer to him.

She ran a hand along the lines of his face and trailed her fingers to his broad shoulders. When she reached his chest, he groaned and pulled her swiftly beside him. He hugged her close, yet didn't wake up.

As she nibbled his earlobe, he groaned again, and she smiled.

"Happy wedding anniversary, darling," she said in his ear.

He mumbled something in reply, and she could feel he was waking up.

"I've got something for you." She took his hand and placed it on her belly.

He opened sleep-filled eyes and stared at her with a confused expression on his face.

But then, his eyes grew wide, and he sat up straight. He returned his hand to her belly and stared her with astonishment, his gaze pleading with hers for an answer.

She laughed softly and nodded.

He brought his other hand up, ran his fingers in his hair as he took in her implication.

"A baby?" he asked in a hushed, reverent tone.

"Yes." She couldn't believe it herself—it all felt like a dream.

Laughter bubbled from her throat when he reached out and hugged her. He crushed her to his chest, and seconds later, loosened his grip.

"Did I hurt you?" Concern rang heavy in his

voice.

Lara rolled her eyes. "Dear husband, I'm only pregnant, and it doesn't make me a fragile doll, you know."

Sinking into his embrace, she settled her head in the crook of his shoulder. As she closed her eyes, serenity washed over her.

She sighed. By his side, she'd found her place ... on the other side.

Thank you for reading The One That Got Away by Zee Monodee. If you enjoyed this story, please leave a quick review on the site of purchase.

Subscribe to our newsletter to find out about book releases, giveaways and more.

www.loveafricapress.com/newsletter

Island Girls: 3 sisters in Mauritius

by Zee Monodee

The One That Got Away
How To Love An Ogre
Falling For Her Bad Boy Boss

Also by Zee Monodee

Be My Valentine Vol 2 Anthology
Unravelling His Mark (The Protectors #2)
The Torn Prince (Royal House of Saene #4)

Other books by Love Africa Press

The Future King by Kiru Taye

A Small-Town Girl by Diana Anyango

Love In The Bar by Maggie Smart

Under The Radar by Stanley Umezulike

Find us on:
Facebook.com/loveafricapress
Twitter.com/loveafricapress
Instagram.com/loveafricapress

www.loveafricapress.com

9 781914 226267